SKYDANCER

Geoffrey Archer is the former Defence and Diplomatic Correspondent for ITN's *News at Ten*. His work as a frontline broadcaster has provided him with the deep background for his thrillers – the bestselling *Skydancer*, *Shadow Hunter*, *Eagle Trap*, *Scorpion Trail*, *Java Spider*, *Fire Hawk*, *The Lucifer Network* and *The Burma Legacy*. A keen traveller, he now writes full time and lives with his wife and family in Surrey.

SKYDANCER

Geoffrey Archer

arrow books

Published by Arrow Books in 1988

19 20 18

This novel is a work of fiction. Names and characters are the product of the author's imagination and any resemblance to actual persons, living or dead, is entirely coincidental

First published in the United Kingdom in 1987 by Century

Arrow Books
The Random House Group Limited
20 Vauxhall Bridge Road, London SW1V 2SA

Random House Australia (Pty) Limited
20 Alfred Street, Milsons Point, Sydney
New South Wales 2061, Australia

Random House New Zealand Limited
18 Poland Road, Glenfield
Auckland 10, New Zealand

Random House (Pty) Limited
Endulini, 5a Jubilee Road, Parktown 2193, South Africa

The Random House Group Limited Reg. No. 954009

www.randomhouse.co.uk

A CIP catalogue record for this book
is available from the British Library

Papers used by Random House are natural, recyclable products made from wood grown in sustainable forests. The manufacturing processes conform to the environmental regulations of the country of origin

ISBN 0 09 945140 9

Printed and bound in Great Britain by
Cox & Wyman Ltd, Reading, Berkshire

Chapter One

The strengthening south-westerly wind scooped the slate-grey waters of the Gare Loch into small foam-crested peaks. To his right, towards the open sea, the angler watched a stubby naval launch butt its bows into the waves. At the sight of the white ensign streaming from its stern, he turned his head to one side and spat on to the ground in a private ritual. It was still early in the afternoon, but the sky had darkened as if it were dusk. Rain threatened.

The fisherman pulled up the zip of his drab-green waterproof to shut out the early autumn chill, and settled himself on to the canvas seat. His twelve-foot glass-fibre rod reached out from the tree-lined bank, the float cast well out on the water. His tackle box was well stocked, and a small bucket of maggots seethed by his side.

The man seemed curiously inattentive to his float, however, and before casting he had omitted to bait the hook.

'Crawford' was the name the angler used in the seedy drinking places that passed for bars on the Clyde Estuary. He had lived in the area for years, though no one seemed sure of his ancestry. He owned a small motor-boat and sometimes attended lobster-pots – with little enthusiasm.

Crawford found fishing a tough life, and a hard one in which to make money. But he had long since ceased to work at it, apart from for appearance's sake. He had found an easier way to earn the price of a drink – just by watching the comings and goings on the other side of the loch.

The Royal Navy's shore base at Faslane is the home of the 3rd and 10th Submarine Squadrons. To Crawford the vessels that slipped silently to and from the quayside, with its towering cranes, were like iron sharks piloted by silent and secretive men with arrogant eyes.

At first the boats had all looked the same to him, black and sleek with smooth, square fins; but he knew better now, thanks to a man he had met one night in Kath's Bar in Helensburgh. 'Donald' was what he had called himself, but Crawford had not been fooled; the man's accent was foreign.

They had met again the next night and had talked about the sea. Crawford had begun his habitual slander of the men of the Royal Navy, 'toffee-nosed pansies' as he called them. He had loathed them since leaving school, when the Navy had rejected him for service. It had been a bitter blow not to have been accepted; from a young age he had boasted to his classmates that he would be a sailor when he grew up. He had never forgiven the callous indifference of the recruiting officer who had turned him away.

What the foreigner had offered him that second time they met was a chance to get even with the men in dark blue – and an easy way to make money took. 'Donald' had given him pictures of the different submarines that visited Faslane, showing him how to tell them apart. Crawford had agreed to phone London at prearranged times to report what he had seen, and for his trouble 'Donald' came north once a month to hand him an envelope full of banknotes.

The vessel Crawford was studying now, through a small but powerful pair of binoculars focused half-a-mile across the water, was the most deadly submarine of all, a Polaris boat, HMS *Retribution*. Behind the fin, the long blunt-ended casing housing the sixteen nuclear missiles made its identification unmistakeable.

Suddenly he was startled by a noise. He snatched at the bucket of maggots and slipped the glasses under the recess of its base. On the road just twenty yards behind him, a vehicle slowed to a halt, its rattling diesel sounding alarmingly like a police patrol from the dockyard opposite.

Checking that his float was still bobbing freely, he pulled a small square tin from his pocket, and began to roll a cigarette. His heart was pounding, fearing that his trick with the maggot bucket had been spotted. He felt the steely glare of the security men on the back of his neck, and he shivered.

It seemed as if they watched him for a full five minutes. Then he heard the crunch from the gearbox and the judder of the engine as the police van moved on again. When the noise faded he chanced a glance after it, confirming that his identification of the motor had been correct.

The police were ignoring him. He whistled with relief, then drew on his cigarette. The smoke bit sourly into his throat.

There was nothing illegal about fishing in the loch, nor about looking at submarines through binoculars, but if the security men took an interest in him and learned what he did with the information he gathered, he would be in trouble. Crawford did not know exactly who the foreigner was, but he knew damned well where the information went.

He did not consider it *spying*. There was nothing secret about the information 'Donald' wanted. After all, the Navy did not try to hide the comings and goings of their ships. But by ensuring that the 'other side' knew what those self-satisfied submariners were up to, his need for revenge was beginning to be fulfilled.

His brief use of the binoculars was enough for his purposes. He had seen fresh food being taken on board. HMS *Retribution* was making ready for sea. High tide was in two hours; Crawford guessed the submarine planned to sail when it ebbed.

Two days earlier he had watched *Retribution* emerge from the enclosed dock at Coulport, on the other side of the spit of land that separates the Gare Loch from the open sea. He knew it was there that the missiles were stored: the Polaris rockets with their nuclear warheads. 'Donald' had told him the submarines never go to Coulport during normal routine because their missiles are kept on board, sealed beneath deck hatches.

But *Retribution* had gone there, so something was up – something out of the ordinary. 'Donald' had been most interested in that particular news when Crawford had phoned the London number to tell him about it. He had asked him to ring again as soon as the submarine had sailed.

Crawford shivered as the water gusted across the open water. That police patrol was certain to come back again before long. There was only one road around the loch.

He reeled in his line. The hook spun and danced in front of him. He grabbed for it and impaled a pair of maggots on its barb. He would have to be there for a few more hours yet, and the best way to curb the suspicions of the police was to catch some fish.

Two weeks later, in north London, General David Twining, British Army retired, struck out across

Parliament Hill Fields for his early morning constitutional, sucking a throat pastille to counter the effects of the cold, damp air.

The dog at his feet looked ridiculously small to belong to such a tall man. Short-haired and almost legless, the bundle of wiry brown fur darted backwards and forwards across the path, tracing complex and invisible smells.

Mist clung firmly to the ground. It was late October and wet leaves made the path slippery where it passed under the almost bare trees. The sun had only recently risen, and showed no sign yet of burning through the grey.

Twining's bearing was unmistakeably military, his back parade-ground straight. A brown felt hat covered his balding head, and he wore a dark green loden coat, acquired during his days commanding a division of the British Rhine Army. Most mornings he could be seen striding up this path on Parliament Hill, but only by the few who arose as early as he did. Recently his wife had urged him to choose a less lonely route for his morning walk; Hampstead Heath had become a haunt for muggers in the past few months. He had scoffed at her worries, but had to admit to himself that this morning the gaunt branches of the old oaks did look curiously menacing in the fog.

Suddenly his scurrying dog stopped dead in its tracks. Hackles raised like a worn scrubbing brush, the animal began to growl.

'Ollie, you fool! What's the matter?' snapped the retired soldier. He shared some of the dog's alarm, though, and strained to identify the vague noises he could hear above the dull dripping of the wet branches.

His walking stick had a heavy handle carved from bone, and he reversed the cane in his hand, ready to use as a weapon if necessary. The sound was eerie in the gloom – the rustling of paper and the clatter of tin cans. The general's pulse quickened; he was not as young as he once was, and felt unsure whether he could defend himself against determined muggers, whatever blustering assurances he had given his wife.

The dog, still growling, had taken up a position behind his master now, as Twining walked cautiously forward towards the source of the noise. Slowly, through the mist, he began to make out a dark figure rummaging through the contents of a litter bin.

'Huh! It's a bloody tramp!' Twining muttered to himself, slightly ashamed at having allowed himself to fear something worse.

The dog darted forward, hurling a torrent of barks at the figure wearing an oversized black coat, who pulled back in alarm from his investigation of the rubbish. The tramp's face was obscured by upturned lapels and, with a curse and an ill-aimed kick at the dog, he turned and shuffled hurriedly off into the mist.

Ollie made as if to give chase to the departing itinerant, but after a sufficient show of bravery he scurried back to his master, wagging his tail in anticipation of praise.

'Good boy, Ollie! Good boy!' the General murmured, patting the animal as much to steady his own nerves as the dog's.

'Look at this mess!' he exclaimed, as he straightened his back, and stared at the litter bin. In his eagerness to find something of interest, the tramp had strewn its contents all over the path. Twining swore angrily; he loathed litter, and would frequently clear up after untidy tourists on summer evenings here. He bent down and began slowly to collect the rubbish and return it to the bin, taking care there was nothing unsavoury amongst it to foul his pigskin gloves.

Halfway through his task, he suddenly stopped in surprise. In his hand he held something that had been tediously familiar during his military career – a buff-coloured folder with the letters MOD. stamped on it. The initials stood for Ministry of Defence, and the cardboard file looked fresh and clean.

Startled, he opened the folder and took out the single sheet of paper it contained. He had left his reading glasses at home but, holding the document at arm's length, he could still make out the words 'R.V. Separation Mechanism', and the acronym AWRE.

'Good God!' he exclaimed under his breath. 'That's the Atomic Weapons place.'

A small group of protesters had been camping outside the gates of Aldermaston Research Establishment for several years now, on and off. Banners denouncing the evil of nuclear weapons hung on the chain-link fence – next to the camp washing.

Every morning and evening, the protesters' numbers were augmented by a dozen or so local women, who came to wave their placards and to stare in stony reproach at the thousands of Aldermaston employees entering or leaving the establishment. These protesters saw themselves as part of an international sorority struggling to save the world from nuclear destruction. From time to time their activities would feature in the national newspapers, and though the reports were frequently insulting, this only served to strengthen their sense of alienation from the Establishment.

Peter Joyce drove up to the gates of Aldermaston soon after eight o'clock on that particular October morning. He had taken to making an early start in recent months, to cope with the colossal workload that had built up for him. Joyce headed the project to which most of the Aldermaston's extensive facilities were currently devoted – the creation of an advanced new nuclear warhead for the Polaris missiles that Britain had maintained operational for over twenty years.

The design team had been assembled almost overnight two years ago, following a dramatic Government decision to cancel plans for replacing Polaris with the much larger and more sophisticated American Trident missiles. Faced with the danger that new Soviet Ballistic Missile Defences might make the ten-billion-pound Trident obsolete early in the next century, the Government had suddenly decided to save money by modernising Polaris instead.

Peter Joyce was a physicist by training and had developed a knowledge of military electronics that was unequalled in Britain. In his late forties, he looked fit and energetic. His square jaw gave him the appearance of a 1950s cricketer. Several major armaments manufacturers both at home and in the USA had tried to buy his talents over the years, but he had always resisted them. Working for the Government at Aldermaston did little to swell his bank account, but it gave him access to the most advanced technology in the world, the 'cutting edge' of research, with the use of vastly more comprehensive scientific facilities than any commercial arms manufacturer could afford to maintain.

Hundreds of millions of pounds had been spent on buying the most powerful computers in the world, including the massive number-crunching Crays. They had been worked around-the-clock to fulfil the Government's latest requirement: to develop a deception system that would enable the Polaris warheads to penetrate any defences the Soviet Union could devise this century.

It had been no easy task; packing the advanced electronic deception systems into the small nose-cone of a Polaris missile was 'like squeezing a Rolls-Royce engine into a Mini', as Peter muttered to his colleagues whenever the problems seemed insurmountable. But that task had now been nearly completed; unarmed warheads together with their decoy systems were about to be fired off in a Polaris test rocket, for the first time later that week.

Countless times each day, as the test launch drew nearer, Peter ran through his mental checklist, for fear some vital component of the system had been overlooked. To him the development process had been like a chess game, using his brainpower and ingenuity to outwit his Russian opponents. The weapons that he was developing may have the ability to slaughter millions of people, yet for him the exercise of designing them had been almost academic. It was inconceivable, he felt sure, that human beings would ever be mad enough to actually use them.

As he drove in through the gates of Aldermaston, the few dozen placard-waving protesters on the roadside had a rather less optimistic view of human nature. Few of those watching knew the identity or particular importance of the man behind the wheel of the grey Vauxhall. But one woman certainly did – she was his wife.

Sharp at nine o'clock, the Permanent Undersecretary at the Ministry of Defence was at his desk on the sixth floor of the bleak, grey military powerhouse in Whitehall. Sir Marcus Beckett was a punctual man, steeped in the ethic of professionalism and academic excellence by which the British Civil Service likes to think it is characterised.

He was a short man, not quite five feet nine inches in his socks. Self-consciousness at his stature had fuelled his determination to succeed in a career where a height of more than six feet seemed a requisite for rapid promotion.

His last job had been at the Treasury, and he had arrived at the Defence Ministry fired by determination to cut the ever-growing cost of Defence, undaunted by the limited success his predecessors had enjoyed in that same task.

The phone rang just as he was saying 'Good morning' to his secretary. The caller was an anxious clerk in the main reception area downstairs.

'She says there's a retired general called Twining standing at the desk,' the secretary whispered to the PUS, covering the mouthpiece of the phone with her hand. 'He insists on talking to you personally; says it's a matter of national security. She's checked his ID, and he seems genuine.'

Beckett frowned. The country seemed to be full of retired generals, and his own connection with Defence had been too short to give him any memory of a man called Twining.

'Better get him escorted up here,' he muttered eventually, but added sharply, 'Be ready to have him thrown out if he turns out to be a nutter!'

Three minutes later, as General David Twining was ushered into his office, Beckett scrutinised him critically, concluding that the man certainly looked genuine. In two short sentences, the general summarised his military career by way of introduction, then, with a distinct sense of drama, he placed on the civil servant's desk the buff-coloured folder he had found that morning.

'I found this in a rubbish bin on Hampstead Heath.

Parliament Hill to be exact,' he intoned, narrowing his eyes to observe Beckett's reaction.

The civil servant frowned as he opened the folder and stared at the single sheet of paper inside. Suddenly his eyebrows shot upwards in undisguised horror.

'Good Lord!' he exploded. 'In a rubbish bin? Are you sure?'

Twining looked affronted.

'Well of course you're sure. Otherwise you wouldn't be here!'

Beckett swung round sharply to press the switch on his office intercom, asking his secretary to send immediately for the head of security.

'Sit down. Sit down please, General,' he gestured to a chair, while taking a longer and closer look at the document. After a moment he groaned softly. 'This does *not* look good.'

He put the folder down again.

'Anyone else know about this? Was anyone with you when you found it?'

Twining shook his head. 'Only my dog.'

Sir Marcus winced.

There was a respectful tap at the door.

'Come in!' Beckett yelled. 'Ah, Commander Duncan! We've got some work for you, I'm afraid.'

After brief introductions Sir Marcus slipped the buff folder across his desk towards his head of security.

'What, er . . . what do you make of that then?' he asked, after allowing the commander a few moments to study it.

'Well, sir,' Duncan answered grimly, 'I know what it is, and I know which security vault it's come from. What I don't know is what it's doing up here.'

'*He* found it! This morning! Lying around on Hampstead Heath! General Twining here!' Sir Marcus spluttered in his anger and concern. 'How could it have got there, Commander?'

Duncan looked uncomfortable.

'There's clearly been some sort of lapse . . .' he began lamely. 'Clearly a major breach of security. And er . . .' – glancing uneasily towards the retired general – 'I think it's something we should discuss in *private*, if you don't mind, sir.'

'Yes, of course,' Beckett nodded. 'General, would you like to explain to Commander Duncan just exactly what happened this morning, and then we won't need to detain you any further.'

The security man pulled a pad from his pocket and began to take a careful long-hand note of Twining's description of events. Then, with a request that the general keep himself available at home to help investigating officers later, Sir Marcus shook him warmly by the hand and thanked him profusely for his discretion in bringing the document to the Ministry directly.

'Right! Tell me the worst!' Sir Marcus barked as soon as the door had closed behind their elderly visitor.

'It's project Skydancer, sir. Here's the identification code in the bottom right-hand corner. This paper is one of a set of engineering plans – classified "top secret". This is probably a photocopy, but the originals are under the custody of the Strategic Nuclear Secretariat, down on the fifth floor. Must be only a handful of people with access to such a document.'

'Bugger!' Beckett exploded. 'How the hell could this one have got loose?'

Commander Duncan felt a prickling at the back of his neck. By his tone the Permanent Undersecretary almost seemed to be blaming him for it.

'I don't know, sir. Give me a little time and I'll try to find out,' he answered as coolly as he could.

Sir Marcus paced over to the window and stared down at the passing traffic.

'We'd better call a conference, right away,' he decided, turning back towards his desk. 'The key people in Skydancer – I'll get them here, so we can evaluate the seriousness of this business. I mean . . . God Almighty! The whole bloody project might be compromised! It has to be the bloody Russians!'

Peter Joyce squealed the tyres of his car as he turned through the gates of Aldermaston in his hurry to reach the motorway for London. The gaggle of protesters had dispersed by now. The permanent residents of the 'peace camp' were settling down to their morning chores, while the other protesters – including his wife – had gone off to their daily work.

On the insecure telephone line from the Ministry of Defence, Sir Marcus Beckett had been understandably vague about the exact nature of the security breach. But his voice carried an edging of ice which had made that vagueness additionally disturbing.

The road from the atomic weapons plant wound through picturesque villages and over bridges, which were a pleasure to pass on any normal day. But Peter cursed them as he struggled unsuccessfully to overtake a slow-moving lorry. Eventually, with a surge of relief, he swung his car on to the motorway and, pressing his foot to the floor, raced towards the capital. He leaned forward in his seat, concentrating on the road ahead, his dark eyes focusing far in front. Occasionally he lifted a hand briefly to push back the hank of straight brown hair that fell across his forehead.

In less than two hours he had reached the Defence Ministry in Whitehall. In the PUS's office he found himself joined by Alec Anderson, the civil servant at the head of the Strategic Nuclear Secretariat. Unsuspectingly, Anderson had arrived a little late for work that morning, and now looked shocked and confused. He was a policy man, not a technician, and like Sir Marcus Beckett was waiting anxiously for Peter Joyce to reveal whether General Twining's discovery was as significant as they feared.

Several pairs of eyes focused on Joyce's tall figure as he scanned the page of secrets.

'Christ Almighty!' he breathed after the first glance. 'This *is* a page from the Skydancer plans. Shows the re-entry vehicle separation mechanism. The full set describes precisely how the decoy system works, how it can defeat the Soviet defences. This page on its own is sensitive enough, but if someone's given the Russians the full set . . . it'll be a disaster!'

'Well let's not jump the gun,' Beckett countered hurriedly. 'It may not be as serious as that.'

As a personal friend of the Prime Minister, the civil servant was dreading the public outcry and political uproar that could result from a full-blown security leak in his Ministry. The previous government had been brought down by a top-level Soviet infiltration of the security service MI5.

'Commander Duncan,' Beckett turned hopefully to his security chief. 'What have you been able to find out?'

'Well, sir, I checked in the documents register and I've found there are only two sets of these papers in existence, one kept here and the other at Aldermaston. While Mr Joyce was on his way up here, I took the liberty of ringing George Dogson, head of security at AWRE, and got him to check the vaults. Hope you don't mind, Mr Joyce,' he added, looking across.

'Of course not. What did he say?'

'All in order. Nothing missing there. Now, as for the other set, the ones here in MOD, they are kept in a strictly controlled security room, but a room to which dozens of people have access. All of them with top-level clearance, of course. But the nuclear papers are kept in a special filing cabinet there, and the only people with keys to that cabinet are Mr Anderson here and his secretary Miss Maclean.'

'Well.' Alec Anderson felt sweat breaking out on his forehead. 'We'd better go and look, hadn't we?'

Now a deeply unhappy man, he led the commander down to his office, to check the file. Mary Maclean, an attractive dark-haired woman in her late thirties, looked up in surprise at the sight of her principal being escorted into the room by the stern-faced security chief. She blanched when Anderson asked her to collect the Skydancer technical file from the secure room. Closing her eyes momentarily, she seemed to hesitate as if struck by some painful realisation.

The two men watched closely as she slowly opened her desk drawer, took from it a key, then stood up and walked rigidly from the room. Anderson and the commander looked at one another with silent alarm.

'Do you always keep that key in your desk drawer?' the policeman asked her icily when she returned with the file.

'Yes, I do,' Mary Maclean replied defensively. 'But I keep the drawer locked whenever I'm out of the room. And I keep the key to the drawer in my handbag. It's always with me, I can assure you.'

The Commander's heart sank. This simple lapse of security procedures meant that his list of suspects had grown dramatically. Literally dozens of people could have attained access to the vital papers.

He watched intently as Anderson opened the file and checked through the sheaf of papers. The thirty sheets of paper were all numbered – and they were all there.

Duncan then took hold of the file and thumbed through the pages himself, until he found the one that matched the photocopy in the buff folder. Each sheet had been hand-stamped with a Ministry seal. He checked the angle of the imprint on the original and on the copy. They matched perfectly.

'No doubt about that,' he muttered to himself with a certain satisfaction.

'May I . . . may I enquire what this is about?' Mary asked uneasily.

'Someone's got at the file – and copied it,' Duncan responded bluntly.

She gasped. 'And you think it's because . . .' her voice faltered.

'We're not thinking anything yet, Mary,' Anderson interposed as gently as he could.

'Well I should hope not,' she remarked almost indignantly. She had put in long service at the Ministry and was proud of her record. Skydancer had played a significant part in her recent life, and it was not solely because of her professional involvement. In the last three months there had been personal reasons why she found it painful just to hear mention of the project.

From the look on Alec Anderson's face it was beginning to hurt him too.

'Would you mind, Mary?'

Anderson was handing her the file.

'Would you mind putting this back in the vault?'

*

As the two men re-entered the office of the Permanent Undersecretary, Sir Marcus Beckett's face expressed his heartfelt wish that they could have solved the mystery. But the Commander's brooding scowl and Anderson's look of shocked bewilderment soon dashed his hopes.

'How the hell could this have happened?' he demanded when they had told him what they had learned. 'These are about the most sensitive documents in the whole bloody building, for Christ's sake! How on earth could someone make copies without your knowing?'

Anderson made as if to speak, but no words emerged.

'What do you know about this, Anderson?' Sir Marcus continued, looking ready to launch a physical attack on anyone he could hold responsible for the disaster.

'Nothing at all, PUS,' Anderson half stammered in reply. His face was flushed. 'I'm shocked . . . utterly.'

'I'll start a review of procedure immediately, sir,' the security man broke in, eager to press on with a detailed investigation.

'It's a bit bloody late for that!' Beckett snapped. 'The bird seems to have flown!'

He strode across the room to glare angrily out of the window at the Thames Embankment below. Peter Joyce stared at the Undersecretary's hands clasped tightly behind him. The fingers of one hand turned white with the pressure of his grip, and then began to colour again as the sight of the slow-moving river traffic seemed to exert a calming effect.

'All right,' Sir Marcus said eventually, breaking the uneasy silence, 'let's look at the worse case scenario.'

He sat himself at his desk, and drew a blank sheet of paper from a drawer. Then he wrote the figure '1' at the top left-hand corner.

'We have to assume that every page of the document

has been photocopied,' he began. 'There would be little purpose in doing just one, unless someone is simply trying to make a point.' He paused to look round at the expectant faces of the three men opposite.

'Well? Is someone trying to make a point?' he demanded. 'Someone who knew there was a weakness in the security system, and wanted to show it up?'

His enquiry was greeted by murmured denials and frowns.

'What about your secretary, Anderson? Could she be up to something? Any odd behaviour lately? Change of life, that sort of thing?'

'Oh . . . I hardly think so, PUS,' Alec Anderson answered hurriedly. 'She's a bit young for that, and although she's been careless with the keys, I'm sure her loyalty is not in question.'

Anderson cast a furtive glance at Peter Joyce, but the scientist stared back impassively.

Sir Marcus began to write.

'Then we have to assume we are talking about espionage,' he declared. 'The assumption must be that someone had copied the Skydancer plans and is feeding them to the Russians. But why was this single page found in a rubbish bin? Were the Russians meant to pick it up from there? It's damned odd; I mean there must be dozens of safer places to make the handover – why choose a rubbish bin?'

'I've already got someone observing the place, sir,' the Commander interjected, 'in case someone comes looking for the document. But I agree it's an odd place.'

'The big question,' Beckett continued, as if he had not heard what the security man had just said, 'is whether this bungle occurred at the start of the handover process, or whether the Russians already have all or most of the rest of the papers.'

There was no sure answer to that question, but as Peter Joyce had explained, the Skydancer plans were of critical national importance, and if the secrets were already largely in the Russians' hands, several hundred million pounds of taxpayers' money could now have been totally wasted. A political hornet's nest of huge dimensions would be stirred up the moment news of this security leak emerged.

There was a chance, just the slightest chance that the mystery could be solved rapidly, Beckett thought to himself. In which case it might never need to become public knowledge, and the Prime Minister could be spared the damaging publicity and the taunting from the opposition in parliament. He would have to call in the security service immediately, that was clear, but he would hold back from telling his Secretary of State about it in the hope the matter could be quickly resolved, without the politicians' involvement and the inevitable and damaging attention of the media that would follow.

Bringing the meeting to an abrupt end, he instructed his officials to return to their duties, and to discuss the matter with no one other than the men from the security departments. After they left the sixth-floor office, Alec Anderson and Peter Joyce paused in the corridor outside to look at one another uneasily. Each recognised alarm and suspicion on the other's face. Then they nodded at one another and walked off in different directions, without speaking.

Peter Joyce hardly noticed the road as he motored back to Aldermaston. From time to time he touched his forehead to push back those strands of hair that stubbornly refused to grow any way but forwards. His usual air of confidence had largely evaporated that morning.

He was driving back at only half the speed he had maintained on his journey up to London, his mind in turmoil as he began to assess what a devastating blow this security leak was about to deal him. For the moment he was less concerned by the critical national issue of the leakage of nuclear secrets; he was gripped instead by a personal foreboding, a fear that it could emerge that indirectly and unwittingly he himself had been somehow responsible for the leak – and that those closest to him would see this as just retribution on him.

He vividly remembered the day, three months earlier, when he had first taken that set of vital documents up to London. They were to form the core of a top-level briefing of Government ministers who demanded to know in detail what this vast amount of public money had been spent on. He remembered the occasion with painful clarity, because it was the last time he had spent an evening with Mary Maclean – the night on which he had to tell her that their relationship was over.

Their love affair had lasted two years. It had begun almost by accident, and had blossomed freely, without strains and complications, at a period when his marriage to Belinda was proving increasingly stressful. But eventually Mary had begun to make assumptions about their future together, assumptions involving steps he was not prepared to take.

She had been devastated when he had told her their affair must come to an end. It was the night before the ministerial briefing; and he had visited her flat. Guiltily he remembered now that the top secret plans had been in his briefcase all the time. The crazy – but not so crazy – thought now passed through his mind, that she could have copied the papers later and given them to the

Soviets in an act of revenge. 'Hell hath no fury . . .' But no – he could not really believe that.

Peter stamped on the brake pedal and swerved into the left-hand lane, as he realised he was about to overshoot the turning off the motorway. He cut in front of a lorry which hooted loudly.

'Damn!' the scientist hissed. He would end up crashing if he was not more careful. Heading for the country lanes leading back to Aldermaston, he slowed down further, and continued to ponder how events might develop.

His secret affair with Mary Maclean was bound to be uncovered. The security men would question him closely on his care of those secret papers, and be alarmed by what they learned. They would also talk to his wife, and discover she was a confirmed anti-nuclear activist – and an associate of political groupings well to the left of the normal British political spectrum. They might begin to speculate whether it really was only now that those secrets had gone missing, and not months or even years previously.

And what would they say to Belinda? Would the security men ask her how much she knew of her husband's affair with Mary? She had not known anything – Peter was certain of that. But how would she react when she found out? Would she walk out on him? And what of the children, for whose sake he had finally chosen to reject his mistress and preserve his marriage – would he lose them after all?

'What a mess!' he muttered as he finally turned the car through the gates of Aldermaston.

Once back at his desk, he instructed his secretary to discourage telephone callers. Peter Joyce was a methodical man who had spent his working life confronting apparently insoluble problems. Pulling out a thick notepad, he sat back and forced his brain to concentrate. First he had to list and analyse the dangers that both he and the Skydancer project now faced. Then he had to think of ways to counter them, or at least to limit the damage.

Three thousand miles away the surface of the western Atlantic heaved and surged in a long, lazy swell, the aftermath of a depression which had moved off to the east to dump its rain on the soft green hills of Ireland.

Five hundred feet below that surface, the dark, still waters were unaffected by the weather above. It was down there that HMS *Retribution* slipped silently westwards, her 8,400 tons of sleek, black steel propelled by the tireless energy of her nuclear reactor. Longer than a football pitch, the leviathan of the Clyde was in her true element down there, amongst the other weird creatures of the deep that relied on sound, and sound alone, to protect themselves from predators.

And predators there were, in increasing numbers, for these boats and their crews who lived under water for two months at a time. The normal role of ballistic missile submarines like HMS *Retribution* was to lie in wait, lurking in the Atlantic depths far enough from the Russian coast to go undetected, but close enough for the sixteen Polaris missiles on board to stay within range of their targets. To lie in wait in the fervent hope that the very existence of her weapons would deter a war, and that they would never have to fire the rockets that could destroy several Soviet cities and slaughter tens of millions of people.

The predators for HMS *Retribution* were the Russian hunter-killer submarines, whose task was to scour the oceans for Western missile boats. If a war was ever to start, the Russians would try to sink *Retribution* before her deadly missiles could be fired.

The navies of Nato had the reverse task of tracking the Soviet missile boats, and in peacetime the roles of hunter and hunted were constantly rehearsed in a sophisticated game of hide-and-seek.

Evenly placed along the smooth flank of *Retribution*'s hull were small, flat plates, the ears of the submarine which could hear other vessels hundreds of miles away. Trailing behind the boat's fan-like propeller, a cable hundreds of yards long towed an array of hydrophones which could listen for distant sounds, unencumbered by the tiny noises generated by the movement of the submarine itself through the water. This was the most powerful tool of all in the electronic armoury that had enabled the Royal Navy's 'bombers' – as the Polaris boats were called – to stay ahead of the game, to hear the Russians before the Russians heard them, and to remain undetected on their Atlantic patrols.

In the belly of the submarine's massive carcase one hundred and forty-three men lived their lives, apparently oblivious of their great depth under water, the pressure of which was such that, without the protection of the steel hull, it would crush them to death within seconds.

It had been nearly two weeks since they had last seen daylight, and Commander Anthony Carrington, the captain of *Retribution*, was looking forward to smelling fresh air again. He had just announced on the boat's public address system that they were due to dock in Port Canaveral, Florida, the following day. An air of anticipation and readjustment had immediately swept through the boat.

Cut off as they were from the regulating influence of the sun, the crew's time on board was broken into periods of work and periods of rest, rather than of day and night. Men found it easy to lose their sense of time. Now, though, with the prospect of shore leave imminent, they began to adjust their watches from Greenwich Mean Time to the hours observed in the girly-bars of Florida.

Information about the submarine's activities was strictly rationed on board to those few who needed to know. On a normal patrol the majority of the crew would have no knowledge whereabouts they were in the world's oceans. On this voyage, though, the entire company had been informed they were heading for America, and all knew from past experience that meant they were going to use the American Eastern Test Range, and fire a missile. Only a handful of officers and specialist technicians, however, knew that the missile would be carrying the new Skydancer warhead, on which hundreds of millions of pounds of income tax had been spent in recent years.

'What's the latest from the sound room?' Carrington quietly asked the officer of the watch, as he prepared to leave the control room and return to his cabin.

'Plankton are being a bit noisy, sir, but not much else,' the young lieutenant joked. 'Oh, about an hour ago we heard a Benjamin Franklin boat passing us in the other direction. About a hundred miles south of us. Presumably heading for her patrol area over our side of the pond.'

The Benjamin Franklins were American submarines carrying Trident missiles, and the signal-processing computer on board *Retribution* had automatically identified the vessel from a library of acoustic signatures. Analysis by microprocessors meant that almost every vessel could be positively identified from its individual sounds, and all but the very latest Russian submarines had their tell-tale noises recorded.

'All right, OOW., I shall be in my cabin,' Carrington told his junior as he weaved his tall shape past the shiny periscopes which had not been raised from their rests since *Retribution* left the Clyde two weeks earlier.

Moving from one part of this submarine to another was easy compared to the traditional diesel-electric boats with their narrow gangways, claustrophobic hatches, and bunks amongst the torpedo tubes. Being six feet four inches tall, Carrington was grateful to have command of a nuclear-powered vessel which was almost as spacious as a surface ship. His cabin, though, only had room for a small desk apart from his bunk, and he found it cramped for his tall frame.

He sat at that desk and turned the pages of his log, reflecting on a voyage which had been exceptionally full of incident. The problems had started the moment they had left the Clyde. A Russian submarine had been heard nosing around just outside the estuary, clearly hoping to tail the Polaris boat out on to patrol. The Royal Navy still made the proud boast that none of their 'bombers' had ever been successfully tracked by the Russians, and they were prepared to go to extreme lengths to maintain that record.

Another British nuclear-powered submarine – a hunter-killer boat similar in size and sound to the *Retribution*, but carrying torpedoes rather than ballistic missiles – had been called back from patrol near Iceland to act as a decoy. Using the cover of a noisy cargo ship to drown its own propeller sounds, the submarine had slipped unnoticed into the Clyde, and had then immediately turned out to sea again. Pretending to be the *Retribution*, it had led the Russian shadow on a wild-goose chase round the Scottish islands, while the Polaris boat itself had slipped unnoticed into the deep waters of the Atlantic.

Two weeks was much longer than was needed to cross the ocean, but HMS *Retribution* had just been modified and refitted, requiring a long series of tests and sea trials to be undertaken. These had been the cause of Commander Carrington's second major headache.

The *Retribution* was over twenty years old, and so was most of her missile-launching equipment. The grafting of new systems on to old often produced teething problems, and with the vital test launch of the new Skydancer warheads coming up, Carrington had been determined that if the firing failed, it would not be because of inadequate practice with the systems beforehand. During their journey across the Atlantic they had repeatedly run through the complex countdown procedures. On the first four successive runs, four different electronic faults had appeared which could have caused an abort if the launch had been for real. The engineers had sweated and cursed as they grappled with the printed-circuit panels. Eventually they had solved all the problems, but only after four perfect tests did the captain consider they were ready.

'Can I bring you a cuppa tea, sir?' the chief steward poked his head round the cabin door, which had been left half open.

'Ready for the rock shrimps?' the commander asked, when the tea was brought in. They were a speciality around Cape Canaveral.

'Er . . . well, I'm a steak man myself, sir,' the steward answered with a grin of anticipation of his run ashore.

'You should try 'em. They steam them in beer, you know.'

'Yes sir, I know. Some of the lads go for them, but me . . . well, I know what I like.'

*

When Alec Anderson arrived home that evening from one of the most harrowing days he had ever spent at the Ministry of Defence, he had timed his return to the house in North London to coincide with the moment when his wife Janet would be too preoccupied with the children to bother him with questions. He knew he could not disguise his anxiety, and if he had to tell her what had happened that day, she would make matters worse with her worrying.

Anderson was aged thirty-seven and had been doing very well in his career as a civil servant. He had enjoyed a succession of good promotions through a wide variety of departments – just what was needed if he was to succeed in reaching the top of the professional tree, and he was an ambitious man.

The position he now held as head of the Strategic Nuclear Secretariat had been one of the ripest plums on that tree, and he had plucked it eagerly when offered to him some six months earlier.

'Hullo. You're early,' Janet called from upstairs. The sound of running bathwater and the high-pitched chatter of his two small daughters told him that his return had been well timed.

'Had to bring some work home,' he shouted up to her. 'I'll be in the library.'

'Library' was a somewhat pretentious word for the front room of their suburban Edwardian house, but it was the place where he kept his father's old roll-top desk and the few possessions that he really valued. On the shelves of a glass-fronted mahogany cabinet there were rows of leather-bound volumes in varying states of repair, and most of the Latin text-books from his schooldays. On the walls hung his most prized items of all, miniature paintings that he had collected over the past fifteen years – delicate watercolours of lakes and castles painted by Victorian artists making the Grand Tour of Europe.

He rolled open the lid of the desk and switched on the brass lamp that shone down on to the tooled green-leather interior, marked with the ink stains of past decades. From his briefcase he pulled a file, and spread it open before him. His eyes did not focus on the printed pages, though; the file was there only to provide an excuse for the seclusion that he sought.

Anderson had always favoured Britain being a true nuclear power. Having developed the technology in the first place, it would undermine the country's stature to abandon it, he believed. He had always argued his case forcefully in the Ministry with those of his colleagues who considered a British nuclear deterrent redundant alongside the massive American arsenals. His fluent advocacy of the case had clearly played a part in his selection for his present job.

He even used to expound his arguments regularly at the dinner table when they had guests round, much to Janet's annoyance. She hated to think of the horror that would be unleashed if such weapons were ever used, and preferred to shut her mind to the whole issue. To her there were innumerable more pleasant topics of conversation, and secretly she rather regretted that Alec had gained his last promotion.

Nevertheless Janet adored her husband, devoting all her energies to him, their home, and their two girls aged seven and nine. She had never been academic by nature; much of her education had been directed towards learning the social graces. She knew she was in no way an 'intellectual' companion for Alec, and she loathed 'women's-libbers', because they made her feel guilty at being so satisfied with the life she had chosen.

Although content to have an adoring wife – and to an

extent his ego demanded that his female companion should be his intellectual inferior – Anderson occasionally found that the mundane level of their conversation and her clinging lack of independence grated on his nerves. He longed secretly for the mental companionship he had experienced in his boarding-school, something he had never been able to recapture in his adult life. The closest he ever came to that now was his regular escape from domestic claustrophobia on Friday nights, when he would visit the local pub and relax with a group of male friends, drinking draught bitter and playing bar billiards.

Suddenly, however, the world had become threatening. He was under suspicion. Friends were becoming enemies, and the bright future he had envisaged was now clouded by uncertainty. As he stared absently at his father's old gold-plated pen-stand, and fiddled nervously with a bottle of ink, he realised how important to him were those three members of his family splashing the bathwater upstairs. Whatever their inadequacies, they were devoted to him, and he needed that devotion more than anything else.

'I'm sorry, darling. I had to see to the children,' Janet bustled into the room, her sleeves rolled up and her arms still red from their immersion in the hot water. 'Can I get you a drink or something? And how awful that you have to work this evening . . .'

She stopped in mid-flow when she saw his face so drained of colour, and the haunted look in his eyes.

'Alec, you look dreadful,' she exclaimed. 'What on earth's happened?'

For a few seconds he stared at her without answering.

'Oh, it's nothing much,' he answered eventually, trying to smile confidently. 'Just some papers that have gone missing from the office, and I've got to try to figure out how it happened.'

Peter Joyce turned the car gently into the driveway to his house, anxious for the wheels not to scatter gravel on to the lawn, where it would blunt the blades of his mower. Built in the previous century, his home had originally been a small farm, but when Peter had bought the property it had been left with just over an acre of ground. During the years of their occupancy the Joyces had developed the land lovingly.

At the side of the house he had built a double garage, one half of it occupied by a small sailing boat on a trailer, which Peter raced at a nearby lake during the summer months. The other garage space was empty. The Citroën was not there, so Belinda would not be at home to greet him. He parked his own car next to the boat, swung the jacket of his grey herring-bone tweed suit over his shoulder, and walked through the back door of the garage into the large rear garden. In the flower bed to the left, under the partial shade of an oak tree, the buds on the azaleas were setting well, ready for the following spring. He looked beyond them to the half-completed greenhouse at the far end of the lawn, and wondered when he would next find time to continue with its construction.

'Daddy!' A yell of enthusiasm burst through the kitchen doorway as thirteen-year-old Suzanne ran out to greet him.

'Sylvie and I are doing our homework, groan, groan!' She reached up to hug him. 'And Mark is out playing football. But Mummy's late as usual.'

Peter put his arm round her shoulder and they walked back into the house. Suzanne adored her father, whereas at fifteen her elder sister had grown more circumspect – involved with boyfriends of whom her father disapproved and holding rebellious young views about the Establishment which he represented.

'Shall I make you a cup of tea?' the thirteen-year-old suggested.

'No, I think it would be better if I made it myself and you got on with your homework,' Peter replied kindly, patting her gently on the backside. She smiled selfconsciously, pulling her shoulders back so that her developing breasts gave shape to her school blouse, and set off back to her bedroom, grumbling quietly.

Peter found it both pleasing and sad to see the second of his daughters turning from a child into a woman. He wondered how long it would be before she too began to find fault with him, like her elder sister.

He filled the electric kettle at the sink and plugged it into the mains. While waiting for it to boil, he eased himself on to a chair at the kitchen table. A cork pinboard on the wall opposite was plastered with 'Ban the Bomb' posters, and notices announcing the dates of forthcoming protest meetings.

Peter was forty-eight and had been married for nearly twenty years. Staring at those posters which criticised his lifetime's work, he reflected on how much had changed since he had first met Belinda.

Brought up in a middle-class district on Tyneside, he had moved south after graduating, to take up a research post at Imperial College London. Belinda had been working there as a laboratory assistant.

She had undoubtedly been one of the most attractive women in the college; he had first spotted her in the canteen. A frequent focus of attention when students and lecturers gathered for lunch, her face was oval and her chestnut hair shoulder-length. He remembered how her skin had looked so perfectly smooth, without need of make-up, her lips wide and sensual. Her dark brown eyes had seemed to extend an invitation, yet promised a challenge too.

The third time he had seen her there, she was sitting alone at a table. He had stifled his shyness and had carried his tray across the room to join her. She had smiled at him encouragingly, and it had been easy to chat to her. She was sharp and witty, yet with an attractive sense of reserve. In those days he had tended to express himself in bursts of wild enthusiasm, and she had found that exciting.

A relationship had developed quickly. They had become lovers within a few days. It was the 1960s, when the moral climate was newly liberated, and before long they had been sharing a two-roomed flat together.

There was a click as the boiling kettle switched itself off. He stood up, dropped a tea bag into a mug, and extracted a milk bottle from the fridge. Giving the tea a few moments to brew, he looked through the window into the garden. He loved his home; it was peaceful, secure and permanent. Those early days with Belinda seemed like distant history to him now. They had been carefree in some ways, he supposed, but uncertain too. The relationship had begun so quickly that he always suspected it could end just as suddenly.

Life with Belinda had been fun then, and that fun had lasted for a long time. They had lived together for over a year before marrying. The ceremony had been brief and simple, one Saturday morning. They had invited only their closest relatives to the register office, and had not bothered with a honeymoon. They had felt no different after the wedding, which had somehow seemed wrong at the time, and they had spent the next few days fearing the marriage had been a mistake. Before long, though, their relationship had developed a new sense of security. Peter went on to establish his career at Aldermaston, and Belinda decided to become pregnant.

For the next ten years or so she had devoted herself almost exclusively to motherhood, immersing herself in its ethos. Breast-feeding the three babies had come easy to her; she had studied manuals on child-rearing. She also turned her hand to horticulture, and a large corner of the garden had been cultivated to make the family self-sufficient in vegetables. She had baked bread enthusiastically, had woven and knitted. But this total involvement with creation had produced a traumatic and unexpected effect on her relationship with Peter. Originally they had seen eye to eye on most issues, but motherhood had changed Belinda; her concept of morality had grown radically different from her husband's.

The crunch had come five years ago when Belinda had grown bored and dissatisfied by her 'earth-mother' role and decided to find a job.

As he drank his tea, Peter could still sense the surprise he had felt when she had confronted him with this. What a fool he had been for not anticipating it. He had been away for a few days attending a conference, and had returned home to find her in a state of obvious agitation.

'Peter, we've got to talk,' she had announced while he was still hanging up his coat. There was a tremor in her voice.

'Why? What's happened?' he had answered instinctively. He feared some family catastrophe. The children were nowhere to be seen.

'Where are they all?'

'They're staying with friends for the night – I thought it best.'

'What are you on about, love?' he pressed, seizing her by the shoulders and peering anxiously into her hostile eyes.

Belinda had twisted herself from his grip.

'I can't go on like this anymore!' she had burst out theatrically, tears brimming. 'This lie! We're living a lie, don't you see?'

Stunned, he had followed her into the kitchen.

'Don't be so bloody melodramatic! What are you talking about?' He was tired and unready for a confrontation.

'You . . . your work . . . what you're doing at Aldermaston . . . it's wrong, it's criminal. It's immoral! You're planning genocide . . . mass murder. You spend your days working out how to do it. It's evil, don't you see?'

Peter then shook his head in disbelief. His work had never before been an issue between them. They had hardly ever discussed it.

'Don't be daft!' he had countered cautiously. 'You know bloody well that isn't true!'

His wife had clenched her fists in a gesture of controlled fury.

'Don't you tell me what I do or do not know to be true! I'm not one of your damned computers! You haven't programmed me, you know!' She began to shout. 'You've no idea what I think about most things – things that are really important.'

'And that's my fault?' he snapped back.

'Yes! . . . well, partly.'

She had been thrown for a moment, then continued.

'You gave up being interested in my views years ago. And I . . . well, I suppose I just kept them bottled up.'

He had stared at her blankly.

'Oh boy,' he finally breathed. 'What brought all this on? Have you joined CND or something?'

She glared at him defiantly.

'Yes. As a matter of fact I have.'

Then he had begun to pace round the kitchen.

'Okay, okay. Let's talk then. Let's get it over with. Firstly, let me make it clear that there's nothing immoral about my work. Everything I do is aimed at *preventing* people from killing one another – *stopping* them going to war. I . . . I'm not planning genocide, for God's sake!'

'I know that that's what you believe, Peter,' Belinda answered, controlling her voice with difficulty. 'But I am also very, very sure that you are wrong, terribly and fatally wrong. When a weapon gets invented, eventually it gets used. That, sadly, is human nature.'

'Except the nukes! For over forty years the world has had nuclear weapons and never used them!'

'Hiroshima?'

'It's because of Hiroshima that they've never been used since!' he had shouted in exasperation.

Belinda's shoulders slumped. Her eyes had filled with a great sadness.

'You're wrong, Peter.' Her voice trembled. 'One day, perhaps not very far in the future, mankind will prove that you're wrong. Millions will die, and you and people like you will be responsible.'

Her words had felt like a kick in the stomach.

Suddenly, though, her resolve had crumpled. She rushed towards him, flinging her arms around his neck and sobbing against his chest. For several minutes she clung to him, weeping uncontrollably.

Eventually her tears had subsided.

'I didn't want to hurt you, darling,' she stammered, strands of hair sticking to the tear-stains on her cheeks. 'I love you, you see. I love you as much as ever. Which is why it hurts so much to feel what I feel.'

She had begged him to change his job, to take up some other scientific work not involved with weaponry. But he had dismissed her appeal, and instead had sought to change her new-found attitude by reasoning – then by pouring scorn on her ideas.

But soon he realised that to be self-defeating. She was not susceptible to his arguments any more. A deep rift seemed to have opened up between them, and as the ensuing days passed he realised it was permanently to affect their relationship. Worse still, the lack of consensus on this fundamental issue had spawned disagreements on other subjects too.

They had nevertheless tried to be 'adult' about it, assuring one another there was no need for their relationship and their love to change just because of differing viewpoints That had not worked out either. Belinda had already set up for herself a job at a local craft workshop, learning to turn wood on a lathe. She had made friends there with a group of militant feminists deeply involved in radical anti-nuclear protest. The house had begun to fill with posters and books describing the horrors of Hiroshima and Nagasaki, and they had soon begun to argue over the effect this dispute would have on their children.

Peter was brought back to the present by the sound of car tyres on the drive, and the spluttering engine note of Belinda's ancient Citroën 2cv. He walked to the front door and saw that their eleven-year-old son Mark was sitting in the car with her. She must have called in for him at the sports-field on her way home.

'Just look at this creature,' she called to no one in particular as she entered the house, holding the boy at arm's length. 'The school showers have broken down again. Ever seen anything so disgusting?'

Peter could see the broad grin half-hidden by the mud on his son's face, a grin that seemed almost attached to his prominent ears. The blue and white football kit was caked with mire.

'Playing in goal again?' he asked.

''Sright. Only let one through, too,' Mark answered proudly, stripping off his clothes and dropping them on the kitchen floor.

'Straight into the bath with you,' his mother replied, pushing him towards the stairs.

Belinda walked past her husband and headed for a kitchen cupboard.

'Like one?' she asked over her shoulder, holding up a bottle of red wine.

'Why not,' he replied, taking two glasses down from a shelf.

Belinda found some peanuts in the larder and poured them into a bowl which she placed on the table.

'Why the special treats?' he asked with irony.

'Thought you might need them. I have a feeling you've had rather a busy day.'

His arm froze, halfway through lifting the glass to his lips. What did she know, and how did she know it?

'You were seen leaving the base in a very great hurry this morning,' she continued, smiling at his consternation. 'Looking rather anxious, according to witnesses.'

Her insistence in calling the research establishment 'the base' annoyed him intensely. It sounded so military.

'I thought your lot were all washing their smalls at that time of the day,' he countered. She raised an eyebrow warningly. 'I had to go to London at short notice,' he countered, wondering how much to tell her at this stage.

'Trouble at mill?' she asked flippantly.

'You could say that. Security scare. I, er . . . ought to warn you,' he went on hesitantly, 'that we may get some security people coming round here asking questions.'

Belinda stared at him in astonishment, a mouthful of wine unswallowed. She gulped hard, and placed her glass back on the table.

'What sort of security scare,' she questioned.

'Papers,' he answered vaguely. 'Seems as if someone has copied some classified papers and left them lying around.'

Belinda frowned. 'Is that serious? And what do you mean "lying around"? Where exactly?'

Peter hesitated. He was not supposed to discuss the matter.

'In a rubbish bin,' he stated flatly.

Belinda eyed him thoughtfully for a moment, then she began to laugh.

'It's not funny, love,' he growled.

'Oh, yes, it is,' she exploded. 'I've been telling you to put your work there for years!'

He stared at her forlornly. This woman for whom he still had so much affection, despite the distance that had grown between them, had no concept of the seriousness of the situation, no idea of the thunderstorm of unhappiness likely to burst over their heads at any minute. He agonised whether to tell her about Mary Maclean before she learned about his affair from someone else.

Belinda stopped laughing abruptly. Peter's face normally expressed a self-confidence bordering on cockiness, but there was no sign of that now. Instead she recognised an emotion she'd rarely seen there before. Fear.

'Can't you tell me more about it?' she asked with sudden concern.

'Not yet,' he replied firmly.

Anyone observing the MI5 man since he arrived at the Defence Ministry late that morning could have been forgiven for thinking that he did not seem to be reacting very quickly to the disastrous situation confronting the Strategic Nuclear Secretariat. Commander Duncan of the Ministry police had telephoned the Security Service as soon as that morning meeting in the Permanent Undersecretary's office had concluded. John Black had arrived within thirty minutes of the commander's call, and to Duncan's annoyance, had insisted on turning one of the senior secretaries in the police section out of her office so that he could use her desk and telephone.

It was as if Black was setting up camp, Duncan thought to himself as he watched the MI5 man unload the contents of his briefcase, including a plastic sandwich box, a vacuum flask and, most extraordinary of all, an ashtray.

'Can't stand those chipped-glass things the Civil Service provides,' Black explained.

His own had a porcelain base and a chromium-plated lid with a knob which, when pressed, spun the cigarette end out of sight.

'If I conceal the evidence I feel less bad about the amount I smoke,' he joked.

Duncan reckoned Black was in his late forties. He had a square, featureless face, greasy hair cut short at the back, and skin of the grubby grey colour and dead texture that characterises a heavy smoker. His eyes were contemptuous and mocking.

'How much have you uncovered so far, then?' John

Black demanded eventually, his lunch safely stowed away in a drawer.

The Commander was senior in age and rank to the MI5 man, but now felt more like a junior constable as he reported all that he knew of the affair and detailed the investigations he had already set in motion.

John Black was the head of a counter-espionage section at 'C' Branch in the Security Service, dealing with Government ministries. To his colleagues at the Curzon Street headquarters he appeared a bit of a loner and rather antisocial. A good investigator, they would concede, but he seldom drank at the pub after work or partook of the in-fighting that was normal life for MI5.

Recently, Black's reticence and secretiveness had even made him a suspect in an internal investigation at MI5. A defecting 'trade counsellor' from the Soviet Embassy in London had revealed the KGB had a highly placed agent in MI5. Circumstantial evidence had seemed to point to Black after three successive cases that he had been working on were broken by the Russians at an early stage. He had been suspended from duty for several weeks. Eventually Black's name had been cleared, however. A Russian double agent in Moscow had identified Black's own head of department as being in the pay of Moscow for over ten years. The affair had caused such political uproar that first the Home Secretary and then the Prime Minister had resigned.

Early that evening Black sat on his own in his office at the Defence Ministry. Most of the thousands who worked there daily had left for home. He inhaled deeply from a cigarette whose glowing end was nearly burning his fingers, savouring the bitterness of the smoke, and then ground the butt into the ashtray. As he slammed his palm down on the knob, the metal plate spun unevenly; the realisation that the bowl was nearly full caused him to wince.

The pocket notebook open in front of him had its pages half covered with untidy geometric patterns, subconsciously sketched as he had repeatedly pondered the circumstances of this curious case.

There was nothing normal about it; it did not have the 'feel' of a professional espionage operation. Yet for copies of the missile plans to have been made at all, it must have taken organisation and a treacherous intent, he concluded. But a rubbish bin? Why on earth did *one* page of the plans turn up in a rubbish bin? And what about the other pages? Why weren't they all together?

He had not been at all surprised when Duncan informed him that the Ministry policeman watching the spot on Parliament Hill had reported no sign of anyone subsequently searching there for the file. The vital clue that could crack this case did not lie out on the ground – of that Black was certain. It lay in someone's mind.

In a space still left between the angular shapes on his notebook page, John Black wrote the name 'Mary Maclean', and underlined it. The woman had been as white as a sheet when she was summoned into his office for an interview, and desperately contrite. She clearly expected instant dismissal from the Civil Service for her carelessness with the secret file keys. Mary Maclean had given every appearance of wanting to co-operate, he remembered, and yet her answers to his questions had seemed hesitant and incomplete. There was something she was holding back, of that he was certain. The woman had a secret, and he did not care for people with secrets.

Black took another pen from his inside jacket pocket. In ink of a different hue, he drew a frame round the name he had written, and then began to colour the letters, in such a way that the words 'Mary Maclean' cast a red shadow.

For Mary Maclean the click of the door closing firmly behind her in her garden flat in Chiswick was the most comforting sound she had heard all day. She leaned her head against the door in relief at being home, and snapped the lock shut, holding her finger against it for several minutes as if afraid it might slip open again. She swallowed hard and clenched her teeth against the tears she could feel welling up – tears of anger and self-pity.

Then pulling herself together, Mary Maclean headed for the kitchen. She reached up to the cupboard over the sink and took down a bottle of gin and then another of tonic. She was in a state of shock after the day's events, and was finding it hard to think clearly. She had felt like such a criminal to be interrogated first by Commander Duncan and then by that sinister security man, John Black.

Dropping an ice-cube into the full glass, she took it into the living room and collapsed on the small sofa facing the French windows. The leaves of the flowering cherry-tree outside were deep red and gold, and they were beginning to carpet the lawn. She loved her garden and could sit gazing at it for hours. The autumn colours were so beautiful, yet in a way she dreaded seeing them each year; they reminded her that time was passing and that she faced a lonely future.

'How could I have been so stupid?' she murmured bitterly.

Keeping that key in her desk drawer had seemed sensible enough at the time. She had dreaded losing it if she had carried it around with her as she was supposed to do. Carrying the key to the desk instead had seemed a lesser risk somehow. If she lost that, at least the secret papers would still be safe – or so she had reasoned.

The two policemen were clearly unimpressed by this logic, however, and had treated her with scorn and contempt. They had not actually accused her of stealing the documents, but had implied it was primarily her fault that someone else had been able to.

She had mixed her drink with almost as much gin as tonic, and now felt the alcohol spread its comforting relaxation through her limbs.

Mary Maclean was thirty-eight years old and had never married, though there had been a couple of opportunities when she could have done. Each time she had hesitated, unable to make the final commitment. The intensity of feeling she wanted had not been there. She longed for contact with men she could admire, forthright and intellectually dynamic, but those who actually approached her tended to be the opposite, looking to her to inspire and direct their lives.

She had a pleasant face, more attractive for its character than for outright beauty. Her brown hair had a natural wave, and she had concealed recent grey strands by judicious application of henna. Her grey eyes had a look of intelligent intensity which some men found appealing and others unnerving. She wore bright, plain colours and she would not stand out in a crowd, but then she never wanted to.

The beginning of her love affair with Peter Joyce had been totally unexpected. For several years she had known him only on an official basis, whenever he visited the Ministry for meetings. She had assumed he was already married, and had never particularly considered whether or not she found him attractive.

But then, two years ago, Peter was in Whitehall for a routine conference one afternoon when a sudden drivers' strike had paralysed the railways. He had come up to London by train, and in the chaos of the emergency the Ministry had no official car or driver spare to take him home. It was already late, and since he had to be in London again the following day, he had decided to find a cheap hotel for the night. By chance he had asked Mary to help him, and she had successfully found him one among those listed in the yellow pages. He thanked her profusely and was on the point of leaving her office when he turned back on impulse.

'Why don't you join me for dinner this evening?' he had asked hesitantly. 'I hate going to restaurants on my own.'

To her own surprise she had accepted immediately, and then became embarrassed by her eagerness.

They chose a busy little Italian restaurant in Bayswater. Inevitably their conversation had centred on common ground at first, the Ministry and its curious workings. He had been amusingly indiscreet about the way politicians could be manipulated by the technical departments, and she had found her own humour growing waspish as she talked of the odd personalities she encountered in her work. Their conversation had ranged widely after that. They had laughed a lot, and been reflective too. They had compared their upbringings, his in the steely clamour of Tyneside, hers in the quieter comforts of a London suburb. The food had been passable and they had been well into their second bottle of Valpolicella by the time the bill arrived.

It had still been daylight outside, on a fine summer's evening, and they had decided to go for a walk; their second bottle only half consumed, Peter had taken it with him, she remembered. Strolling along the railings by Hyde Park, Mary had burst out giggling.

'Just look at you with that bottle sticking out of your

pocket!' she had exclaimed. 'If you're not careful I'll ring the *Daily Mirror* and get them to come and take a picture of you. It'd look good on the front page with "Britain's Mr H-Bomb" beneath it!'

'But they'd brand you as a Russian spy!' he had countered, smiling.

She had slipped her arm through his, and before long they headed to his hotel to finish the wine. There had been just one glass in his room, so they shared it. It had been years since she had felt so at ease with a man.

'I want to make love to you,' he had said suddenly.

The hotel bedroom was cramped, and had smelled of stale pipe-smoke. She had blinked at him in momentary surprise.

'I . . . I think I'd like that.'

It had seemed as if her voice answered without her brain instructing it. His invitation had been so casual and so natural that it appeared simple, yet quite unlike her to agree so readily.

She had already known he was married – he had talked about his family during dinner – but on that evening such knowledge seemed no barrier. Normally she would never have considered such spontaneous intimacy with a man – particularly a married man. But somehow this had not felt like adultery; simply a natural conclusion to an extraordinarily pleasant evening.

It had not stayed so simple however. Perhaps it might have done if they had merely said goodbye the following morning, and returned to their previous official relationship across the desk in the Defence Ministry, but everything had been too good that evening for them not to want to repeat it.

Peter had arranged to stay in London again a few weeks later, and he contacted Mary discreetly a week in advance. On that second meeting she had asked him more about his wife. She had not intended to at first, but she felt she had to know more.

At first he had joked about his continuing disagreements with Belinda, and the irony of a nuclear weapons specialist being married to an ardent disarmer. Mary had seen behind the humour, though, and realised his marriage was in serious trouble. Instinct had told her to be cautious, but already she was in the grip of a sexual longing the strength of which she had never experienced before.

'Damn you, Peter!' Mary cursed in retrospect, tightly pinching the bridge of her nose to try to hold back the tears now relentlessly filling her eyes. 'It's all your fault!'

She picked up the glass from the coffee table and downed the rest of the gin.

'Oh hell!' she shouted out loud, tempted to hurl the glass across the room.

Three months had passed since he had told her their affair must end, but that still hurt. Feelings of hatred for him alternated with a passionate craving to win him back again. She had been trying to put it all behind her, but now she would not be allowed to. The investigators were starting to pry – and sexual indiscretion would attract them like bees to honey. Her affair with Peter had been so private and secret; now it would become public knowledge.

Mary clasped her arms tightly round her chest and shivered. She stared at the silent telephone, willing it to ring, willing it to be Peter at the other end.

Chapter Two

Following a day of acute anxiety, Sir Marcus Beckett had just fallen into an uneasy sleep at his Buckinghamshire home. The telephone woke him abruptly soon after midnight. His wife groaned and pulled a pillow over her ear.

'Great Middleton 2367,' he mumbled automatically into the mouthpiece.

'Sir Marcus?' came a crisp voice. 'Downing Street here.'

'Oh? Oh yes!' he answered, adrenalin pumping into his veins.

'I have the PM for you, sir. Just a moment,' the telephonist continued smoothly. There was a click and the sound of an extension ringing.

'Marcus? Are you awake?' a familiar voice bellowed into his ear.

'I am now,' he answered quietly, struggling to guess the significance of the call.

'What the hell's going on, Marcus? Have you seen the *Daily Express*?'

'We, er . . . we don't get the papers until morning out here, Prime Minister,' he winced, dreading what was to follow.

'H-bomb secrets in litter bin. Defence Ministry secrets probe! That's what the bloody thing says! First edition. All over the front page!' the head of the Government was yelling down the line.

Beckett guessed that a few whiskies had been consumed that evening before the early copies of the Fleet

Street papers had been delivered to Downing Street.

'Oh, dear God!' Sir Marcus groaned. 'How the hell did that get out?'

'More to the point, why the hell didn't I know about it?'

'I . . . I'd hoped it was a minor matter, a mistake . . . and could be cleared up without bothering you,' he explained lamely.

'Minor?' the PM shrieked even louder. 'Doesn't sound minor to me! Bloody retired general spouting his mouth off to the papers about how he found a diagram for the new missile warheads on Parliament Hill. You call that minor? What's the matter with you, Marcus?'

'General Twining talked to the press? I don't believe it!' Beckett gasped.

'Well, you'd better believe it, Marcus! So get your finger out of Doris's bum, and come over here right away!'

With that, the phone at the other end was slammed down. That man could be disgustingly crude at times, Beckett brooded to himself as he pulled on his clothes.

It was raining hard as he drove himself towards the capital. Normally he would be conveyed by a Ministry chauffeur, but there was no way of getting his driver to come round to collect him in the middle of the night at such short notice. He was driving his wife's rusty old Fiat, which he now realised had a decidedly worn exhaust. He would take some pleasure in driving it straight into Downing Street and parking right outside Number 10, something normally unheard of for private cars. He hoped the racket of the exhaust would wake up the whole of Westminster.

His mind had fully cleared now, and he had determined to counter the PM's anger with aggression. After all, he had been acting in his friend's best interest, trying to keep this business out of the political arena. The man should be grateful instead of downright rude, he thought.

'Good morning, Sir Marcus,' exclaimed the policeman at the Whitehall end of Downing Street, looking uneasily at the car the civil servant was driving. The officer had been warned to expect this late-night visitor, and reluctantly agreed that he could park outside Number 10, but not for too long. He winced at the throaty roar that proceeded on down the street.

In the event, two hours passed before Beckett emerged again, a chastened man. The Prime Minister had been totally unconvinced by the arguments for keeping him in the dark, and he was summoning a full-scale crisis meeting later that morning. It was nearly 4 a.m., and Sir Marcus decided there was no point in returning to his bed. The PM wanted to see all his top officials immediately after breakfast, so Beckett drove across Whitehall to the slab-sided building which controlled Britain's defences. He went straight up to his office on the sixth floor to prepare for the meeting. There were several phone calls he would have to make before long.

By 7.30 a.m. that same newspaper headline had also caused consternation at the Royal Navy's Headquarters at Northwood. Polaris missile submarines are sent their orders from inside a deep concrete bunker there, hidden in the leafy suburban hills north-west of London. The Commander-in-Chief of the Royal Navy Fleet read the *Daily Express* over his toast and marmalade, sitting at breakfast under the carefully restored

Adam ceiling of his elegant official residence a short distance from the command centre.

Scalding his mouth on coffee sipped too eagerly, he hurriedly scanned the rest of the paper, but found no other reference to the story.

The admiral was acutely concerned to know more, remembering that HMS *Retribution* was now approaching the final proving trials of the new Skydancer warheads. Rising from the table, he strode to his study to telephone the First Sea Lord at his official residence in Admiralty Arch overlooking the Mall.

'Good morning, First,' the C-in-C began. 'I hope I'm not disturbing your breakfast.'

'Don't worry,' Admiral Baker replied. 'Had my breakfast ages ago. Been up for hours. Got a morning call from Marcus Beckett at six o'clock. I suppose you're ringing about the same thing.'

'The story in the *Express* – I assume you've seen it?'

'Certainly have!' Admiral Baker confirmed. 'The PM is calling a crisis meeting at 9.30, so it looks serious. Whatever you do, don't let them go ahead with that test until you've found out how bad things are.'

The Royal Navy was extremely proud of its role as keeper of the British Strategic nuclear deterrent. If the weapon's secret new ability to penetrate the strengthened Soviet defences had been lost to the Russians, it could be like cutting off Samson's hair, the two admirals agreed. If that happened, the damaging effect on the Navy's status could be dramatic.

Precisely at half-past nine, eight men sat themselves down at the table in the Cabinet Room at 10 Downing Street. The angriest of them was Michael Hawke, the Secretary of State for Defence, who was clearly furious that his most senior civil servant had failed to inform him of such a monumental security breach. Hawke had entered politics late in life, and was fiercely ambitious. The fact that the Prime Minister had learned of this security leak before he had would not look good on his record.

The most unhappy man at the table was the Permanent Undersecretary himself, whose efforts to keep the politicians out of the investigation had failed so dismally.

They all stood up as the Prime Minister stormed in. It was the sort of formality he expected in his efforts to show that he was as tough and domineering as the woman who had preceded him in office.

Sir Richard Sproat, Director of MI5, was the first to be called on. Conscious of heading an organisation for which he was still struggling to regain public confidence, he looked uncomfortable as he admitted their investigations had made little progress.

'We have learned one thing,' he assured the meeting. 'The *Daily Express* got their story from some anonymous caller with a well-spoken voice. An English voice at that. He rang their defence correspondent. The quotes from General Twining were then elicited by a newspaper reporter posing on the telephone as someone from the Defence Ministry seeking clarification on precisely where the document had been found. The general was most indignant to find himself quoted all over the *Express* this morning, and he is demanding that the Government refer the matter to the Press Council.'

Most of those sitting around the table had felt themselves to be victims of the media at some stage in their careers, and there was a murmur of agreement.

'It's still far from clear what this security leak amounts to,' Sproat continued. 'Some or all of the plans for the new Polaris warheads have apparently been photocopied, and one page has mysteriously found its way in a Defence Ministry folder to a rubbish bin on Hampstead Heath. Now this may well have been a dead-letter box, and the handover to some foreign power may have been aborted by the tramp – we haven't traced him yet, by the way – and by the general taking his morning constitutional. We don't know that for sure – but there could well be some other explanation, too. We're putting out feelers both here and abroad to discover if the Soviets are really behind it, and whether or not they've already received other pages from the blueprint.'

'The point is this,' the Prime Minister broke in, aggravated by the lack of firm information, 'we *have* to assume the Russians have acquired the papers – all of them. It's simply not safe to assume anything else. And we've got to make plans to counter whatever advantage the Soviets might now have over us.'

The PM turned to study the faces of the other men present. The Home Secretary and the Foreign Secretary were there from his Government, joined by the head of MI6, the First Sea Lord, and the Chief of the Defence Staff. None of them, though, was fully qualified to assess exactly what was at risk in this affair.

'It's time to call in that chap we've got waiting outside,' the PM then announced. 'Would you mind, Marcus?'

Beckett crossed the room to the door and called down the corridor, 'Would you come in now, Mr Joyce?'

As he entered the room, Peter Joyce noticed a look combining both expectation and hostility on the faces of the various politicians. He knew they needed him to tell them precisely what was what – since they were ignorant of the technology – but that they resented the power that his knowledge now gave him. He quietly took the spare chair that Beckett gestured him towards.

'Now then, Mr Joyce,' the Prime Minister continued, 'we need your technical expertise so that we can judge the seriousness of this affair. Would you be so good as to explain, in the simplest terms possible, just what the stolen plans revealed. And please remember that most of us in this room are laymen when it comes to the business of ballistic missiles.'

Peter stood up so that he could get a clearer view of the nine other men around the table. He looked from one face to the next, to see who he recognised. Despite what the PM had just said, four of the men were from the Defence Ministry, so had already been briefed on the project. The security men were the only ones unfamiliar to him.

'Well, gentlemen, as you know, the document found on Parliament Hill was part of the secret plans for Skydancer,' he began. 'Perhaps the first thing I should do is remind you why Skydancer was set up to start with. About five years ago, the Soviet Union began to spend a great deal of extra money on Ballistic Missile Defence – literally defences against incoming ballistic missiles. The Americans had already launched their own BMD programme, the Strategic Defence Initiative, the one the media called Star Wars, and, as you will remember, the 1972 ABM treaty between the two countries, which had limited BMD systems, rather fell by the wayside as a result of the technical advances being made.

'We in Britain were faced with a dilemma. We were investing ten billion pounds in the Trident system to replace Polaris, but suddenly faced the danger that the new Soviet Defences might make Trident obsolete early in the next century, only giving us a few years use of it as an invulnerable deterrent. As a nation, Britain cannot really afford defences against Russian missiles, so not only could we not defend ourselves against nuclear attack; we soon wouldn't have been able to deter one either.

'Well, faced with all this, the Government, as you remember, took a crucial three-pronged decision. The first factor was to cancel Trident as being a waste of money. The second was to launch a new investigation into what form of nuclear deterrence might still be feasible in the twenty-first century. And the third – and this is where I came in – was to instruct Aldermaston to make further modifications to the old Polaris missiles to enable them to penetrate Soviet defences for the next decade or so. And to do that as cheaply as possible.'

Michael Hawke glanced at his ministerial colleagues and winced, knowing full well that Skydancer had been anything but cheap. The expenditure of hundreds of millions of pounds on the project had been the source of constant complaint from other ministers in the Cabinet.

'So we set up the Skydancer programme,' Joyce continued firmly, 'to design and build a new front end for the Polaris rockets, which would be clever enough to get through the Russian defences.'

'I think we all know the history bit, Mr Joyce,' the Prime Minister interjected impatiently. 'Perhaps you would get to the point now. What we want to know is how much of the project may have been compromised.'

Peter turned to the PM and nodded. He smoothed back his hair and continued.

'Very well, then. The Russian defences consist of a mixture of technologies, both missiles and high-powered lasers. The key to those defences lies not in the weapons themselves, but in the radar and electro-optical detection systems used to spot the incoming missile warheads, and to track them accurately so that the defending weapons can attack them. Our task with Skydancer was to devise new gadgets that would deceive, blind or mislead those Russian detection systems.'

He paused to scan the faces of his audience, to see if they were still following him.

'Skydancer itself is what we call a "space-bus", something that sits on the front end of the missile and separates from the rocket part after it's been launched from the submarine and gets outside the earth's atmosphere. This "bus" can manoeuvre in space and change course in a way which makes its future path difficult for observers on the ground to predict, hence its name "Skydancer".

'Now, into that "bus" fit the re-entry vehicles, the six objects that will eventually plummet down from space towards the target on the ground. Some of those RVs are warheads with nuclear bombs inside them, but the others carry an assortment of electronic and mechanical devices designed to help make the warheads themselves "invisible" to the scanners on the ground. Once released from the space-bus, those re-entry vehicles are in free fall; they just drop straight down. So, as you can imagine, the accuracy of the weapon depends entirely on the position and attitude of the space-bus when the RVs are ejected from it. And the plans that seem to have been stolen describe with mathematical precision the pattern for the ejection of those RVs.'

He paused there and waited to see if there were any questions.

It was the Home Secretary who was the first to speak. He harboured a deep suspicion of scientists in the defence industries, always suspecting them of inventing new problems in an effort to suck more money out of the public purse for their projects. He half suspected the Aldermaston men of setting up this whole spy scare for their own ends.

'Are you trying to tell us, Mr Joyce,' he whined sarcastically, 'that all these clever inventions of yours have suddenly become worthless – if the Russians have learned how your bus scatters its goodies over the earth?' He glared at the scientist with the icy stare he had perfected during years of withering interrogation of civil servants.

'No, I'm not saying that, Home Secretary,' Peter Joyce replied. 'It's not that easy. The problem is this. Suppose one of our missiles is fired at Moscow; the observers manning the Soviet defences round the city would see four objects falling very rapidly out of the sky towards them. Only there wouldn't be four objects, in fact. There would be six, but two would be invisible, do you follow? So the Russians would most probably attack those four "warheads" and destroy them; but seconds later the two real bombs would have detonated and flattened most of Moscow.'

The Home Secretary's brow knitted in a frown.

'So,' Joyce continued, 'if the Russians know how many objects they should be seeing, and know the exact pattern in which they started their journey downwards from space, they might just be able to do some very clever calculations. With a high-powered computer they could feed in the positions and the trajectories of the objects they *can* see, and calculate the exact positions of the ones they *can't*.'

He could sense that his message had struck home painfully.

'And if they can calculate where the bombs are, they can shoot them down even if they can't actually see them?' the Prime Minister asked incredulously.

Peter Joyce nodded uncomfortably. 'It *is* possible, Prime Minister,' he conceded.

'Good God!' the First Sea Lord muttered under his breath. Admiral Barker had a sudden vision of his prized new weapon, designed to keep the Royal Navy's proudly-held nuclear deterrent viable, being humiliatingly still-born.

'And if the Russians believe they can defeat our nuclear deterrent,' the Prime Minister continued, still thinking through the implications of what he had been told, 'then it won't be a deterrent any more. It won't stop them launching a nuclear attack on us if they feel like it.'

'And it'll be a complete waste of hundreds of millions of pounds of tax-payers' money,' the Home Secretary grunted. The political implications of that would not be lost on the Prime Minister.

'Now, look here,' intervened Field-Marshal Buxton, the Chief of the Defence Staff, annoyed at the panic around the table and the paranoia of his naval subordinate, who appeared to fear most the loss of a role and the consequent diminution of his own service. 'You're assuming one hell of a lot from the Russians, Mr Joyce. If they did decide to develop a counter to Skydancer, it would cost them a packet, wouldn't it?'

'Well, it wouldn't be cheap,' Peter conceded.

'And they're already up to their eyes in financial problems, building the BMD system to defend against the older missiles, so they'd have to be pretty certain they could beat our new warheads before they decided to spend the money on it.'

'You could be right,' the scientist nodded.

'So, what are you saying, Field-Marshal?' the Prime Minister interjected. 'You think we should forget all about it?'

'Certainly not, Prime Minister. What I'm saying is

that the Russians would need to be convinced that the Skydancer plans they have, if they have them at all, are the right ones. Before they pour money into new computer systems, they'd need to be certain that the problem the computer is intended to solve is the right problem, if you get me.'

'In other words,' Peter Joyce chipped in, 'if we could persuade them that they've been sold a pup, that the plans are fakes, then they wouldn't be prepared to waste their money.'

'Precisely. Ivan's so short of the readies at the moment, he's only going to want to bet on certainties,' Buxton concluded with a smile.

'Aah!' the Prime Minister exclaimed, slamming the flat of his palm down on the table. 'Now we have the makings of a plan, I think. How about some counter-intelligence, Dick?'

Sir Richard Sproat stroked his chin uneasily. 'Well, I'm not so sure. It seems a bit early to launch into that sort of game,' he cautioned. 'I mean, at this stage we don't even know if the Russians are involved, let alone whether or not they've actually got hold of the plans.'

'I tend to agree with Dick,' the MI6 chief added. 'But if we do set something up, it should be too difficult to sow doubts about the stolen papers in the appropriate quarters, when the right moment comes along.'

'I've had a thought,' Peter Joyce announced. 'The first test of the Skydancer warheads is due to take place a few days from now. The Russians will be watching that trial shot very closely indeed from their spyships and satellites. If they do have the plans, they'll be trying to check that the re-entry vehicles behave as the blueprint says they should.'

'Ah, yes,' the CDS muttered, guessing at what was about to be suggested.

'Now, it is possible to re-programme the missile, to get the space-bus to do something that utterly contradicts the description in the drawings. It would pretty well invalidate the test for us from a scientific point of view, but it would also certainly confuse them in Moscow,' he concluded with the hint of a smile.

'But how would you ever be able to test the thing properly, without giving the game away?' Michael Hawke demanded.

'That could be a problem,' Peter conceded, thinking hard. 'But if its main purpose is to deter, rather than to be used as a weapon, what matters most is that the Russians should be convinced the missile works properly. So as long as we express confidence and satisfaction with Skydancer, even if it's never fully tested, that might be enough.'

There was a snort of derision from the Home Secretary. 'And a bloody convenient way of avoiding being held to account if the thing's a flop,' he muttered.

'Don't you think we should just wait for a while, until we know if the Russians have got those papers?' Sproat persisted with his caution.

'We may never know that for certain, judging by the past performance of our intelligence operations,' the Prime Minister countered bitterly, remembering how his predecessor in Downing Street had finally lost the post he now held. 'No. We must assume the worst case,' he continued, 'and I suggest that Mr Joyce should make immediate moves to set his deception plan in motion. All agreed?'

The intelligence men shrugged their shoulders. In the face of the concurrence of the politicians with their leader, there was no more they could say.

The Prime Minister then insisted that Joyce's mission should be kept a total secret. No one outside that room should learn about it unless it became absolutely essential.

As the meeting broke up, Peter Joyce took Field-Marshal Buxton to one side.

'Look, I could be ready to move this afternoon if I really work at it,' he confided. 'If you can fix me a plane, I could fly over to Florida and do most of the work during the journey. Should have everything ready by the time I get on board *Retribution.* I'd need to take an assistant with me, and we'd want a power supply for our portable computers.'

'You're on,' Buxton agreed. 'I'll get Brize Norton to provide the flight. The sooner we get this moving, the better.'

Peter hurried out through the front door of Number 10, and into the back seat of the official car that had brought him to London earlier that morning. There was much to do if he was to keep the deadline he had set himself.

As his uniformed driver sped down the motorway towards Aldermaston, Peter began to consider the enormity of the task ahead. He was certain that the deception plan he had described at the meeting was indeed possible, but exactly how to carry it out was another matter.

He closed his eyes to concentrate, and his mind's eye began slowly to focus on a face. The square-jowled features were a composite, belonging to a man whose name he did not know, but a man of whose existence he was certain. He had often focused on this face in the past, whenever he needed some encouragement to overcome seemingly impossible difficulties. He thought of the face simply as 'the Russian'.

The primary motivation behind his work at Aldermaston had been to outfox 'the Russian'. With a combination of information from intelligence sources and guesswork based on an understanding of the way he expected 'the Russian' to think, Peter had calculated what Skydancer would need to be able to overcome the new Soviet defences around Moscow. To him it was an exercise in scientific theory rather than a plan for fighting a war; he well understood the disaster that would ensue if the weapons were ever used in anger, and he was convinced 'the Russian' did too. He likened his work to a game of chess, calculating how to avoid the traps his opponent had set for him. Now, however, he was facing an additional problem. 'The Russian' seemed to be cheating.

He had met several Russians in the flesh at international conferences on such 'non-military' subjects as computer technology. Many of those attending were in fact military scientists looking to learn something from their competitors. Scientists from the West were usually open about the nature of their employment; the Soviets were not, disguising many of their top weapon designers behind academic titles. It gave them a certain advantage.

Peter felt certain that some Soviet scientist he had already met must be the man behind the new batteries of defences round Moscow; and that the man whose skills he believed he had beaten with Skydancer was now seeking to gain an advantage, to achieve by theft what he could not through his own skill. He did not know the Russian's identity, of course, but he was determined not to let him win.

Even though his Ministry was only a few minutes' walk from Downing Street, Michael Hawke climbed into the back seat of his official Jaguar when he left Number 10, and allowed himself to be driven the short distance back to his office across Whitehall. As a vociferous proponent of Britain's nuclear might, the Defence Secretary was a potential target for attack from some of the more violent anti-nuclear groups, and the police insisted he should be driven wherever he went.

Before leaving Downing Street he had secured a quiet word with the Prime Minister, eager to ensure that the blame for failure to inform the PM of this spy scandal the previous day was laid firmly at the feet of his Permanent Undersecretary, Sir Marcus Beckett, and that none of it would stick to him personally. It had been a tricky conversation on two accounts: Beckett was a personal friend of the PM, and he himself was strongly disliked by his chief. It seemed to have gone all right though: he was assured that Sir Marcus had been given a thorough roasting for his misdemeanour.

Back in his sixth-floor office, he stood for a moment behind the antique mahogany desk at which innumerable defence reviews had been planned. Waiting for his attention was a fat folder labelled 'Long-term Costings'. The Ministry had a ten-year rolling plan for expenditure, which was constantly updated and adjusted to cope with the delays and cost-overruns which seemed endemic to weapons production. There were key decisions to be taken over which programmes they should axe to keep within budget, and until that morning this task had seemed likely to absorb all his time for the next few days. This secrets scare would change all that, he reflected.

Behind the thick stone walls of the GRU headquarters in Moscow's Znamesky Street, General Novikov was betraying signs of unease. The normally poker-faced head of the military intelligence-gathering network had just replaced one of his four telephones on its rest – the one that linked him directly with his civilian counterpart, the KGB.

The news from London was alarming. For an operation to appear to have become unstuck, almost before it had begun, was an embarrassment that was hard to conceal. The GRU worked in collaboration with the KGB, but since the intelligence to be gathered in Britain was purely military in nature, the operatives were under his control. There was a long history of rivalry between the two organisations, and the KGB never lost an opportunity to launch sniping criticism at its military counterpart.

The problem for Novikov was that he had heard nothing from his operatives in London. He remained optimistic that the blueprints would soon be in Moscow. But the KGB had been demanding clarification, and he had no idea when he would be able to provide it.

He was well aware how important those British missile plans were. The air defence forces, the PVO, had just spent billions of roubles modernising their rocket systems to defend against ballistic missiles, and wanted reassurance that their money had not been wasted. Also the Department of Military Sciences, which was continually devising measures to counter the enemy's countermeasures, was desperate to learn of the latest twist added to the spiral.

One man in particular had applied acute pressure on the intelligence services to find out what the British were up to – a man whose true role in Soviet life was known to only the most senior personnel in the military and intelligence communities.

*

Across the other side of Moscow, Oleg Kvitzinsky had just arrived home. The small name-plate on the door of his apartment described him as a professor of mathematics, which his neighbours believed him to be. He was a tall, burly man in his late forties, with straight, rather lank hair held in place by a light coating of oil.

'Katrina?' he called out as he headed for the bedroom of his apartment, which was spacious by Moscow standards. His wife had decorated it in styles she had selected from the shops or copied from the magazines of Europe and America.

There was no reply, and he guessed she must be visiting a friend in a neighbouring apartment in their block, which was reserved for the administrative elite of the Communist state. The women always had plenty to talk about; they lived in the small, self-protective circle of privilege at the top of Soviet society, with its own services and shops, where there were no queues and virtually no shortages. At their level, the men were usually free to travel abroad with their wives, and they did so at every opportunity, returning to Moscow laden with possessions that most of their fellow countrymen could never dream of owning.

The large Japanese transistor radio which Kvitzinsky now switched on in the bedroom was one such object. He had obtained it in America as being the most refined and sensitive radio that money could buy. He spun the dial until the needle reached a familiar resting point: the BBC World Service. He looked at his Swiss watch, and smiled at the good fortune of his timing. He had not heard any news that day, and the London bulletin would begin in precisely one minute.

He hummed to himself as the familiar signature tune blared through the apartment – but the news headlines soon wiped the smile from his lips. For the third item mentioned was the discovery of an apparent attempt to steal British nuclear missile secrets.

'It can't be true!' he howled.

Impatiently he paced the room, waiting for the full details to be read out.

'The idiots!' he hissed, when the newsreader had finished. 'They can't have fouled that up so soon!'

Angrily he turned off the radio and marched into the living-room with its fine view over the Moskva River. He poured himself a glass of vodka and drank it quickly. Then, shuddering at the oily warmth of the liquid, he filled the glass again and took it into the kitchen to lace it with ice.

Staring out through the picture window at the city, Kvitzinsky reminded himself of what was at stake. In his hands lay the responsibility for the protection of Moscow if there should be a nuclear war – at least that was more or less how the Military Committee had put it when they appointed him. As chief scientist for the Ballistic Missile Defence modernisation programme, it was his special responsibility to ensure that the technology of their defences could match that of the missiles aimed at them.

Trying to stop any small nuclear warhead hurtling out of the sky at thousands of miles per hour was a brainstorming problem. The idea of defending an area the size of the Soviet Union against such an attack was nonsense. What mattered to the leaders in the Kremlin, however, was that Moscow itself should never be destroyed. Without its capital, the nation would cease to exist, they believed. It was for that reason, when the first Russian anti-ballistic missiles were built in the 1960s, they were concentrated in a ring round the city.

Until a few years ago, those ABMs all carried nuclear warheads. If the city was attacked, these would have been fired into space and detonated in the path of the enemy rockets, hoping to destroy the incoming warheads through blast and radiation, even from a considerable distance. Accuracy had not been so easy to attain in those days; Kvitzinsky had thought of it as trying to crack a nut with a hand-grenade, and feared that much of Moscow could be destroyed by the defences themselves.

New technology had changed all that, though. New radars and infra-red detectors had made it easier to pinpoint and track objects in space, so that new super-accurate missiles and ground-based lasers could destroy attacking warheads individually and with great precision.

But to every measure there was a counter-measure, as Kvitzinsky knew well. The new American approach would be to saturate the defences round Moscow – to fire so many missiles at the city that eventually all the defences would be exhausted. An ever-increasing expansion of the number of defences was the only effective answer to that.

With the British it was a different matter. They could not afford the massive numbers of weapons the Americans possessed, and had resorted to guile to achieve their aims. With a nuclear force of just sixty-four missiles, Kvitzinsky knew that the British had one main target in mind, the capital itself.

The British scientists at Aldermaston had been assiduous in their efforts to ensure their Polaris H-bombs would be able to penetrate Moscow's defensive ring. At the end of the 1970s they had started an improvement programme called 'Chevaline', hardening the Polaris warheads so that they could withstand the blast and radiation effects of Moscow's nuclear-tipped ABMs. Chevaline also involved the firing of several missiles in rapid succession so that their warheads and decoys would arrive over the target at the same time, causing the maximum of confusion and difficulty for the Soviet defences.

At the end of the 1980s, Chevaline's potential effectiveness had been almost negated by the Soviet introduction of new radars and infra-red detectors, and a massive increase in the number of defensive missiles round Moscow.

Inevitably, the game had not ended there. The British had decided to follow the American lead and go for massive numbers of warheads. The Trident system was to be bought, with eight bombs per missile. Moscow had resigned itself to expanding its defences yet further.

But suddenly, two years ago, the British had changed their minds again. They had cancelled their expensive Trident plans, and resorted to guile once again.

'Skydancer!' Kvitzinsky spat out the English word. He had to know what tricks of technology the British had invented this time, tricks the Military Committee had designated him to counter.

Standing by the window, hands deep in his pockets, he looked across the roofs of Moscow to the onion domes of the Kremlin in the distance. There had been snow flurries earlier in the day, and he saw that it was now beginning to rain.

It would be raining in London, too, he guessed. He had visited the British capital several times and liked his stays there. It was an unprotected city, though, he mused: if there was a nuclear war, London would have no means of stopping Soviet missiles raining down to destroy it. Curious, he thought: the British talked with vague optimism about surviving a nuclear war, yet they made no effort to protect their centre of power.

'Perhaps they are right,' he murmured. 'Perhaps protection is indeed a waste of time.'

He tossed back the remains of the vodka. This would not do: those were negative thoughts. His orders were to keep Moscow safe. The trouble was that to learn how to do it, he needed those people in London to get him the Skydancer plans, and in that they seemed to be failing.

The day in Britain was three hours younger than in Moscow; and in Florida, where the big grey RAF VC10 jet was now heading, it was five hours earlier still. As the aircraft strained upwards into the clouds over the wet grasslands of Oxfordshire, Peter Joyce breathed in deeply, eager for the seat-belt sign to be switched off so that he could press on with his work.

He sat in an executive section of the cabin: two pairs of deeply padded seats facing each other, and a large table top between them. Opposite him sat a young woman with curly blonde hair and brown eyes. Her pretty face was turned towards the window, and she made no effort to conceal her excitement as she peered through the window.

'Ever been to America before, Jill?' Peter asked.

He did not know the girl well but had been assured she was one of the best computer programmers at Aldermaston.

'I've never even flown in an aeroplane before!' she confided, blushing with embarrassment.

'What? Never even been to Majorca?' he joked.

She shook her head. 'I'm an outdoor girl. I prefer hill-climbing to lying on a beach.' Her accent was broad Yorkshire.

'Well, there won't be time for anything like that

where we're going. I'm sorry to say.'

As the aircraft began to level out, Peter looked up and saw the sign was finally off. As he unclipped his seat-belt and stood up, a steward came forward from his place near the rear galley.

'The flight engineer's laid on a power supply for you from a socket in the galley, sir,' the man announced, glancing at the girl and wondering where these scientists were from. He had been told their mission was secret.

'Would you like me to bring the cable along right away?'

'Yes, please,' Joyce replied. 'Then perhaps you could give us a hand with these.' He pointed across the aisle to where the components of two microcomputers had been carefully strapped in to protect them from the jolting of the takeoff.

They lifted the heavy boxes and placed them on the table, plugging in the leads that linked the components together. The flight engineer had reappeared from the cockpit by the time the steward had uncoiled the cable from the galley, and he supervised the final connection of the equipment.

'Do you have everything you need now?' the engineer enquired, standing back and looking with satisfaction at the green glow emanating from the VDUs.

'Yes, thank you,' Joyce replied. He could see curiosity on the RAF men's faces, but he wanted them out of the way. 'We'll press the call button if we want anything.'

The engineer and steward returned to their posts.

Peter drew across the blue curtain which shut off each end of their 'suite' from the rest of the aircraft.

'Right, Jill. Now with luck we won't be disturbed.'

They sat down opposite one another at their

keyboards. Peter fumbled in a jacket pocket for the spectacles he wore for reading, and placed the tortoise-shell half-moon frames on the end of his nose. They gave him a somewhat bookish appearance, slightly at odds with his square features.

'I finalised the parameters in the car on my way to Brize Norton,' he declared, passing a sheet of paper across the table to his junior. 'It's only a compromise. We could have made Skydancer turn cartwheels, and that would really upset Moscow; but we can't be too clever or they'll realise it's an expensive leg-pull. I think I've got it right,' he continued, pointing to the paper which the girl was now studying. 'But if you don't think so, for God's sake say so now. If you can work on the programme for the manoeuvring, I'll get on with the ejection routine.'

The operation of the missile was controlled by computer software; a variety of programmes could be selected, containing subtle differences to enable the warheads to cope with both short and long ranges. Completely changing the character of the missile would require a massive rewriting of the programmes, to be fed into the missile's control system when they went on board the submarine in Florida.

Peter could not help feeling apprehensive about what he was doing. Having spent most of the past two years refining and perfecting a complex electro-mechanical device, he was now about to sabotage its first operational test. Instead of demonstrating to himself and the keepers of the public purse that the money had been well spent, he was about to obfuscate the issue, possibly for ever.

Sitting in that aircraft, with the blinds drawn so the afternoon sun would not reflect from the computer screens, Peter found it difficult to get started. An image of 'the Russian' was firmly fixed in one corner of his brain, as if the man was peering over his shoulder at the keyboard. The face of Mary Maclean filled another corner, provoking in him a deep sense of guilt.

At the end of his second full day of enquiries into the nuclear secrets case, John Black had decided the whole business stank. British agents in Moscow had not been able to detect any KGB or GRU activity over the missile plans; and GCHQ had not intercepted a single communication between the Soviet Embassy and Moscow that seemed to relate to it. Nothing but routine reporting back to the Kremlin on what the newspapers were saying.

Yet somebody was definitely up to something, that much was clear. It either meant the Russians were being unusually cunning, and exceptionally clever at concealing their activities, or else that all this had nothing to do with Moscow at all. He had a strong suspicion that the missile document had been deliberately dumped in that rubbish bin for the express purpose of being found. Some mysterious person had certainly made sure that the world got to know about it by tipping off the *Daily Express*.

Thanks to the carelessness of Mary Maclean in leaving that vital key in her desk drawer, up to about thirty people within the Defence Ministry with access to the secrets room could have 'borrowed' her key to the nuclear weapons filing-cabinet, and copied those papers. If he had to check all thirty of them, it would make his investigation long and tedious, but he somehow felt that would not be necessary. His instinct told him that the culprit was someone who knew precisely what the papers were about – and what a stir it would cause if one of them was found in the wrong place.

On his desk lay the personal security files of three people. The one he had been studying for the past few minutes referred to Mr Peter Joyce. He could see that the scientist had had an impeccable career pattern. The report on his family life looked unremarkable too, except perhaps for a small admission at his last positive vetting, when he volunteered that his wife had become a supporter of the Campaign for Nuclear Disarmament.

On the surface this looked innocent enough: CND was a perfectly legitimate organ of protest, and there was nothing unusual about husbands and wives having differences of opinion over such sensitive issues. But the timing was curious; his admission about the wife's membership of CND had first been made three years ago. John Black had now learned it was just one year later that Peter Joyce had begun an adulterous affair with Mary Maclean. There was no mention of *that* liaison in the security file, and there damn well should have been. The sequence of events intrigued him. First the scientist's wife turns against the work he is doing, then the scientist takes up with another woman - events which could well be the tip of an iceberg of stress, intrigue and blackmailable goings-on that spelled SECURITY RISK in large letters.

The positive vetting system to which all officials in sensitive posts were regularly subjected was something of a joke as far as Black was concerned. Successive governments had been so nervous about 'invasions of privacy' or 'infringing the civil rights of the individual' that a vetting procedure had been allowed to continue whereby individuals were able to nominate their own referees, and security-clearance officers had no power to make inquiries of other people. Over the years the system had allowed the concealment of countless personal weaknesses and misdemeanours which had then been exploited to great effect by KGB blackmail and bribery. In John Black's view, people in high-security positions should be subjected to regular investigation with the same intensity as suspected criminals.

He pushed back his chair, stretched out his arms, and let out a muted belch. The Defence Ministry office which he had occupied for the past two days was beginning to depress him. The walls were a dirty cream colour and seemed designed to induce sleep in the most wakeful of civil servants. He would move back to his own office in Curzon Street the next day, he decided, squeezing the square flabbiness of his chin. He had time for one more cigarette before he set out for his evening visit.

It was Alec Anderson who had tipped him off about Peter Joyce and Mary Maclean. The man had pretended to find it awkward and embarrassing to discuss the subject, but had found it his duty to mention it under the present circumstances. Black had detected a distinctly vicarious flicker in Anderson's eyes; the man must have been quite a sneak at school, he decided.

Anderson's own file had revealed nothing out of the ordinary. He had lived in the same house for seven years, regularly ran up a modest overdraft, but had never defaulted on his debts or been involved with the police except for a parking offence three years earlier. The referees he had nominated during the vetting process had all spoken of him in glowing terms. He seemed a typical civil servant on the way up, well educated, alert and efficient, happily married with a devoted wife and two children in private schools. Yet the man from MI5 was suspicious by nature, always on the look-out for dark secrets behind the facade of normality.

He had given Anderson quite a grilling that afternoon, starting gently by taking him through all he could remember about the secret documents, from the moment they had first arrived in his department for the Ministerial briefing three months earlier. He asked precisely who had been shown the papers since then, and how often they had been removed from safe-keeping to be studied. Anderson claimed he had never looked at the papers since their first arrival, finding the technical details difficult to comprehend.

Then Black had turned to personal matters, questioning the civil servant about his normal routine, who his friends were, how often he went out, what was the state of his marriage, and so on. On those questions he had found Anderson less than satisfactory, but then he had not expected anything else from someone so stereotyped. The man's somewhat chubby features had twisted themselves into an expression of indignation at the intimate nature of these enquiries. His eyes had seemed occasionally to cower behind the lenses of his spectacles, but the trace of perspiration that broke out on his brow could have indicated simple nervousness rather than any effort at concealment.

When the interview had ended, Black continued to watch his subject closely as he stood up to leave the room. Anderson was tall with an unathletic gait. His dark hair was greying at the temples; there was a slight ruddiness to the cheeks and a somewhat bibulous mouth.

Mary Maclean scraped the edge of the record as she aimed the gramophone needle for the groove. The wine she had been drinking since she returned home had unsteadied her hand. Her second attempt was more successful, and within moments the crackling from the loudspeakers had given way to the opening choral blasts of *Carmina Burana.* She wanted the intensity of Carl Orff's work to blow the dark thoughts from her mind like a March wind.

She had just been watching the BBC nine o'clock news with its report on the Prime Minister's statement to Parliament, in which he had insisted there was no evidence yet of any loss of vital secrets following the discovery of the document on Parliament Hill two days earlier. The opposition parties had howled derisively, believing themselves on the scent of a security scandal as had helped unseat the current Prime Minister's predecessor.

Mary's day at the Ministry had been long and painful. Wherever she went in the rectangular labyrinth, she imagined once-friendly eyes staring after her with curiosity and suspicion. No one referred directly to what they had all read in the paper that morning, not wanting her to think they were putting blame on her. But Mary felt accused by their very silence.

The music reverberating round the apartment began to work its usual therapy. Mary felt herself start to unwind.

Suddenly the rapping of the door knocker startled her. From the small sofa she stared fearfully at the door, as if trying to peer through it and see who was there.

It was probably that nosey old bat who lived at the front of the house, Mary thought. Come to complain about the loudness of the music, no doubt. Mary turned down the volume before peeping through the spyhole in the door. But it was not her neighbour; it was John Black. She opened the door on the security-chain.

'I'm sorry to disturb you, Ms Maclean,' he smiled through the narrow gap.

To her the way he used the term 'Ms' always sounded offensive, as if he was mocking her unmarried status.

'I wonder if you would let me in. I have some important new questions to put to you.'

It was more of a demand than a request, and she slipped the chain from its runner and opened the door fully.

'I don't know what more I can tell you, Mr Black,' she began uneasily, leading him in. 'Nothing that's relevant anyway.'

The investigator settled his heavy frame into an armchair and smiled in a manner calculated to be reassuring but which managed instead to be both patronising and belittling. His eyes focused on hers with disconcerting steadiness.

'Do you mind if I call you Mary? It's so much easier, and I'd prefer our conversation to be informal.' He raised his eyebrows inquiringly.

Mary shrugged in reply. She did not consider she had any choice in the matter.

'My first name is John, but you can call me whatever you want,' he continued with a self-deprecating smile. 'Yes. You said *relevant*. That's a very *relative* word, don't you think?' He chuckled at his own attempt at word play.

'I mean, what *you* as an ordinary citizen consider relevant, and what *I* do, as an investigator into a crime which in wartime would be a capital offence, those are of course two completely different things, don't you think so, Mary?' He stopped, with his eyebrows raised again, as if insisting on a reply.

'I, er . . . I'm sure you're right,' she replied, determined not to be seduced into an informality which could lead to her dropping her guard. The man was spinning a web in her path, the threads of which she needed to keep in focus.

'I mean, let's just take an example,' he continued, looking theatrically round the room and then settling his eyes on the glass still clasped in her right hand. 'Well, for example, I happen to notice that you have a half-consumed glass of red wine in your right hand. Now . . .'

'Oh, I'm sorry. Would you like . . .' Mary cut in, but he dismissed her offer with a wave of an arm.

'No, thank you. But take that glass, for example. Now you would say, I feel sure, that it has no relevance to my inquiries at all.'

He leaned forward in his chair, like a school-teacher trying to ensure that his class was following his argument.

'But I have to ask myself, how often does she have a glass of wine? How many glasses a day? What else does she drink? Whisky? Gin?' He paused for a second in his rapid flow.

'Vodka perhaps? And when she drinks, does she start to talk about things to strangers? Secret things, personal things. Does she expose those little skeletons in the cupboard, which when she's sober she keeps firmly locked away? Give away secret documents even?'

'That's preposterous!' she burst out in indignation.

'Of course, it is. Of course, it's preposterous,' Black replied softly, sitting back in the armchair and clasping his hands over his broad stomach. He smiled at her almost benignly. 'But I have to ask these questions. I have to think of outrageous motives for people who are caught up on the fringes of espionage, and see if they just happen to fit. It's not a part of my job that I enjoy,

Mary, and that's why I've come round here tonight to ask for your help. Would you like a cigarette?'

He pulled a packet from his pocket, flipped back the lid and held it out towards her.

She shook her head, allowing a flicker of distaste to cross her face. 'I don't, thank you,' she answered crisply.

'Do you mind if I smoke?'

'Well . . . I,' she hesitated.

'You do mind. I can see that. And of course you're absolutely right. It's a filthy habit.' He put the packet carefully back in his pocket.

'But have I made my point? Have you understood how you can help me?'

Mary was confused. The man had not been specific. She had understood the drift of his argument, but what exactly did he want to know? Most crucial of all, what did he know already? Did he know about her relationship with Peter Joyce?

'You'll have to forgive me . . .' she ventured timidly. 'Sometimes I'm a little obtuse. I'm really not entirely sure what I can tell you that would be of any help.'

The faint smile disappeared from his flabby lips, and his eyes grew cold and expressionless. He stared at her for a few moments before continuing.

'I want to know some personal details, Mary. We've already talked in the office, haven't we, but, as I'm sure you will remember, the only ground we covered there was on things like office procedure, routines, access to documents, and so on. Well, to be frank, that didn't clarify anything very much, so I want to learn a little bit more about your personal life, just so that I can put my suspicious old mind at rest and cross you off my list of people who need investigating.'

'Yes, well, of course, that sounds perfectly reasonable,' Mary replied uneasily.

He smiled briefly, as a reward for her answer, then waited for her to continue.

She looked back at him anxiously, hoping that he would ask her questions and so reveal his hand. He did not however.

'Well, there's not a lot to say,' she began uncomfortably. 'I er . . . I lead a pretty quiet sort of life. I er . . . live here alone, as you can see, but I have lots of good friends whom I see from time to time.'

She stopped and shrugged her shoulders as if there was no more to be said. Black looked at her icily.

'How much do you drink?' The question was hardly audible.

'What?'

'One bottle of wine a day? Two?'

'Oh, nothing like . . .'

'Whisky? Gin?'

'Well, yes. From time to . . .'

'How much? Two glasses a day? Half a bottle?'

'Now, look here . . .'

'Ever had treatment for it? Alcoholism?'

'No!'

'Are you sure? I can easily check.'

She shook her head in disbelief, but found herself putting down the wine glass she had been holding.

'Go to pubs, do you?'

'Sometimes, but . . .'

'On your own? Sitting in a corner hoping someone will come up and talk to you and buy you a drink?'

'No! I . . .'

'Is that how you get your men? Pick them up in the pubs, do you? Tell them they can come home with you if they bring a bottle of scotch?'

'For God's sake! You can't just come round . . .'

'Don't you like men then?'

'What do you mean?'

'Lesbian, are you? A student of Sappho?'

Mary found herself trembling uncontrollably. She was dumbfounded, and felt that at any minute she would be sick. Through the mist of tears clouding her eyes she could no longer clearly see the monster of a man who was taunting her. Part of her wanted to get up and run away, escape from her own home, but the rest of her felt incapable of movement, like a rabbit mesmerised by a stoat.

She was aware that Black had stood up from his chair and was now wandering round the room. She heard the click of a cigarette-lighter behind her, and then smelled the Virginia tobacco smoke that swirled around her head.

'Interesting books you've got, Mary.'

The man's voice was softer now, less aggressive.

'You've done a bit of travelling in your time, judging by the number of guide-books on the shelf here. France, Spain, Morocco. Oh, and here's the Soviet Union.'

Mary was breathing deeply, trying to steady her racing heartbeat and to bring herself back in control of her voice. She knew the interrogation had a long way to go.

'You have been to Russia, have you?' Black asked pointedly.

'Yes, I went to Moscow and Leningrad in 1984. It was a holiday organised by a civil-service travel club. We looked at museums and art galleries.'

She breathed a silent sigh of relief at having given the answer without a quaver in her voice. She heard Black chuckling to himself behind her. Another cloud of smoke swirled past her head. He is doing it deliberately, she thought to herself.

'Interesting titles you've got here, though, Mary.

Marxism Today must make good bedtime reading. *The Spread of Socialism in the 1980s* can't be a bad yarn either. Good heavens, we've got a whole shelf of such treats here. *The Long Road to Freedom*, *Socialist Progress*, they're all here.'

She heard him take first one book from the shelves and flip through its pages, then, with the occasional chuckle and a whistle through his teeth, he would replace it and take another.

'I'm sure there's something you'd like to tell me about all this, isn't there, Mary?' he asked with amused resignation.

'I've always been interested in political philosophy,' she answered flatly. 'I read PPE at university. And I am a supporter of the Labour Party. I have been for many years. But that will be in your file on me already, I'm sure.'

She heard him breathing heavily. His lungs must be coated with tar, she thought to herself. She found herself praying that he would die from cancer.

He was standing at the end of the sofa now, looking straight down at her.

'It's still the policy of the Labour Party to scrap British nuclear weapons, isn't it?' he asked innocently.

'Yes. But not all members of the party support that policy,' she answered coldly, looking straight ahead. She reached for her glass, and swallowed the remains of her wine.

'Good God!' he exclaimed in disgust. 'It amazes me that we have any secrets left in this country. There you've been for the past God-knows-how-many years, sitting in the nuclear weapons department of the Ministry of Defence, with top-security clearance, and all the time you've been an alcoholic, lesbian, left-wing anti-nuclear activist!'

'Look, you evil pig of a man!' Mary exploded in rage, rising to her feet so that he could not dominate her. 'I've had quite enough of your vile insinuations and lies. I am not a left-wing anti-nuclear activist! I happen to believe in nuclear deterrence, and in Britain keeping the bomb. I couldn't possibly have done the work I do if I didn't believe that. Also, I am not an alcoholic, and above all I am not a lesbian!'

Her voice had risen to a penetrating crescendo, and she was trembling again. This time with anger at the faint expression of amusement discernible on John Black's face.

'Oh,' he nodded amiably. 'Oh well, you should have said that before. Would have saved a lot of trouble.'

With that he turned away from her and studied a watercolour on the wall. Sighing gently he moved on to examine some prints, and stopped by an antique walnut-veneered bureau, on top of which were two photo-frames. One contained a picture of an elderly couple in a country garden. They looked to him as if they could be her parents. Next to it was a more recent colour print of Mary with her arms round two young children.

'Nice-looking kids,' he commented sincerely.

'They're my brother's.'

'Sort of substitute for not having any of your own, are they?'

Mary ignored the remark and bit her lip.

'You've never been married, have you?' he persisted.

'No,' she answered softly.

Suddenly there was a squeak from the hinges of the old bureau.

'You can bloody well keep out of there!' she shouted furiously. 'That's private!'

'I know,' Black murmured without turning round.

'You've got no right to look in there!' she screamed, striding across the room and grabbing him by the arm, to pull him away.

'Rights?' he mocked, swinging round and brushing her hand from his arm. 'Rights? This country's most precious nuclear secrets are being stolen by some self-interested sneak-thief, and you talk about rights!'

His outrage blazed from his eyes.

'What is it you want? A warrant? I can whistle up a search warrant in half an hour, if that's what you want. But along with the warrant will come three of my heaviest-handed men who will not only search this place from top to bottom, they'll slit the very elastic out of your knickers to check that it hasn't got code-words written on it. Those are you rights, Miss Maclean!'

Mary knew that she could not stop her tears anymore. Her privacy was going to be violated, and there was nothing more she could do to prevent it happening. Turning back to the French windows, she pressed her head against the glass and hugged her arms tightly round her chest in an effort to hold herself together.

She heard him rustling through her private papers, which were stuffed inside the cubby-holes of the bureau. Suddenly the rustling stopped, and she assumed he had found what he was looking for. Inside a tattered brown envelope were the snapshots she had taken during her two-year affair with Peter Joyce, together with the three letters that he had written to her during their relationship.

She flinched as she felt John Black's hand on her shoulder.

'Don't you think the time has now come, Mary, for you to tell me about Peter Joyce?'

*

It was after midnight when John Black eventually left the garden flat in Chiswick. The air smelt of fog, and the street lamps looked like orange-headed sentinels glaring sullenly down through the mist. Black sniffed at the air, finding it curiously refreshing after the despair-laden atmosphere he had just left.

He was not proud of the methods he had used to make her tell him what he wanted to hear, but he knew no other way. He shivered in the cold air, hurriedly climbed into his car, started the engine, and set off for home. He failed to notice the large Mercedes parked on the other side of the road.

Chapter Three

Midnight in London was seven o'clock in the evening Florida time. The sun was low in the sky and painted the endless beaches with a wash of golden orange, as the RAF VC10 banked for its final turn over the coast and settled smoothly down towards the runway of Patrick Air Force Base. Beyond Patrick, a few miles to the north, the pilot could see the towers and gantries of the Kennedy Space Center pointing challengingly at the stars.

Peter Joyce looked down at the long oblongs of the cars cruising slowly up and down the coastal boulevards. The pilot had sent back a note to say the temperature on the ground was a humid seventy-five degrees. It certainly looked hot down below, and Peter was grateful he had remembered to wear a lightweight suit.

Jill Piper's face was glued to the window, her eyes drinking in their first sight of the USA. Suddenly Peter remembered he had meant to warn her of something. He glanced down to check, and cursed himself. The girl was wearing a skirt.

'Christ, Jill! Have you brought a pair of trousers with you, by any chance?' he enquired, embarrassed.

She turned from the window, a knowing smile on her lips.

'For the submarine, you mean? Don't worry, I was warned! A friend of mine went on one last year in a skirt, and had ten sailors round the bottom of each hatchway looking up at her as she came down the ladder! I'll change as soon as we've landed.'

Peter smiled; the girl was quite sharp. He was very tired, but satisfied that they had managed to complete the writing of the new programmes. It had been a full eight hours' work, but he was as confident as he could be that the deception plan for the missile test would be convincing.

The plane bounced once as it touched the tarmac; then the nose levelled out and the four engines shook and roared as they went into reverse thrust. Peter glanced across the aisle to check that their microcomputers, packed away in their boxes, were still firmly strapped in the seats and cushioned against the force of the landing. When the plane stopped moving, he left Jill on her own in the compartment to change.

As they stepped out on to the steps the warm air enveloped them. The naval officer standing below was wearing a crisply starched white shirt and shorts. He looked up at Peter with recognition.

'Good evening, Mr Joyce, and welcome to the US of A,' he smiled. 'Phil Dunkley. We met last year.' He extended his hand. 'I'm the PSO, the Polaris Systems Officer from *Retribution*.'

Peter was grateful for the reminder, but pretended he did not need it. 'Of course. I remember you well. Nice to see you again.'

The smile on the Lt. Commander's face broadened as he turned to greet the second visitor from Aldermaston.

'Ah, Miss Piper, is it?' With a quick all-over glance he took in her blonde hair and the shapely figure clad in blue cotton blouse and slacks.

'Jill will do!' she smiled back.

The equipment was loaded carefully into a US Navy van. Then they climbed into a large black automobile, with the officer from HMS *Retribution* sitting next to the US Navy driver in the front. During their forty-minute journey up the coast, Dunkley gave them a running commentary on the local attractions of Florida.

Once through the gates of the US Navy Base at Port Canaveral, Peter felt a sense of anticipation and unease. The smooth black hulls of several submarines lined the quayside – in harbour for maintenance, or waiting to conduct missile tests out in the Atlantic. The sight of this most sinister of military hardware brought him down to earth; the hours spent re-writing the missile warhead programmes had been an academic challenge, but the sight of the slim fins and opened missile hatches reminded him of the monstrous destructive potential of the weapons he designed.

At the end of the quay, the White Ensign fluttering limply in the light evening breeze distinguished HMS *Retribution* from her lookalike American counterparts. As the car pulled to a halt, two sailors on her deck snapped to attention, while a third spoke urgently into a microphone connected by cable to the inside of the hull.

Within seconds the tall, bony figure of the submarine's captain had emerged from a hatchway, and he stood at the head of the gangway with his hand outstretched in greeting.

'Nice to see you again, Mr Joyce,' Commander Carrington exclaimed. They had also met the previous year, when the scientist had attended the test firing of early prototypes of the Skydancer warheads.

'Likewise,' Peter answered, smiling politely. 'And this is Jill Piper, my assistant. She knows much more about using that stuff than I do,' he explained, pointing at the computers that were being unloaded from the US Navy van.

Carrington bowed his head respectfully. 'I'm afraid that usually when ladies come aboard we give them tea and show them the wardroom,' he grinned. 'It's a new experience to have a woman tell us how to programme our missiles.'

His words had sounded pompous even to his own ears, and he covered his embarrassment by leading the way down into the bowels of the submarine.

'Now, how much have you been told about all this?' Joyce asked, once he was alone with Carrington and the Polaris Systems Officer. Jill was elsewhere, supervising the stowage of equipment.

'Not much,' Carrington answered. 'They said there was no need for us to know the details.' The injunction to secrecy was a restraint they were well used to, but the two Navy men were clearly burning with curiosity.

'I'm sorry, I can't explain much to you, as secrecy is terribly important in this matter,' Joyce went on, his eyebrows arched in apology. 'And I'm going to need your help, please, in damping down speculation among the crew. Many of them will remember me from my last visit, but if anyone asks, could you simply say I'm here to make minor adjustments to the missiles?'

The two officers nodded.

'Unfortunately what I have to do is not really minor at all. It involves extensive re-programming of the warheads. Your test launch procedures won't be affected, but the changes will make a big difference to what happens at the other end of the range. And I shouldn't really have told you that much!'

'Don't worry, it'll go no further,' Carrington reassured him. 'Now when do you want to start work? Tonight?'

'No, I don't think we can do any more today,' Peter sighed, drawing a hand round his chin and feeling the stubble of nearly twenty-four hours. 'I'd rather get some sleep and start fresh in the morning. With any luck we might be finished by lunchtime.'

'Fine,' the Commander replied. 'We've booked a couple of rooms for you in a motel down the road. Nothing very special, I'm afraid, but it's on the beach and you should be more comfortable there than on board. We don't have proper facilities for ladies anyway!'

Peter nodded. He suddenly felt a desperate need to sleep; he had been concentrating solidly for the past sixteen hours.

The equipment they had brought from Britain had now been carried carefully down the metal ladders and into the missile compartment in the heart of the submarine. As the PSO led him down there, Peter was pleased to notice sentries standing in the corridors leading to the chamber. He would want complete privacy the following morning.

He stood for a moment looking along the two rows of missile tubes, sixteen in all. Their white casings, over five feet in diameter, looked clean and clinical, and bore large red identification numbers on their sides. Inside each one was a weapon ten times as destructive as the primitive bomb dropped on Hiroshima in 1945.

On this occasion however one tube did not contain a bomb. The one he would have to work on the following day held the product of his recent efforts, a warhead of dummies and complex electronic creations, the testing of which was of vital concern both to London and to Moscow.

Satisfied that the equipment was safe, Peter escorted Jill up to the black steel outer casing of the submarine, and down the gangway to the shore. The US Navy driver was still waiting there to take them to their hotel.

It was mid-evening Florida time, though three in the morning by Peter's body-clock. Large convertibles cruised lazily up and down the boulevards, and the bars, motels and arcade houses competed for attention in garish neon. The air smelled of seaweed and grilled meat, and it still retained much of the humid warmth of the day.

'It's just like on television, only worse,' Jill commented in surprise. 'Do they *only* eat pizzas and hamburgers?'

'Just about,' Peter sighed.

The Navy car turned into the driveway of the Cocoa-Beach Lodge, and pulled up by the hotel entrance. The two Britons climbed out, carrying their small suitcases, and arranged for the driver to collect them at eight the next morning.

Peter entered the reception uneasily; American motels all looked alike to him, but there was something familiar about this one. It was only after checking in, and after he had bid Jill a weary goodnight, that he remembered. As he let himself into his room, he realised this was where he had stayed on his last visit, a year ago, the visit when Mary Maclean had accompanied him.

He exhaled sharply, cursing the coincidence that was stirring memories he preferred to keep buried. It might even have been the very same room; above the king-sized bed was an identical cheap print of a space-shuttle launching from Cape Canaveral.

Peter took off his sweaty clothes and lay back on the bed, listening to the surf pounding on the sand fifty yards away. His affair with Mary had begun in London, but it had been here in Florida in a room like this that it had become more than a casual flirtation.

He had surprised himself that first evening of the

train strike when Mary had joined him for dinner in London. He had not been looking for an affair, he was certain of that, but suddenly the opportunity was there. At the time, neither of them had expected the relationship to develop, but it had, and his occasional visits to America had given them the chance for a week on their own.

He clearly remembered their first night here. They had both experienced a childlike excitement at being able to walk around together openly, without the constant secretiveness they had learned to practise back home. They had enjoyed shrimp and lobster at a restaurant on a tumbledown jetty, with a view up the coast to the launching towers of the Space Center, and then they strolled down the beach as the sun set. At the first onset of a chilly evening breeze, they had hurried back to the hotel.

Once inside their room, they had looked at one another and hesitated. There was something unsavoury about this motel.

'What's this room smell of to you?' he had asked, frowning. 'They must spray it with something.'

Mary had made much of sniffing the air.

'No. It's the smell of adultery!' she'd proclaimed with a wicked smile. 'Now stifle your conscience and get on with it!'

He had snorted with laughter, and then nudged her attention towards the phallic photo of the space-shuttle above the bed. She had turned the picture to the wall.

That week had changed their relationship irrevocably. Until then, neither of them had defined precisely what their affair meant to them. Peter had considered it little more than a flirtation, a compensation for the erosion of his relationship with Belinda. Not in any way an alternative to his marriage, he was determined it should not affect his family. But Mary had brought a new dimension to his life, and that week in Florida had turned the affair into something much more serious. For the first time Peter had realised he was deeply involved with Mary, and that she was intensely in love with him. But warning bells had soon rung in Peter's mind, and he had known instinctively that the end was already in sight.

On their third evening, Peter remembered, they had revisited the restaurant on the tumbledown jetty, and something he said had caused Mary to giggle uncontrollably. Suddenly she looked twenty years younger. All traces of spinsterishness had vanished. Her face had shed its worry-lines and her eyes shone softly.

Peter knew she had not had many relationships with men; her inexperience was clear to him in the way her body had moved against his with hesitancy and uncertainty when they made love. That evening, however, when they returned to their motel, her reserve had evaporated, and she had given herself to him with a totality that was almost sacrificial.

Suddenly everything had changed. His desire to be with Mary was becoming overwhelming. The possibility of leaving Belinda – separation and divorce – had begun to haunt his thoughts.

In Mary's heart a spark of hope had been lit. She had finally found the love that she had always been seeking, and it seemed to her there was now a chance that it could last for ever. In the months that followed their week in Florida, that spark had grown into a flame, eventually so bright and visible that Peter made his painful but inevitable decision. He could not inflict the misery of a break-up on his children. He had to extinguish the flame for ever.

Now he was back in the very place where his real

love-affair with Mary had begun – and where its end had first been signalled.

Could Mary have taken the Skydancer blueprints in revenge, desperate to hurt him? It would be so unlike her, yet was it really impossible?

Rising, he closed the glass door to the balcony, shutting out the sound of the sea, and began to unpack his suitcase. There was much to do the following day; he had to try to sleep.

In London the following morning, John Black looked at the date on his newspaper to remind himself it was Wednesday. It was the third day of his investigation and he still had no clear leads. He was glad to see that the newspapers were turning cold on the story, with no fresh revelations to keep them going.

His first cigarette of the day came before breakfast, and the second immediately afterwards, while he finished his coffee. That done, he set off for Reading – not far from the Atomic Weapons Research Establishment at Aldermaston. It was easy driving out of London at that time of day. As he sped westwards and saw thousands of commuters jammed on the eastbound carriageway, trying to get in to the capital, he was relieved to be heading the other way.

He drove directly to the main police station in Reading, where he had arranged to meet the local Special Branch man. Tom McQuade was an old mate; Black knew he would get help there. This part of Britain was a focal point for anti-nuclear activists, what with the Aldermaston complex and the Greenham Common cruise missile base as well.

'Well, you old poacher, what are you after this time?' McQuade asked suspiciously as they greeted one another. His voice bore the merest trace of an Ulster accent.

'What, me? On the scrounge? Whatever gave you that idea, Tom?' Black countered with a smirk.

Though good friends, there had always been a certain reserve in their relationship. To some extent MI5 and the Special Branch were rivals as well as collaborators.

With the door of McQuade's cramped office firmly closed, John Black lit up another cigarette and slumped in a chair.

'Got a little problem with Polaris, have we?' McQuade needled.

John Black explained the circumstances of his visit. He wanted information on the activities of one woman in particular. At the mention of her name, McQuade smiled wryly and reached for the drawer of a filing cabinet. Extracting a green folder, he opened it and browsed through the pages it contained.

'Ye . . . es,' he mused, 'we seem to know the name of Belinda Joyce quite well.'

Without letting go of the file, for fear perhaps of losing the power over John Black that its information gave him, the Special Branch officer began to explain.

'Quite a successful little operation this one,' he said, tapping the folder. 'Young woman detective on the force here – quite a star. Jenny Ward – good operator. A few months ago Jenny turned herself into a radical feminist, at my request. She signed up with a women's militant anti-nuclear group locally, and penetrated their organisation pretty thoroughly. Usual set-up; you know the form. Lesbians most of them. Not our Jenny though – I can vouch for that personally!' he concluded with a grin.

'Tch, tch. Man of your age, you ought to know

better!' John Black chuckled indulgently.

'Well now,' McQuade continued, smiling with self-satisfaction, 'our Jenny made a very interesting discovery. The group in question is called ATSA – stands for Action To Stop Annihilation. And one of the leading lights turned out to be none other than the wife of one of Aldermaston's most senior and respected scientists, Belinda Joyce. Quite a prize for ATSA. Make quite a fuss of her, they do.'

'Now then, there's an element in the group that I would call basically anarchist, a bit of a throwback to the 1960s. And one woman who fits into that category is called Helene Venner. Definitely a dyke, she is,' McQuade added, wrinkling his nose in distaste.

'We don't know much about Venner. She doesn't seem to be on record anywhere, but she's certainly one of the prime movers in ATSA. It was she who recruited Belinda Joyce. There's a craft co-operative in one of the villages – trendy-lefty sort of place where they make pots and country furniture. That's where they met. They both work there.

'Well, at one of ATSA's evening meetings which Jenny Ward attended, Helene Venner came up with a plan which was a bit of a stunner. She wanted Belinda Joyce to get hold of some of her old man's secret plans for the new Polaris warheads, and hand them over so that Venner could get them published in some left-wing newspaper. She argued that with the weapon's secrets made public, they'd become useless, and they could successfully campaign for the missiles to be scrapped.'

John Black whistled softly. None of this appeared on Peter Joyce's security file. There had been an appalling failure of communication somewhere within the security services.

The scheme itself, though dangerous, sounded absurdly naive – and rather like putting the paper on Parliament Hill deliberately to be discovered.

'And Mrs Joyce went along with all this?' he asked attentively.

'Apparently not,' McQuade continued. 'She got pretty annoyed at the ATSA meeting when all this was suggested. Obviously those behind the idea were depending on her to get hold of the plans for them, but she insisted it was a ludicrous idea. She claimed her husband never brought secret documents home, and she was in no position to ask him to do so. Apparently she flatly refused to take part in anything illegal.'

'Hmm,' John Black mused, stroking his chin with a nicotine-stained hand. 'This ATSA mob, do they discuss everything at these general meetings, or does the real action get decided by one or two individuals privately? I mean, could your girl Jenny have missed out on what was really being planned?'

'It's possible, although they certainly make a show of being ever-so democratic – you know the sort of thing: insistence on a full-scale debate and then a vote to decide what to do, with the result that they hardly achieve anything in the end. But perhaps that Venner woman continued to work on Belinda Joyce over at their craft workshop.'

'Your undercover girl hasn't tried to get a job there, then,' Black pressed.

'Not exactly arty-crafty, our Jenny. Bit clumsy with her hands, you could say.'

'Clumsy hands, eh?' John Black chuckled. 'You want to watch that – she could do you an injury!'

McQuade smirked.

For nearly two hours the two men continued their conversation, with several other files being taken out of the Special Branch man's cabinet, to be studied at length.

It was nearly half-past eleven by the time Black swung his vehicle into the visitors' car park outside the gates of Aldermaston. In the security office he proffered his pass, which identified him as an official from the Home Office.

'Do you have an appointment with Mr Joyce?' asked the guard, checking through the messages list to see if this visitor was expected.

'No. It's what you might call a surprise visit,' Black answered. 'But if you put me through to him on the phone, I'm sure he'll be happy to see me.'

The guard dialled Peter Joyce's number, and spoke to his secretary. Then he put the phone down and looked up at Black coldly.

'He's not here. Gone away for a few days.'

'That's impossible!' Black was irritated. 'Put me through to Mr Dogson, the head of security.'

Dogson was a man he had dealt with frequently in the past, and whom he had consulted when he was first assigned to this case. Reluctantly the guard dialled the new number, and then passed the phone across.

'John Black here. Just arrived to talk to your Mr Joyce, only to be told that he's away for a few days. Know anything about it?'

Dogson did, and expressed astonishment that John Black did *not*. Peter Joyce's visit to America had been sanctioned at the highest level, he said, and that must have involved MI5, surely?

Black felt a hot flush colour his face, and he turned away from the guard so as not to be overheard.

'But I'm in the middle of the investigation, for

God's sake,' he hissed into the phone. 'How the hell can he be allowed to go swanning off to America for a few days?'

'It's not – unrelated, shall we say?' Dogson answered mysteriously.

Black climbed back into his car and slammed the door angrily. He felt humiliated, and he hated that feeling more than anything else in life. It reminded him painfully of commencing his National Service, aged eighteen. He had been fat and breathless as a teenager, and had been thoroughly victimised during the start of his two years in the army.

He picked up the receiver of his radio-telephone, with its built-in encryption device that prevented his words from being deciphered if the call was intercepted. On the keypad he punched out the secret direct-line code to the office of the MI5 director, Dick Sproat. When a secretary answered, Black identified himself and insisted that he talk urgently to his boss.

'Yes, John, what is it?' Sproat's voice crackled in his ear.

'I'm sorry to bother you, sir, but I'm down here at Aldermaston and have just been told that Peter Joyce has left the country for a few days. Seems a bit odd when he's a central figure in my investigation. I gather you know something about it, sir.'

'Oh,' Sproat grunted. 'He, er . . . he'll be back in a day or two. You can talk to him then.'

'But, with respect, sir,' Black continued, his voice rising, 'don't you think that as investigating officer I should have known about this?'

'Normally, yes,' Sproat snapped back, 'but this is not a normal case. Its secrecy classification is so high there are some things you don't need to know, and this is one of them.'

The line clicked, and a dialling tone returned. Sproat had hung up on him.

'Bloody ridiculous!' Black exploded, as he snapped the receiver back into its rest. 'It's like trying to fight a gorilla with one hand tied behind your back!'

To console himself while deciding his next move, he sought a pub for some lunch. He did not have far to drive, and pulled into the crowded car-park of a half-timbered roadhouse advertising bar food.

Following a couple of pints of bitter and a steak pie and chips, he felt reasonably more comforted. He had even positioned himself on a stool close to two young technicians from Aldermaston, so he could eavesdrop casually on their ill-informed speculation about the stolen nuclear secrets.

After relieving his bladder of most of the beer, he then returned to his car and took out his road atlas.

It took him some time to find the Joyces' house, which stood on the very edge of their village. Black stopped his car in the road a few yards from the gateway on to the drive, and he studied the building. It was an attractive red-brick house with a slate roof. A golden-yellow climbing rose covered a side wall, still bearing a few late blooms. In the garden stood a magnificent oak tree that had shed most of its leaves for the coming winter. The tree and the house might well be about the same age, he speculated; early nineteenth century perhaps.

'Must be worth a bit,' he pondered suspiciously.

This part of Berkshire was prime commuter country. Could a government scientist afford to live here without earning a bit extra on the side? Of course, if they had bought the place some time ago, the price might have been more reasonable, he conceded.

Tom McQuade had said Belinda Joyce worked at a craft co-operative, but he did not know whether that was just part-time. Black locked the car door and set off up the gravel drive to check if she was at home. An old, rusting Citroën 2cv stood outside the large garage, and some of the ground-floor windows were open. Through one of them he could hear the rumble of a washing-machine, and he saw the figure of a woman working in the kitchen.

Belinda Joyce looked startled when he introduced himself, but Black was used to that.

'I'm enquiring into some problems to do with your husband's work, Mrs Joyce. It's a matter of national security. I'd like to come in and ask you some questions, if you don't mind.'

The woman was exactly as he had pictured her, dressed in faded grey jeans and an oversized hand-knitted sweater of an indeterminate 'country' colour. Her oval face was framed by straight hair hanging down to her shoulders, brown hair that was streaked with grey and needed a wash. Her dark eyes showed an intelligent intensity, but radiated hostility when he asked to come inside. He had seen a thousand other women who looked like Belinda Joyce, middle-aged and losing their looks, women who had committed themselves fervently to a cause late in life and were now determined to change the world. He knew the way their minds worked and he did not like them much.

Lieutenant Robert Simpson was the supply officer on board HMS *Retribution*. He found it odd walking through the empty passageways of the submarine when half the crew were on shore leave. The lower-ratings' recreation area was almost deserted, and whole compartments of bunks had not been slept in that night. It reminded him uncomfortably of one summer during his childhood, when he had had to spend the half-term holiday on his own at his boarding-school because his family had been abroad.

Today would be busy for Simpson; he had to complete his inventory of foodstocks and other supplies, and place orders for the rest of their voyage, allowing a generous reserve for emergencies. Known in naval jargon as the 'Pusser' or Purser, his job was more like that of an hotel manager than a sailor.

In the galley the leading chef handed over his list of the most urgently needed food items, and asked Simpson how many of the officers would be at lunch that day. Simpson told him that six were on shore leave, but there would be two visitors on board.

As he headed back towards the middle of the submarine, where lay the control room and the officers' accommodation, he began to wonder about those visitors. At breakfast in the wardroom that morning, the captain had refused to be drawn on the purpose of their visit. Simpson had resented the look of cold dismissal in Carrington's eyes when he had asked. It was as if the captain did not consider him a real officer, and certainly not one who could be trusted with secrets.

The visitors were due aboard soon after 8 am, and Simpson was loitering close to the forward hatch then. For Robert Simpson was not just the ship's 'Pusser'; he had a personal mission of his own to carry out, one that he had been planning and dreaming of for a full five years.

He had been a member of *Retribution*'s crew for less than a year, so did not recognise Peter Joyce as he climbed down the ladder. One of the petty officers did, however, and remarked within Simpson's hearing that the stranger was 'that bloke from Aldermaston' who had been on board the previous autumn.

Simpson followed, as casually as he could, while the visitors were escorted by Lt. Commander Phil Dunkley towards the stern. But, in the passage leading to the missile chamber, he saw his way would be blocked by the unusual presence of an armed sentry, and so he turned back.

'Curious!' he muttered to himself. 'Never seen that before.'

The submarine crew had been told they were to perform a routine missile test within the next few days, but Simpson knew from hints dropped in the wardroom that the test was to be far from routine – the missile in question being the first to be fitted with the new Skydancer warhead system. He had also read the news summary from Britain which came through to the submarine by telex, and which included a report on the missing Polaris papers in London. With the sudden clandestine arrival of the scientists on board, he began to divine a connection here.

Peter Joyce was not feeling his best after a night of little sleep. He removed the jacket of his light-grey suit and hung it on a hook next to the launcher control panel, whose lights and dials would reveal whether the missile gyros and arming mechanisms were operational when the weapons were fired. Hanging from the same hook was an old baseball bat, to be used as a cudgel by the missile technicians in case any member of the ship's company suffering from mental derangement or troubled conscience should ever try to interfere with the countdown.

'Let's check those boxes, Jill,' Joyce said, looking to see that the seals had not been broken overnight. His assistant ticked off the contents against an inventory.

As Peter turned to the Polaris Systems Officer to explain what they had to do, he spoke directly, aware that Dunkley was one of the few members of the crew of HMS *Retribution* who had been trained in the workings of the new warheads.

'I'll need my assistant with me for this,' Dunkley said soberly after Peter had described the task ahead. 'We operate a two-man rule when doing anything to the missiles. It's in the regulations. It avoids mistakes as well as keeping the security people happy.'

Peter nodded. On the side of each of the sixteen launch tubes was a circular access hatch about two feet in diameter, secured tightly to withstand the colossal pressure inside from the gas used to eject the missiles at the start of the launching process. With his assistant watching his every move, Dunkley wrenched at the two-handed brass key that released the securing bolts, and swung the hatch open. The curved skin of the missile with its matt-grey radar-absorbing paint could be seen inside.

'Have you got the tray there?' Dunkley asked. They had to take great care when the hatch was open so as not to drop anything down between the missile and the side of the tube. The assistant PSO passed him a tray which bridged the gap precisely.

The task which Peter had outlined was complex. After opening the launch tube, the PSO had to unscrew a second panel on the missile itself, uncovering the rotating 'bus' on which the warheads were mounted. Each re-entry vehicle in turn would have to be rotated in line with the opening, so that a printed-circuit memory board could be withdrawn from its internal computer for reprogramming. The components would then need to be replaced with the greatest care.

It was half an hour later before the engineer handed over the first board of microchips to the scientists. The magnetic bubble memories on the card looked like miniature tablets of Swiss chocolate. Jill Piper slotted the board into a test socket mounted on a programmer, which in turn was connected to one of the microcomputers they had brought with them from Aldermaston. Her fingers flew expertly across the keyboard, and row upon row of data rolled across the screen, signifying that the circuitry was functioning correctly. With a few more deft key-strokes, she ordered the equipment to erase the data in the memories and replace it with the programme written on the flight over from Britain.

After comparing a printout of the new data with the original, Peter Joyce was satisfied, and returned the board to the engineer for fitting back into the warhead. Six times this process was repeated before the scientists could make their final check. They connected a lead to a test socket on the 'bus', fed in electronic instructions, and read on the computer screen the responses from the individual warheads.

'I do believe we've done it!' exclaimed Peter, grinning in triumph. He reached across and firmly shook the hands of the two submariners in turn.

'I wish I knew exactly what it was I've just done!' Dunkley joked modestly. 'All I know is I'm damned glad I don't have to tinker with the thing every time we launch a missile!'

Peter observed the look of expectant curiosity on the officers' faces. 'Look, I'd love to tell you what this is all about, but I just can't. It's extremely secret.'

'Something to do with that spy business in London?' Dunkley ventured casually.

'You really mustn't press me. I am sure you'll make your own assumptions anyway. But it really would be best if you didn't speculate too much, particularly not in front of any of your colleagues,' Peter added.

'Point taken. Now, how about a spot of lunch?'

Dunkley answered, putting an end to the conversation.

As they entered the wardroom, Lieutenant Bob Simpson slipped past them.

'I'll tell the captain you're here, Mr Joyce,' he announced.

'Would you like a drink? I'm certainly in need of a pint.' The PSO headed for a small cupboard in a corner and opened it to reveal a barrel of beer.

'Excellent idea!' Peter exclaimed, beginning to relax.

'We don't drink much when we're at sea, but in harbour . . . well, that's a different matter,' Dunkley chuckled, handing out the brimming glasses.

'Ah, Jill, did they find somewhere suitable for you?' he inquired as Peter's assistant was escorted into the wardroom.

'Yes, fine thanks,' she breezed. 'I can't remember having a guard when I've been to the loo before!'

'Well, we couldn't have any of our young sailors bursting in on you, could we?' Dunkley snorted. 'Drink?'

'Just an orange juice, thanks.'

The young supply officer re-entered the wardroom.

'The captain wonders if you could spare him a few minutes in his cabin, Mr Joyce,' Simpson ventured. 'He would like a quiet word before lunch.'

'Yes, of course,' Peter replied, placing his pint mug on the wardroom table.

When he had left the room, Simpson turned his attention to Jill.

'We don't often have the pleasure of having ladies visit the *Retribution*,' he began awkwardly. He had a shy nature. 'Been doing something special have you?'

For a moment her face froze at his outright enquiry.

'Oh no, just checking the sparking plugs,' she answered sweetly.

*

'Just wanted to ask how things have gone this morning,' Carrington questioned when they were alone, keen to know more but not wishing to pry beyond the areas of information he was entitled to know.

'Yes, of course. Well, we've completed our work successfully, thanks to your excellent systems officers,' Peter answered formally. 'The warheads on the test missile have now been reprogrammed, and within a few days you will probably get your orders to launch.'

He paused, and studied the unsatisfied look on the captain's face. He would have to tell him more.

'In absolute confidence, I suppose I shall have to confirm what you are all guessing: this sudden crisis with the test missile *is* connected with that secret document found in a rubbish basket on Hampstead Heath.'

'It did seem the most likely reason for your visit, I must say,' Carrington's thin face creased into a fleeting smile.

Peter puffed out his cheeks, then let out a long steady breath as he lowered his heavy frame into a small armchair covered with the yellow and green floral print that was standard issue for Royal Naval officers' quarters.

'It's a weird business,' he ventured in a half-whisper.

'It's serious, is it? We couldn't tell from the news reports,' Carrington responded in the same hushed tone. 'The Russians presumably?'

Peter shrugged and shook his head.

'That's just the trouble; no one seems to be sure. At least they weren't when I left England yesterday. But we're having to assume the Soviets have got hold of some very sensitive information. Hence all these last-minute changes.'

For several minutes more they talked around the subject, with Peter increasingly careful not to reveal any details of the alterations to the missile warheads, nor of the precise purpose behind them. When Carrington stood up and suggested they return to the wardroom for lunch, he had realised he would learn no more.

The normal Royal Naval routine is for the captain to take his meals in his own cabin, but the tradition is different on a submarine, where there is a certain levelling of the ranks due to the lack of space and a dependence on the reliability of every individual for their joint survival under water.

Over lunch, a naval version of chop suey described on the menu as 'Chinky Nosh', Carrington led the conversation on to the harmless subject of the perils and pleasures of shore leave in Florida. Peter Joyce hardly noticed how the young lieutenant at the end of the table was staring at him with ill-concealed curiosity.

The conversation had not progressed far, however, when a signaller knocked at the wardroom door and handed in an urgent telex from London. It was addressed to Peter Joyce, and an awkward silence descended on the table as the naval men surreptitiously watched the scientist's expression for some hint of what the message contained.

'They want me back in London as soon as possible,' he announced, frowning.

The rest of the meal was hurried and confused, as messages were sent to Patrick Air Force Base to alert the crew of his RAF plane that he must return to Britain that same afternoon.

Two thousand miles south of Cape Canaveral, in the steamy heat of mid-Atlantic, the 21,000-ton Soviet ship *Akademik Sergey Korolev* dropped her speed from the seventeen knots at which she had been steaming for most of her journey from the Black Sea. She had reached her 'station' now, and would simply have to wait and watch, training her massive radar and telemetry antennae on the segment of the upper atmosphere used by the US Navy's Eastern test range.

It had taken two weeks to sail from Sevastopol in the Crimea, down through the NATO-controlled narrows of the Bosporus and Gibraltar and out into the Atlantic. It was a journey the ship had undertaken many times in the past, with her alternate missions of observing and listening in to the latest Western missile tests or of acting as a tracking station and data relay terminal for her own country's extensive activities in space.

Her departure from her home port had been very rushed this time, though, triggered by a message that had originated in Scotland.

At the moment when the *Retribution* had submerged beneath the waters of the Clyde, heading out for the Atlantic, and had escaped the attentions of a Soviet submarine, the *Korolev* had been steaming slowly past the Golden Horn of Istanbul. Her passage had been reported by Turkish naval officers to NATO's Southern naval intelligence headquarters to Gaeta in Italy, and the information had been fed into the central files of Alliance intelligence data, to which the British Royal Navy had access.

A few days later, as the *Korolev* was passing under the eyes of British observers on the Rock of Gibraltar, she had received a coded signal from Moscow reporting the dates that HMS *Retribution* had been allocated on the American missile range off Florida. This had given her little time in which to reach the area of the Atlantic where the missile warheads would splash down into the sea, and where she would be able to observe them with accuracy.

Kapitan Karpov sat in his cabin with his feet up, smoking a cigar. He was happy to have arrived on station on time, and not to have missed the 'party', but the ship's maintenance reports that he was studying did not please him. Most of the air-conditioning plant was unserviceable, and what was left of it had to be used to keep the temperature down in the massive racks of electronics that powered the gigantic dish aerials on the upper deck. He hoped desperately that the British would get a move on with their missile test, so he could steam north again to a climate that was not so uncomfortably hot and humid.

As the pale grey RAC VC10 sped back across the Atlantic carrying its two passengers, Peter Joyce stared absently out of the window at the streaks of cloud below, tinted by the setting sun.

The world was such a miraculous creation, still able to withhold many of its secrets. How strange, he thought, that people should devise two totally opposing concepts of how to prevent it from being destroyed. Particularly strange since both concepts claimed to base themselves on an understanding of human nature.

He had argued this issue so often with Belinda – until the time had come when they could no longer discuss the subject because of the stress it placed on their relationship.

Though Peter admired the eloquence with which Belinda made her own anti-nuclear case, he still could not accept it. There was a logic to both their arguments, but he was convinced his was the stronger. To his mind there was only one nation that posed any real threat to Britain's survival, and that was the Soviet Union armed with tens of thousands of nuclear weapons. But he was not a 'hawk' and did not believe, like so many of those he met in Western military circles, that Russia was hell-bent on world domination. He did consider, however, that the Soviet Union was led by opportunists who would seize anything to their advantage given the chance. So the Western possession of nuclear weapons should prevent the *big* chance from ever arising.

As the VC10 headed east, away from the sun, the sky darkened rapidly, and Peter began to adjust his mind forward five hours, trying to attune to the fact that it was late evening in Britain.

He had lost track of the days, and had to do some thinking to work out it was Wednesday. He swore quietly when he remembered he was due to attend a parent-teacher meeting at the children's school that very evening. He was active on the fund-raising committee, but he hoped Belinda would have gone in his place.

It was odd this being called back to Britain at such short notice and with no explanation. Something else must have happened, some further development in the investigation. It could not be anything very positive, though, or they would have commented about his work on the missile and whether it was still necessary.

He thought again of Mary Maclean, and could not dismiss from his mind the fear that she could somehow be responsible for this crisis. The memory of the last time he had really talked to her still caused pangs of remorse. He felt he had handled it badly, but he knew of no easy way to end a love affair.

Soon afterwards he had taken his family on holiday to the Lake District, where they had sailed and gone walking on the fells. For Peter it had been like a period of rehabilitation; he'd concentrated wholeheartedly on getting closer again to Belinda and his children. He had found extraordinary pleasure simply being in their company, and he had achieved a certain peace of mind that week, an acceptance of how things must be from then on. But now that peace had been shattered by a dread suspicion which verged on paranoia.

Both women had the motive and the means to betray him. Peter winced at the realisation of how careless he had been.

Three months earlier when he had been to London to explain the Skydancer project to the ministers, he had carried the blueprints with him to Mary's flat on the night he had ended their affair, then taken them to the Ministry, and then to his own home afterwards. Two major security lapses in forty-eight hours.

He told himself he had to stop the drift of his thoughts and try to concentrate on sleep. They would be landing back in England in the small hours of the morning. He looked across to the seat opposite where Jill Piper was dozing. The girl had been disappointed at the brevity of her first visit to America, but was oblivious to the complex reasons behind it.

Lieutenant Robert Simpson was now dressed in pale-blue cotton slacks and a striped shirt with short sleeves. He had just taken a shower and washed his hair. Looking at himself in the tiny mirror in his cabin, he decided he was in a fit state to go ashore. The captain had given him a twenty-four-hour pass, and he felt he had deserved it. HMS *Retribution* was as well stocked for the rest of her voyage as she would ever be.

He leaned through the door of the wardroom to see if his fellow lieutenant was ready, the Assistant Polaris Systems Officer, George Grundy. They had decided to sample some of the bars and discotheques together.

'Come on, George, let's get at it before all the talent's snapped up!'

As they hurried down the gangway on to the quay-side, they welcomed the warm freshness of unconditioned air. George had hired them a car for the evening, and it was parked near the main gate.

'You looked pretty busy this morning,' Bob Simpson ventured as they drove down the long straight road through a succession of beach resorts. 'Who were the visitors in the wardroom at lunchtime? The girl was rather fanciable.'

'Oh, they were from Aldermaston. You remember the tall guy from last year, surely?' George answered cautiously. 'Oh no, you weren't on board then, were you?'

'From Aldermaston?' Simpson answered, feigning surprise. 'What were they doing here?

'Adjusting things, I suppose you could say.'

'What, on the new warheads, you mean?'

George tightened his grip on the wheel.

'I can't talk about that, as you bloody well know, Bob!'

'Sorry. Just curious.'

They motored on in silence for a few moments.

'Must have been important, though,' Bob muttered, half to himself.

'Oh, yes.' George turned the car into the enormous parking lot flanking a complex of bars and restaurants. 'You could certainly say it was important.'

He switched off the engine and they stared at the bright neon signs in front of them.

'Well, this is the place the lads came to last night. Two of them got their legs over, so it can't be bad!' George proclaimed.

Simpson laughed uneasily. 'Well, let's get at it then!'

He opened the door and stepped on to the tarmac.

The name 'Millies' in green neon surmounted the doorway which they entered. Inside the air was warm, and sweet with smoke and perfume sprays. Bob Simpson spotted a telephone in the foyer.

'George, must make a quick phone call. Buy me a gin would you, and I'll see you at the bar in a minute. Leave the best one for me!'

His mate gave a V-sign and pushed his way towards the counter.

Simpson took a handful of quarters from his pocket and dialled the operator. Within seconds the number in England was ringing.

The voice which answered sounded extremely sleepy; it was the early hours of the morning over there. But the drowsiness vanished quickly enough when she heard what Simpson had to say.

The VC10 touched down at RAF Brize Norton just after three in the morning. Peter had only managed two hours' sleep on the flight and felt crumpled and unwashed as he stepped carefully down the steps, blinking in the glare of the floodlights.

He had expected an official car to meet him, but not to see the rear seat already half occupied by a large man with a somewhat featureless face that he did not recognise. A door was opened towards him from inside, and a cloud of warm cigarette smoke wafted out into the chilly English air.

'Mr Joyce?' The man's voice sounded tired. 'My name is John Black. I'm from MI5.'

As Peter slid into the free rear-seat he could see even in the pale glow from the courtesy light that the stranger was regarding him with some curiosity. As he closed the door behind him, he immediately found the foul air stifling; and wound down his window.

'MI5?' Peter answered weakly, sensing reluctantly that he was about to be told something deeply shocking. 'It's kind of you to meet me . . .'

'It's not kindness that brings me here, Mr Joyce,' Black answered sombrely.

The driver slammed the car boot. John Black waited until they were outside the air-base and on the road towards London before he spoke again.

'I have some news for you . . . and some of it you will find distressing,' he announced, staring straight ahead. 'The good news is that we seem to have identified who has been playing around with your secret papers.'

'Oh?' Peter turned to look at him in surprise.

'But the bad news *is* bad, I'm afraid.' Black paused and chewed his lip.

Peter felt his heart beat faster.

'The bad news is that Mary Maclean has killed herself.'

'What?' Peter gasped, clutching at the seat in front of him. 'Oh, God!'

'Cut her wrists,' Black continued softly.

'Oh, Jesus.' Peter's voice caught in his throat. His head spun and, as the car lurched round a double bend, he pressed a hand to his stomach.

'Shall I stop the car for a few minutes?' Black asked with sudden concern.

'I . . . I think you'd better,' Peter whispered.

Black tapped the driver on the shoulder and ordered him to pull over. The car slowed to a halt, bumping on the soft earth at the edge of the road. Peter struggled with the handle and pushed the door open. He swung his legs out and stood up, supporting himself against the side of the car, drawing great gulps of cold air into his lungs to try to stem the nausea rising from his stomach.

He struggled to comprehend the trauma and despair that could have been great enough to drive Mary to such a thing. To cut her own wrists! Giddiness overcoming him, he slumped on to the edge of the car seat, leaning out into the air, his head in his hands.

Suddenly it dawned on him what Black had really just told him. Carefully he lifted his legs back into the car and turned to face the man from MI5.

'You said you knew who took the Skydancer plans?' he began with a sense of resignation.

Black nodded, knowing that Peter had understood.

'She wrote you a note admitting it,' he stated flatly. 'It was addressed to you, but I'm afraid we opened it.'

'I can't believe it,' Peter answered. His worst suspicions seemed confirmed.

'She felt herself to be a woman scorned,' Black remarked pointedly.

For a few minutes they sat in silence, Peter shaking his head from time to time in disbelief.

'Are you ready for us to move on now, Mr Joyce?'

'Yes, I think I'm all right now.'

'Perhaps you would take the corners more slowly, driver,' Black called. He slipped his hand into the inside pocket of his jacket and pulled out an envelope.

Peter stared at it silently for a moment, not realising what it was, and not taking hold of it.

'There's a light behind you, if you want to read it,' Black urged him. 'That little white button.'

Peter found the flexible silver tube with a lamp at the end, designed for government officials to study documents while being driven to their appointments.

The envelope was blank, but he pulled from it a folded photocopy of a typewritten letter. He held it in the light and began to read.

Dear Peter,

I've been such a fool. I'm so sorry. I didn't mean to cause all this trouble.

But you hurt me very deep, you know, and I wanted so badly to hurt you back. Causing a fuss over your precious Skydancer seemed the only way to get at you.

It was me who copied a page from your plans and left it on Parliament Hill, just for someone to find it and make a fuss, to get you into trouble. I feel so ashamed now. It was so silly of me and so selfish.

There never were any spies involved, no Russians, plotting against you. Just me.

But I see now what a mess I've made, and I can't go on. I know you can't let me live with you, but I can't live without you.

Goodbye.

Love M.

Peter could almost hear her saying it, see her tear-filled eyes pleading with him as on the last time they had been together. He swallowed hard to keep his own eyes from watering.

Every moment of that night came back to him – that night their affair ended, three months ago. He had been a coward. He should have told her all as soon as he arrived at her flat in Chiswick, but he could not find the courage. She had cooked them some salmon and had bought a bottle of Sancerre to go with it. It had felt so right being there with Mary that evening – so right that he had to fight to hang on to his resolve to end it all.

They had slipped into bed together after their meal. He wanted to make love to her for one last time. He remembered the stunned disbelief on her face when he told her, as they lay together afterwards. He had explained that the preservation of his family and the happiness of his children was more important than his personal feelings.

Disbelief had turned to anger at his deceit in making love to her while knowing he was just about to end their relationship, then to despair when she finally realised they would never be together like this again. Her face looked crumpled and ugly as she buried it in her pillow to sob uncontrollably.

So, now this, he thought to himself, staring hazily at the typewritten note. She had killed herself because of him. He had caused someone to die.

'What . . . what happened exactly?' he asked, without turning to the man on his right.

'She didn't turn up for work yesterday,' John Black explained brusquely. 'There'd been no word from her, and there was no reply from her phone, so in the circumstances we decided to break into her flat. Found her dead in the bath with her wrists slashed. It wasn't a pretty sight.'

Peter took a deep breath, but felt unable to speak.

'And that note was on her desk, in an envelope addressed to you. That's a photocopy; we've got the original in the forensic lab. Just routine checks, of course.'

'It couldn't have been anything else?' Peter asked, clutching at any means to reduce his guilt. 'You're sure it was suicide?'

'Oh, I don't think there's much doubt. Besides it fits in with the evidence. We've not really uncovered anything that points to a Soviet intelligence operation. I'd had a feeling the whole business was "personal" right from the very start.'

The car had now passed Oxford and was heading south towards Aldermaston. Peter was being taken home.

'Have you . . . have you talked to my wife about this?' he inquired a few minutes later.

'Yesterday. Saw her yesterday. Before we got worried about Maclean.'

'What did you ask her? What sort of questions?'

'Oh, just things that were relevant to my enquiry,' John Black answered evasively.

'Including presumably whether she knew about Mary and me?'

'Of course. Your affair wasn't exactly insignificant, after all, was it?' His eyebrows arched in self-righteousness.

'And what did she say?' Peter asked sharply, suspecting the MI5 man took pleasure in invading people's privacy.

'Seemed a bit shocked. Apparently she hadn't known anything about it, or at least that's what she claimed. She got rather uppish after that. Refused to answer any more questions, and even started trying to ring some lawyer or other, so I decided to leave. With women like your wife there comes a point where you just can't get any more sense out of them – but then I expect you know that already. I suppose that's why you went off with Maclean?'

Peter turned to glare at the MI5 man.

'If I were you I would keep opinions like that to myself!' he exploded. 'I don't think you could even begin to understand what that affair was about. Are you married, Mr Black?'

The MI5 man chuckled. 'No, not me. I don't really like women that much. They're all right for just one thing, but when they start expressing opinions, that's when trouble starts.' He paused reflectively for a few moments. 'But between you and me, Mr Joyce, it's *people* that I don't really like, people in general. Life could run so smoothly if it wasn't for people fouling it up, don't you think?'

Peter felt further conversation was pointless. Black's remarks were odious and insensitive. So he sat in silence for the rest of the journey, Mary's agonised face filling his thoughts. As they neared his village in the rolling hillocks of Berkshire, he began to dread how he would cope with Belinda.

Black leaned forward to instruct the driver to pull up outside Peter's house.

'I'd be glad if you would call into my office at Curzon Street tomorrow morning around eleven,' John Black said. 'There are still a number of security details that need clearing up. All right?'

'Eleven o'clock? I'll try,' Peter answered coolly.

The driver retrieved his small suitcase from the boot and handed it to him.

'Goodnight, Mr Joyce,' Black called from inside the car.

The car purred away down the road, and Peter was left with the sounds of the night. It had been raining, and moisture dripped from the branches of the oak tree in his garden.

The clouds prevented the moon from illuminating his path, but that did not matter. Light was streaming on to the drive from the bedroom window. His wife was awake and waiting for him.

Chapter Four

Belinda had just reached the foot of the stairs as he opened the front door. She was in her dressing-gown. She gazed at him for less than a second, her face tear-stained and pained; then, without speaking, she turned towards the kitchen and moved away from him.

He deposited his overnight bag on the hall floor, and listened momentarily to the stillness of the house. He could almost sense the presence of his three children upstairs, sleeping in happy ignorance of the conflict about to engulf their parents.

He heard a kettle being filled, and followed his wife into the kitchen, knowing they could not put off the confrontation. Belinda plugged in the kettle and turned to face him with her arms folded.

'Hello,' he greeted her weakly from the doorway, without even attempting to smile.

She did not reply. She was like a primed bomb of tense emotion, her whole body rigid, not daring to speak for fear the last remnants of self-control would slip from her grasp. Peter watched her uncomfortably, terribly aware that he was the cause of her acute distress. Her skin looked pale grey from lack of sleep, and her straight, streaked hair was uncombed.

'I'm sorry . . .' Peter whispered, his voice catching in his throat. Pulling out one of the rickety pine chairs from under the kitchen table, he sat down staring vacantly into the corner of the room.

'It would help . . . if you were to tell me how much

you know, Belinda,' he ventured, hoping to find a way through to her.

'Huh!' she snapped angrily. 'Of course it would bloody well help you! Help you to decide how little you need tell me!'

She found herself shouting but quickly moderated her tone, conscious of the sleeping children upstairs.

'I'll tell you just one thing, Peter, give you just one clue,' she continued, unable to control the trembling in her voice. 'Yesterday I had a visit from a man calling himself John Black. You know him perhaps?'

Peter nodded.

'Well this man Black tried to interrogate me. He accused me of conspiracy, treason and theft . . . and of *sexual deviation*.'

Her voice rose to a pitch of indignation.

'Then he told me tales about you which I refused to believe – until he showed me things to prove it.'

The kettle came to the boil behind her, and she swung round to turn it off, her eyes filling with tears.

'I'm making some tea. I take it you'd like some?' she offered, struggling to steady her voice.

'Yes, please.'

Peter took a deep breath before continuing.

'I expect,' he began carefully, 'that John Black told you I was having an affair with another woman.'

She stirred the tea noisily.

'He showed me a letter you wrote her,' Belinda choked on the words. 'It was full of . . . of love! You cheated, Peter. I trusted you!'

'Did he tell you that I broke it off three months ago?' Peter asked hurriedly. 'Did he? Did he tell you that?'

She placed his mug on the table, her face contorted with her effort not to cry. She shook her head.

'Well, I did. It was all over. I haven't had any contact

with her since then . . . hadn't even heard any news of her until just now.'

His wife leaned back against the dresser, clasping her mug in both hands to keep it steady. She shivered; it was cold in the kitchen. She was not sure she was ready to listen to his pleas of mitigation.

'What do you mean? What news? What have you heard just now?' she asked cautiously.

Peter pushed away the tea; the feeling of nausea was returning.

'John Black just told me,' he said haltingly. 'He told me . . . that she's dead. She killed herself yesterday.' Finally the words spilled out.

'Oh, Peter!' Belinda gasped. She was shocked, yet deep inside she felt an uncomfortable gladness at the news. 'How dreadful!'

The distress on his face would normally have evoked her sympathy, but at that moment she could feel none. His grief was for a woman who had been her rival, someone she could only think of as a thief.

'Why did she kill herself?' Belinda asked after a pause.

Peter stared down at his tea.

'It wasn't because of you . . . because of your breaking up with her, was it?'

He pulled a handkerchief from his pocket and blew his nose.

'Oh God,' she whispered, 'it was, wasn't it?'

She pulled another chair from under the table and sat down opposite him.

Peter drew in a deep breath.

'I met her . . .' he tried to steady his voice. 'I met her two years ago. It began as . . . as nothing really. Just a little flirtation. There was no particular reason for it . . . it just happened.'

Peter spread his arms in a gesture of helplessness. He badly wanted to avoid a probing analysis of his motives.

Belinda turned her mind back two years trying to guess when he had first been unfaithful to her. Surely she should have noticed something? In bed perhaps? How could he have been making love to another woman and not show it?

'Two years! For two years you've been deceiving me,' she burst out.

Why had it all happened? There *had* to be a reason for it.

'It was about two years ago I started campaigning seriously,' she continued more quietly. 'That's when I got involved at the craft co-operative and began campaigning against your work, wasn't it?'

'Well . . . it *was* about that time,' he conceded uncomfortably.

'So this . . . this was you getting your own back, was it?'

'No! It really didn't begin for any reason that I can explain. It was just – an opportunity that suddenly presented itself; a temptation if you like, and . . . I failed to resist it,' he ended feebly.

He knew his explanation would not satisfy his wife. His fingers fumbled with the peppermill on the table.

'We didn't meet very often, and I didn't really take it very seriously at first, but . . . Mary became more involved than I did. And in the end . . . I mean she knew I was married – always knew that . . . But in the end she seemed to expect me to leave you and the children and set up home with her – and I wasn't having it. So I told her I couldn't see her anymore.'

Belinda eyed him suspiciously. He must have encouraged the woman to fall in love with him.

'And now she's dead . . .'

Peter flinched at the accusation in her tone.

'Yes, she's dead.'

He still found it hard to believe.

'There was a note. She left a note,' he continued with an effort. 'In it she said that she was very bitter . . . that she'd wanted to hit back at me in some way. She said she took a page from a secret file at the Defence Ministry, photocopied it and left it on Parliament Hill . . . expecting that it would be found by a passer-by and cause a scandal which would damage my work at Aldermaston.'

'What?' Belinda gasped with astonishment. 'So *she* was at the bottom of this security scandal? You mean *she* was the one who's had you running round in circles the past few days? Well, she's certainly got her own back!' She shook her head with a certain admiration at the panic the woman had been able to cause.

For a few moments neither spoke, as Belinda took in the seriousness of what had happened. It was not just that Peter had been unfaithful to her; he was now at the very centre of a national crisis over Skydancer. It would be he who would take the blame for all that had happened. He faced disgrace in his professional life and his career would be in ruins.

His handsome face looked crumpled and crushed. She began to feel a little sorry for him, despite her anger and resentment at what he had done.

'She must have been really desperate,' Belinda reflected.

'I still can't believe she did it,' her husband murmured. 'However much she may have got to hate me, I just can't believe she'd have done this. She was too . . . too professional. This is so out of character – it really is. I mean, it seemed obvious the Soviets would try to steal the Skydancer plans. They're bound to want to know what we're up to. So when that paper was found on Parliament Hill, it looked exactly like a drop that had gone wrong. That explanation fitted perfectly. But now . . . Mary.'

He frowned as he tried to recall the exact words in the note John Black had given him. There had been something about that note that did not seem quite right, he thought in retrospect. He puzzled about what that was.

'Is there any doubt?' Belinda asked, curious at the implications. 'There is, isn't there? I can see it in your eyes?'

Peter was concentrating hard, trying to remember exactly what the letter had said. It was still in his jacket pocket, but he did not want Belinda to read it.

The more he thought about it now, the stranger it all seemed. Mary had been such a stable person. Would she really have taken such drastic revenge on him, and then killed herself? He somehow could not believe it. Or was he just telling himself that to lessen the guilt pressing down on his shoulders?

'John Black said there was little doubt that she killed herself. It seemed to fit the circumstances,' he murmured.

'John Black?' Belinda spat. 'You believe that *creature*?'

'He *is* conducting the investigation,' Peter answered flatly.

'Well, God help poor old Britain!' she exclaimed. 'He's an evil man! And, anyway, I thought MI5 were discredited these days. Aren't they all supposed to be Russian moles? How do you know Black didn't murder your . . . friend, to cover up some spy operation being run by Moscow?'

Peter looked at Belinda in astonishment.

Whether meant seriously or not, her words further

stirred the growing doubts in his mind. For the past three days the Defence Ministry's guard had been up, trying to counter the loss of the Skydancer plans. But now, conveniently, it seemed there had been no loss of secrets after all, so they could all relax again. It was very comforting – perhaps too comforting.

Belinda was torn between both a need and a reluctance to know more about the secret life her husband had been leading for the past two years.

'You loved her, didn't you?' she asked eventually.

'What?' Peter was jolted back to the present. 'I . . . I don't really know,' he stammered. 'I suppose I was . . . sort of infatuated . . . *in love* with her maybe, but that's not the same thing is it? We got on together,' he continued carelessly. 'There was no conflict between us until . . .'

'Conflict! So that's it! Conflict. Something you didn't have with her, but you did have with me. But what *was* that conflict, Peter. What was it about? How did it happen? Well, I'll tell you, in case you've forgotten. That conflict only arose because, as I got older, I began to understand the meaning of morality, and you didn't. It all makes sense in a way; it explains your mistress. One immorality begat another!'

'Immorality? What the hell are you talking about?' he rounded on her.

'You know perfectly well what I mean,' she persisted. 'Your work – that's the source of our conflict. It is utterly immoral for you to devote your life to designing means of genocide, building weapons of mass murder! And it is the moral duty of every rational human being to oppose your work and demand that it ends!'

'Belinda, please! Let's not go through that all over again!' Peter pleaded.

'Yes. I can see how nice it must have been for you to

find a woman who didn't object to what you did for a living. No wonder you fell in love with your Mary if she never said anything that would make your conscience trouble you! If it wasn't for the bloody bomb, none of this . . .'

She stopped halfway through her sentence, turning towards the door. Peter turned in his chair to follow her gaze.

'I heard a noise and thought it was burglars.' Suzanne stood in the doorway, rubbing the sleep from her eyes. 'Is it morning or what?'

Peter rose from the table and crossed the room. Putting his arm round her shoulders he led her back towards the stairs.

'No, it's still the middle of the night. I've just got back from America, and Mummy and I were – talking,' he explained gently, taking her back up to her bedroom. 'I'm sorry we woke you.'

He tucked her back under her blankets and kissed her on the forehead.

'You were having a row!' said Suzanne, holding on to his arm.

Peter wondered how much she had heard.

'Well, just a small one, but it's over now,' he conceded with a smile. 'Back to sleep with you now.'

When he returned to the kitchen, Belinda was placing their mugs in the sink.

'That girl has ears on stalks,' she complained. 'Do you think she heard much?'

'I don't know,' he answered, grateful for the unexpected interruption to Belinda's tirade.

She turned to face him with a reproachful look in her eyes.

'I'm sorry for what I said, but you've hurt me deeply, you know – very deeply indeed.'

Those words. The same words that stuck in the back of his mind, and yet they were not quite the same. '*You hurt me very deeply, you know*'. Wasn't that what Mary had written? Not quite. He had to look at the letter again.

Belinda came over to him, as if looking for a response.

'I'm desperately sorry, too. I've buggered things up dreadfully,' Peter admitted.

He took her hands in his own. She snatched them away and turned back towards the dresser, folding her arms tightly across her chest.

'It's not as easy as that.' She was choking back a new threat of tears. 'You can't just say sorry and expect everything to be all right.'

'No, it's not that simple. I know that.'

She looked so vulnerable, struggling with her feelings, that he felt an urge to clasp her firmly in his arms, to reassure her that their own relationship could and should survive all that had happened.

'You may not find this easy to believe but, whatever may have happened in the last two years, I've never stopped loving you,' he insisted.

Although sincerely meant, his words sounded hollow.

'Do you think you might forgive me one day?' he asked softly.

His wife stared hard at the floor for a few moments, before looking him coolly in the eye.

'I shall never forget,' she answered finally.

'No. I don't suppose either of us will,' he answered sombrely. 'Well, we can't stay down here all night. You go back to bed, and I'll follow in a minute.'

As soon as she had left the room and he heard the stairs creak under her tread, Peter pulled from his inside pocket the envelope containing the letter Mary had written. He held the page under the light over the kitchen table.

He stared fixedly at those crucial words: '*But you hurt me very deep, you know.*'

'Hurt very deep'? Mary would never have said that. 'Deeply', yes, but not 'deep'. It was ungrammatical, and even under such stress she would have still written correct English, Peter was certain.

Suddenly he looked at the page with suspicion; so much of it now seemed wrong. The whole letter had been typed, including the '*love M.*' at the bottom. Surely she would have signed it? All the letters she had sent him in the past had been hand-written. He knew she had a typewriter in her flat, but used it only for business letters.

He was stirred by a sudden sense of unease. What had first appeared the tragic last words of a distraught woman now began to look totally different – something altogether more alarming and sinister.

With only two hours' sleep that night, Peter felt worse in the morning than if he had not gone to bed at all. At breakfast he was conscious of his younger daughter's silent stare as she searched for clues to the conflict between her parents that had disturbed her night's sleep.

By 8.30 he was at his desk at Aldermaston, struggling to make sense of his aroused suspicions. A note left by his secretary the previous evening reminded him that John Black wanted to see him at eleven in London, and announced that the Chief of the Defence Staff had invited him for lunch at his club.

Peter felt at a loss about what to do next; Mary Maclean now dominated his thoughts completely. He felt certain now that her death was by no means the end of the Skydancer secrets affair, but more likely just its beginning.

Suddenly he knew what he had to do. Absent-mindedly he had been fingering the keys in his pocket, and realised that one belonged to the door of Mary's flat. He had omitted to give it back to her.

The motorway traffic into London was heavy at that time of day, and it was nearly ten o'clock by the time he drew up outside the large Victorian house in Chiswick where Mary have lived in the garden flat.

Looking at the house, he felt overwhelmed by sadness, remembering the pleasure and anticipation he used to feel when visiting her here, though a pleasure tinged with guilt. Mary had adored him, and to come here to see her had been a rejuvenation for him. But now she was dead. For a few minutes he just sat in his car, staring at the house, weighed down with his grief.

Eventually he walked up the drive, with dread in his heart. He had had to come – to discover more about how she had died.

The big house was divided into six apartments and the door to Mary's garden flat was round at the side. He tried the key in the lock. It did not fit. The lock had been changed.

There was a wooden gate leading into the garden, and he tried to open it, thinking he might see something through the French windows, but the gate was bolted from the other side.

'You won't find her, you know. She's gone,' an elderly female voice croaked behind him.

Startled, he spun round to see the old woman who occupied the flat at the front of the house. She had been living there longer than anyone else and saw herself as something of a caretaker. Mary had considered her a busybody.

'Oh, it's you,' she continued, puffing at the cigarette clamped firmly in the corner of her mouth. She recognised him as the man she had often spotted stealing away from Mary's flat in the early mornings.

'Yes,' Peter answered abruptly, annoyed at the way she had crept up on him. 'Yes, I was trying to get into her flat, but the key she gave me doesn't seem to fit anymore.'

'No, it wouldn't.' She stared accusingly into his eyes. 'They changed the lock after they broke the door down. You know what happened to her, I suppose?'

He nodded.

'Yes, well you would,' she sniffed self-righteously.

She was in her late sixties, with curly grey hair, and a pair of glasses sat crookedly on her nose.

'So you're a scientist, are you?'

'How did you know that?' Peter asked in surprise.

'Policeman told me. His name was Black. Asked me all sorts of questions about Miss Maclean and her visitors. Seemed to know all about you. Even had a photo of you in his briefcase.'

'Did he indeed?' Peter answered as casually as possible trying to control his growing annoyance. 'Tell me, do you by any chance have a spare key for the new lock? I seem to remember Miss Maclean saying you used to keep one for her in case she locked herself out.'

'Want to go in there, do you?' She looked at him oddly, her lower lip quivering. 'No one's cleaned up in there, you know. It was a horrible mess the policeman said. Told me I should keep well out of it. He said some relative of hers would come down at the weekend and sort things out.'

'Do you have a key?' Peter repeated abruptly.

'Well, yes. As a matter of fact Mr Black gave me one so as I could let her relatives in when they come.'

'Then may I borrow it, please? Obviously you know I was a close friend of hers,' he insisted.

She hesitated, looking anxious.

'I suppose it's all right,' she muttered, turning back towards her own flat. 'The police did say they'd finished.'

As Peter waited for her, he was dreading what he might find inside.

After a few minutes she returned and handed him a key. As he went in, she hovered by the door, not daring to enter. He closed the door firmly behind him.

In the small entrance hall he stood still for a few moments, conscious of the silence. Mary had always treasured the way she could cut herself off from the world outside simply by closing that front door. None of the noise of passing traffic or aircraft seemed to penetrate in here. Today, though, that silence seemed unreal, as if any moment it might be broken by the sound of her voice calling out to him.

He looked around; splintered wood on the door frame bore witness to the force used by the police to enter the flat. A rough job of carpentry had been done when the new lock was fitted, and wood shavings still littered the floor.

Peter paused by the door to the living-room. Inside it looked much as always, though the cushions were squeezed into the corners of the chairs, where heavy policemen had clearly been sitting on them.

At the end of the hall, two doors stood ajar. One led into the bedroom, but through the other he could see the edge of the bath and the washbasin beyond. He dreaded entering that room, but knew he had to. As he drew nearer he could see streaky red-brown stains on the bathroom carpet.

Fighting to control his nausea, he forced himself to look into the room. Blood streaks were also daubed round the edge of the bath and a concentrated stain round the plughole had been left where the water that had formed Mary's shroud had drained her blood away.

Peter choked at the sight and backed away. Turning into the neighbouring room he sat on the bed, clutching his head in his hands. He could not believe that she had done such a thing to herself. The sight of that blood made him realise just how violent her death had been. But that was the key to it. She was just not capable of such an act of violence. If Mary had ever contemplated suicide, it would have been by some other means. Gas or drugs maybe, but not to slash her own veins with a knife.

'Somebody murdered you!' he said out loud, astonished at the certainty of his conviction.

And, yet, was he deceiving himself? Was there any real evidence of murder – or was it simply what he preferred to believe?

He stood up. There might be something else, some other clue in this flat that would point to the truth of what had happened, something the police had overlooked. Against one wall of the bedroom stood a small writing table, and on it the portable typewriter on which her final letter was apparently written. Its keys were dusty with fingerprint powder. The police had been thorough, at least.

He looked round the bedroom again, but nothing struck him as out of the ordinary. Then he walked down the hall to the living-room. Standing by the sofa, he rested a hand on it to support himself. A trace of Mary's perfume seemed to linger in the air. He cast his eye round the room, looking for anything out of place – something that had not been there before, or something familiar missing from its usual position. He began with the bookcase, running his finger along the volumes which had meant so much to her. Then he moved into the kitchen; an unwashed wine glass stood on the draining-board, its lip and stem coated with the white powder used by the forensic men. Next to the cooker a rack for kitchen knives was fixed to the wall. He stared at it for a moment, conscious that one knife was missing. There should have been five. He had always noticed the perfect symmetry with which they were arranged there, with the largest knife in the middle and blades of decreasing size on each side. It was the smallest one that was missing, the one she had kept particularly sharp for slicing vegetables.

He shuddered as he realised what it might have been used for. Surely she could never have used that knife on herself. She just could not have done that, he was sure of that. But suppose she had been murdered, who would have done it, and why?

Peter returned to the living-room. The thought of finding something which Black's men had overlooked, something that would point towards murder instead of suicide, began to seem impossible. He furrowed his brow in concentration, and tried to direct his gaze systematically at every detail of the room, from one end to the other. After a few minutes he shook his head in despair; it all seemed just as he remembered it.

The antique bureau with its walnut veneer was a fine piece of furniture, he realised. He had never really studied it before, but now crossed the floor to inspect it closely. He ran his hand over the waxed surface which felt almost warm to the touch. He vaguely remembered Mary explaining it had been in her family for generations; it was her continuity with her past. How much had her family really been told of what had happened, he asked himself? Their framed photographs had stood on top of the bureau. There was now only one of her parents here, but surely there had been two before. He remembered the other picture distinctly; Mary with her arms round two children, her niece and nephew.

He turned his head to scan the bookshelf, in case the photograph had been moved there. Then he walked briskly round the room in search of it, before hurrying back to the bedroom. It was nowhere to be seen.

'That's odd.' His voice sounded like an intrusion in the stillness of the flat.

That photograph had always stood on the bureau – from the day he first visited her, of that he was certain. Its position had never changed. Perhaps the police had taken it, but why should they? It was hardly evidence. He hurried back to the bureau and pulled open the lid.

The compartments inside were empty. All her papers were gone. That must have been the police, he assumed; they would have reason to look through her documents. Closing the lid, he opened the drawers below in case the photograph had been put away, but there was still no sign of it.

Suddenly he peered at his watch. He had almost forgotten his appointment with John Black. It was half-past ten, with just thirty minutes for him to get to MI5's headquarters. He would have to leave immediately, and take the underground. It would be quicker than driving and trying to find somewhere to park in Mayfair.

In the hall he lingered for a moment, looking again towards the bathroom.

'Goodbye,' he whispered softly.

'You were in there a long time,' the old woman commented as he emerged. She held out her hand for the key.

'Was I?' Peter answered vaguely. She was staring expectantly at him through her crooked glasses, trying to assess how he was affected by what he had seen inside.

'It's like you said,' Peter answered her unspoken question, 'a horrible mess.'

'Poor soul. Such a nice girl . . .' She turned her head away.

'Tell me,' Peter asked impulsively. 'The night before she was found . . . do you know if she had any visitors?'

'Oh, I wouldn't know. I never see or hear anything. I'm at the front and she's at the back, see,' she insisted hurriedly.

'No, I'm sure you don't,' Peter reassured her gently. 'But try to remember about the night before last, just in case there was something unusual. It could be important.'

The old woman turned away and made as if she was thinking deeply as she walked slowly back towards the front of the house. Just as they reached the front drive, she turned round with a gesture of sudden recollection.

'Now you mention it, I do remember someone leaving her flat, sometime after midnight. I couldn't sleep because of the indigestion. It's been terrible lately, and the doctors are no use with that sort of thing, are they? Well, I heard some feet on the gravel here, and I looked out of the window. It was a man, quite large he was, with a raincoat. He must have had a car, because I heard him slam the door. Inconsiderate, I call it, making such a noise late at night . . .'

'It's dreadful how thoughtless some people can be,'

Peter agreed patiently. 'But that was it? No other noises that night?'

'Well, no. It went on, you see. I was just dropping off, after taking some Milk of Mag., when he came back. Or *someone* did. I heard feet on the gravel again.'

'Same man again, was it? Did he look the same?'

'Oh, I don't know what he looked like. I was under the covers that time. Didn't see him at all.'

'So you didn't hear anything more after that?' Peter persisted earnestly.

'No. No, I slept like a baby. Didn't know any more about it until the police came yesterday evening.'

Thanking her for her help, Peter hurried away down the drive. As he turned on the pavement, he glanced back and noticed that she was still watching him.

He arrived five minutes late at the Curzon Street office of MI5, with its windowless ground floor. John Black looked aggravated by his lack of perfect punctuality as he pointed him to a chair in a sparsely furnished room used for interviews.

'Make yourself comfortable. We've got a lot to talk about,' he gestured impatiently.

'Really? I thought the case was solved, as far as you were concerned,' Peter replied with an edge to his voice.

'There are a lot of details, Mr Joyce. If you knew the amount of paperwork I have to do . . .'

'I suppose so.'

As if to make his point, the investigator slapped a fat folder down on the table and lowered his over-weight body on to a swivel-chair behind it. The impact with the seat expelled from the man's lungs a blast of air which carried the smell of stale cigarette smoke across to Peter's nostrils.

'You know, Mr Joyce,' Black continued in a voice that was tired and irritable, 'it seems to me that the way you've been conducting your business during the past few years is totally at variance with the high standards of personal behaviour required in a man of your status, a man entrusted with some of the nation's most sensitive secrets. You wouldn't disagree with that, would you?'

Peter was stunned by the suddenness of the attack; he knew he was bound to face official criticism for what had happened, but did not feel ready to cope with it quite like this.

'I think you had better explain what you mean,' he answered defensively.

'Oh, come now, for heaven's sake! Then let me itemise it for you.'

Counting off his accusations on the fingers of his outstretched hand, Black held the scientist with a gaze that was cold and derisive.

'First: your wife takes issue with your work, and joins a subversive organisation whose purpose is to undermine Britain's nuclear capabilities. You knew about this but failed to report it to your security officer at your last positive vetting.

'Second: you start up an adulterous relationship with Miss Maclean, a relationship which lays both you and her open to the possibility of blackmail – a very real possibility considering the secret material to which you both had access. This affair you also failed to report to your security officer.'

Peter made as if to interrupt, but Black gestured him to silence.

'Third: you have flagrantly disregarded the Defence Ministry rules concerning the safe storage of classified documents. Three months ago you left them lying around in your briefcase at the home of the woman with whom you had been having the adulterous affair, at a time when your termination of that relationship might give Miss Maclean the motive to do something foolish and dangerous with those papers –'

'Did Mary tell you about that? Did she admit to you that she had taken the plans?' Peter burst in, seizing the opportunity to divert the criticism that Black so painfully and accurately aimed at him.

John Black's eyelids seemed to blink for the first time since this conversation had started. He looked almost surprised that he himself should face a question.

'She certainly told me that you had the plans in your case that last night you spent in her flat.'

'But did she actually tell you that she'd done anything with them?'

'No, she didn't admit that to me in person,' Black shifted his position on the chair. 'But we have the letter, don't we?'

'Yes. Well, I'm not happy about that,' Peter answered firmly. 'Let me get it quite clear. What you gave me last night was an exact photocopy of what you found in her flat?'

'Yes, it was.'

'And you're convinced it was she who wrote it?'

'Her fingerprints were all over the letter and the typewriter keys, so unless you –'

'Yes, but she never typed letters to me,' Peter insisted. 'They were always hand-written. And some of the grammar – it just wasn't her.'

The MI5 man permitted himself a wry smile.

'People under sufficient stress to kill themselves don't always behave according to previously established patterns, Mr Joyce,' he countered firmly. 'And what exactly are you suggesting by all this, anyway?'

'I'm suggesting that she was murdered,' Peter ventured.

Black heaved himself upright in the chair and sighed.

'I wouldn't want you to think we hadn't thought of that. It was one of the first possibilities we considered. But we have to deal in *evidence*, and there simply isn't any to suggest that someone else killed her. The knife she used had her prints on, and no one else's. The pathologist's report confirms that death was caused solely by loss of blood, and there's no trace of any pacifying or tranquillising agent in her body. As I said before, her prints were all over the suicide note – and, let's face it, she was sufficiently cut up over the way you dumped her to have the motive to do herself in. The business with the document in the rubbish bin fits too, since there's still no sign from any intelligence source that the Russians have got hold of the secrets.'

At the end of his explanation, Black moistened his lips and there was a glint of triumph in his eyes. He extracted the packet from his pocket, wrenched back the flip-top, tugged out one of the cigarettes and placed it between his lips in one smooth movement. Then, as an afterthought, he extended the packet across the table and enquired with his eyebrows whether the scientist would like one too.

Peter shook his head. From Black's slouching, untidy appearance and off-hand manner, he found it impossible to assess whether the man could be trusted. He was conscious of the persisting widespread suspicion about MI5 following its recent disastrous infiltration by Soviet agents, yet the Security Commission had scoured the organisation afterwards and pronounced it clean.

Peter thought back to his conversation with Mary's elderly neighbour. Black was a large man, and could fit the description she gave of the figure who had visited Mary that fatal night.

'Did you call to see Mary at her home the night she died?' Peter asked.

Black looked up sharply. 'Yes, I did. Why do you ask?'

'I went to her flat this morning,' Peter answered casually. 'The woman next-door told me she had seen someone about your size.'

'Oh? Been playing policeman, have you?' he snapped sarcastically. 'Yes, I interviewed Miss Maclean at her home that evening, but I hope you're not insinuating my visit had any connection with her suicide . . .'

'Did you . . . did you remove anything from her flat at any time?' Peter asked cautiously. 'Any documents or papers, for example?'

Black smiled. 'If you mean the letters you wrote to her, then yes, I have them here. They're quite safe.'

'And what about photographs? She had family photographs in frames on her bureau. Have you taken one of those?'

John Black frowned.

'Describe them to me,' he answered evasively.

'There were two. One showed her mother and father, and that's still there; the missing one was of Mary herself, with her young niece and nephew. I wondered whether you'd taken it.'

'No, I've not got any photographs.'

For a moment he looked uncomfortable, as if the question had caught him out.

'But I think you may be a little out of date with your recollection,' Black added hurriedly. 'When I interviewed her two nights ago, there was only one picture on the bureau – one of her parents. I remember it distinctly because I asked her about it. There was only one, then, Mr Joyce.'

His eyes sparkled with innocence, but Peter felt certain he was lying.

'That's odd,' he persisted. 'Tell me one other thing: was it you the neighbour heard leaving after midnight?'

Black did not at all like being questioned. It was like reversing the natural order of things.

'It probably would have been,' he mumbled irritably.

'And did you return to her flat after that? The neighbour heard footsteps coming back again later.'

'She *has* been talkative,' Black exclaimed angrily. 'Now, if you don't mind, I'll have a turn at asking the questions!' But he still looked thoughtful.

Peter realised he would achieve nothing further, so for the next half hour he submitted to a detailed probing of his work routines, his wife's anti-nuclear involvements, and his own private life. By the time the questioning eventually ended, he felt emotionally and physically drained.

It was about three-quarters of a mile from Curzon Street to St James's Square, and Joyce had a brisk walk to reach the East India Club by one o'clock. The exercise was a help in sorting out his thoughts before he met the Defence Chief.

Field-Marshal Buxton was waiting for him in the panelled bar, clutching a whisky and soda.

'What would you like, Peter? Kind of you to join me today. Hope it wasn't inconvenient.'

'I'll have the same as you,' Peter replied. 'It's not inconvenient at all.'

Buxton was dressed in worn tweeds, and looked more like a country gentleman than the head of the nation's armed forces.

'I use this place when I want to get away from my

military chums,' he confided. 'Unlike in the Army and Navy Club, hardly anyone here knows who I am, so it's ideal for private chats.'

He studied Peter's face thoughtfully, trying to assess his general reaction to the events of the past two days.

'You must be jet-lagged!' he exclaimed suddenly. 'How extremely inconsiderate of me to summon you to lunch when you should be getting your head down.'

'Don't worry, I haven't had time to get jet-lagged, and I've just spent the morning with John Black of MI5.'

'Have you, now?' said Buxton. Looking round at the handful of people in the bar, he took Peter by the arm. 'Tell you what, why don't we take ourselves and our drinks to the dining-room. Then we can sit comfortably and natter privately to our hearts' content.'

Seated at a corner table in the palatial restaurant with its gilded ceiling, they were a comfortable distance from anyone else, and the CDS began to talk freely.

'Bad business about that girl Mary Maclean,' he growled. 'Distressing for you, I imagine.' His face expressed a combination of sympathy and disapproval.

Peter glanced at him uncomfortably. He had not yet accustomed himself to the idea that his affair with Mary had become such public knowledge.

'But it's disturbing, too,' Peter replied carefully.

Just then the waiter came for their order. The field-marshal recommended the Dover sole, and Peter concurred with his suggestion.

'Disturbing? In what way?' Buxton probed, when the waiter was again out of earshot.

Peter then explained at length his doubts about the 'suicide', and described the conversation he had already had with Black.

'Sure you're not imagining things?' Buxton

remarked. 'A woman scorned is pretty unpredictable, you know. Suicide is in itself an irrational act, so I feel you're asking a bit much to expect her to behave in any normal way while carrying it out.'

Buxton could see that Peter was taken aback by this dismissive statement.

'Look, I'm sorry. I don't mean to doubt your word, but let's face it, it sounds a little as if you're trying to make excuses. All this has been a hell of a strain for you, and it's obviously personally embarrassing. There's bound to be a full internal inquiry at the end of it all, and inevitably you aren't going to come out of it very well. There's firstly your affair with that poor girl, and then, from what I've been told, you've been pretty lax about security procedures too.'

Peter looked startled.

'Oh yes. I've heard about it, I'm afraid. The Prime Minister is horrified at what's been going on, and is after your blood. The only thing that's likely to save you from his wrath is his need to sweep the whole thing under the carpet in case it damages his tenuous hold on the reins of government. The press haven't yet heard about Mary Maclean's death, but the PM's planning to feed them something this afternoon. He may make a statement to the House of Commons.'

'Good God!' Peter was aghast. 'This is crazy. Don't you see, blaming the whole thing on a woman's revenge is too tidy – too convenient an end to the business.'

He pushed away his half-finished plate, and swallowed a mouthful of the white Burgundy Buxton had chosen.

'Look, if you were in charge of the new anti-missile system protecting Moscow, and you learned by whatever sources that Britain had developed a new warhead enabling its nuclear bombs to penetrate those defences, wouldn't you do everything you could to acquire the details of those new weapons?'

'Probably,' Buxton replied briefly.

'Now, if you were the head of the KGB department responsible for getting hold of those plans, and your agent in the field made a colossal bungle of the operation, what would *you* do about it? You'd try desperately to cover your tracks. And if you were a KGB chief, wouldn't you be ruthless enough to commit murder if it would succeed in throwing the poor old British off the scent?'

Buxton studied his glass of wine thoughtfully.

'It's not inconceivable,' he conceded.

'So, to go rushing in and blame the whole thing on an emotional woman has to be shortsighted, don't you think? At least get the PM to wait a few days before saying anything to the House.'

'Not sure I can do that,' Buxton mused. 'He thinks he's obliged to tell them something. But I might be able to persuade him to keep the details to a minimum. And anyway, come to think of it, if there is substance to your theory, it wouldn't do any harm for Ivan to think we'd fallen for his little trick. Might make him careless, don't you think?'

The waiter was hovering again.

'More to eat, or just coffee?' Buxton enquired.

'Coffee, thanks.'

'What about John Black?' Peter continued as the waiter moved away. 'He seems to be closing the investigation. He maintains there's no evidence that it was anything but suicide.'

'Hmmm.' Buxton dropped a spoonful of sugar crystals into his coffee.

'I suppose . . .' Peter persisted. 'I suppose they *are* clean now? MI5, I mean. The Soviet infiltration seemed pretty extensive. There was something odd in what John Black said to me.'

'That business with the photograph, you mean?'

'Yes. He insisted that picture wasn't in the flat when he interviewed her – yet there was something odd about the way he said it. I'm sure he was lying.'

'Why should he bother to lie about a thing like that?'

'I don't know,' Peter frowned. 'But let's be fanciful for a moment. Let's pretend that Black is a Soviet agent, and that he murdered Mary and fixed it to look like suicide. Supposing there was some sort of struggle, and the photograph was smashed. He'd have got rid of it, wouldn't he? And of course he'd deny it had ever been there.'

'Well, yes, but that's an awful lot of supposing,' Buxton answered doubtfully. 'The curious thing is there is still no word from any of our agents suggesting the KGB are doing anything at all. Our men are pretty well placed, you know. They would almost certainly have heard some whisper of an operation if one was underway.' The Chief of the Defence Staff paused, frowning. 'And yet that in itself is damned odd, isn't it?' he then continued. 'If I was Ivan, I'd be bloody *sure* to be hatching some plot to learn the secrets of Skydancer.'

'That's exactly my point,' Peter interrupted in relief. 'So perhaps the Soviets are deliberately by-passing all their usual intelligence people. Perhaps there's some special team involved, and the reason we've heard nothing about it is that this team includes undiscovered Soviet moles inside our own security services!'

'Clearly we mustn't draw any conclusions too soon,' Buxton determined. 'We'll have to keep an open mind on the matter for the time being. And that leaves a big question-mark hanging over the test launch of Skydancer. You've just set up a complex deception plan to counter a Soviet espionage operation which may or may not exist. If there's no plot, you could put the original programmes back in the missiles and do a proper test. But we don't know that for sure, so for the time being we'd better just do nothing. I'll send the boat back out into the Atlantic just to confuse the Russians, then we'll just sit tight and see what pops its head up out of the trench. Agreed?'

A waiter approached table. 'Excuse me, sir, your secretary is on the phone,' he told Peter.

Peter made his apologies and followed the waiter out of the room.

The message was a summons to the Defence Secretary's office.

In Moscow snow was swirling in great determined gusts round the city squares and along the broad boulevards. It was still early for such intense snowfall Oleg Kvitzinsky reckoned, as he eased his Mercedes saloon into the parking area behind his apartment block. The tyres crunched tracks in the virgin whiteness as he drew to a halt.

He had just returned from the headquarters of the GRU, and could feel a deep depression settling over him. General Novikov had been abrupt and dismissive at his doubts about the intelligence organisation's competence. Novikov was an old-style soldier, a Party hardliner who would never willingly accept criticism. The general considered Oleg a mere scientist, not qualified to comment on his methods.

At the lift entrance he gave his customary smile to the old woman who pressed the buttons. Like all those who acted out this menial role in Moscow, she was a KGB freelance who earned money by reporting the comings and goings of citizens, and taking particular note of any visiting foreigners. Oleg found it painful that the organisations which were essential to providing information for his own work should also find it necessary to spy on *him*.

As he opened the door to his apartment he saw Katrina waiting for him. She was standing in their living-room, framed by the light of the picture window, staring out at the view of Moscow – its stylish pre-revolutionary architecture contrasting strongly with modern concrete slabs and factory chimneys. She turned to face her husband, and folded her arms. She had a round face and thick black hair expensively set in a bouffant style that was chic for Moscow but which would look cheap and clumsy in the West. The intensity of her dark eyes was further defined by thick mascara. As Oleg crossed the room, he saw her heavily lipsticked mouth was clamped firmly shut in an expression of brooding unhappiness.

'Hello, my little dove,' he began sarcastically, knowing he was in for a further round of niggling criticism.

'The Ivanovs are going to Geneva again tomorrow!' she burst out, unable to contain any longer the source of her unhappiness.

'Are you surprised?' he countered, struggling to remove his heavy overcoat. 'Igor is an adviser on our mission to the United Nations.'

'Well, why can't *you* get a job like that?' she called after him as he returned to the hall to hang up his coat.

'Katrina, don't ask questions to which you already know the answers!' he called back with forced patience.

Until two years ago, Oleg had nothing to do with military affairs, specialising instead in the extension of the use of computers and industrial robots in the Soviet

Union's heavy engineering plants. Such a senior civilian post had given him the right to foreign travel and, much to Katrina's satisfaction, he had taken full advantage of it. Switzerland, West Germany, Japan and the USA had all been frequent destinations on their overseas itineraries.

But all that had ended when he was summoned by the Academy of Military Sciences to take control of the Ballistic Missile Defence modernisation programme, which had found itself in deep trouble because of lack of coordination between the missile makers and the electronics and radar industries. Working for the military had its attractions – funds were almost unlimited, for example – but its great disadvantage was the refusal of the authorities to allow military scientists to travel to the West for fear they could be compromised, kidnapped or seduced away with the secrets they held inside their heads.

His salary had increased dramatically with this military job, and they now had the use of one of the finest apartments in Moscow – but Katrina was increasingly miserable. She had moulded her lifestyle round the acquisition of Western possessions for the home. She had once cultivated friends who had similar tastes and ambitions, but now she felt increasingly like a leper, rejected socially because her access to these foreign pleasures had been cut off.

Having removed his snow-scuffed boots, Oleg slipped his feet into a pair of sheepskin moccasins bought in Canada, and headed for the heavy oak sideboard where the drinks were kept. He pulled out a bottle of Scotch whisky and poured a two fingers' measure into a cut-crystal tumbler. Without turning round, he swallowed it in one gulp. As the spirit burned his throat, he shook his head like a dog that has just emerged from a swim in the river, and refilled his glass.

'Aah!' he sighed. The alcohol was already beginning to numb his nerves, and he turned to face his wife with a tolerant smile on his lips.

Kvitzinsky was forty-six, and had a pleasant face with a long, thin nose and those arched brows and childlike Russian eyes that always looked poised halfway between laughter and tears. His bald scalp was covered by long strands of straight hair combed up from the side and carefully held in position by a light coating of hair-oil.

'Irina showed me a photograph of the dress she's going to buy in Geneva,' Katrina persisted. 'It was in *Vogue* magazine. She's started dieting again to fit into it.'

'Well, at least that's something you won't have to worry about,' Oleg laughed. Katrina had been fighting a losing battle against fat in recent years.

'I could lose weight if I had a good reason to,' she retorted sourly.

'Then do it for *me*,' Oleg whispered half-audibly into his glass.

'I heard that! Even if I looked like a Hollywood film-star it wouldn't make any difference to your capabilities!' she snapped back. Seizing a glossy magazine from the glass-topped coffee table, she dropped angrily into an armchair with her back to him. 'And don't get drunk tonight. We're going to the dacha tomorrow, remember?'

He had forgotten that, but was not going to admit it. The way things were going, he would not be able to leave Moscow that weekend, but he decided to keep that news to himself for the time being.

Peter Joyce. Peter Joyce. He muttered the name of the British scientist over and over again in his head. What had Joyce been doing on board that British submarine the previous day? General Novikov had received a report from Florida that the scientist was seen making last-minute alterations to the test missile. But had he been altering the warheads so that the forthcoming test would be deliberately misleading, or simply making the final adjustments that any complex weapon system demanded? Oleg desperately needed to know.

Kvitzinsky clearly remembered meeting this Peter Joyce three years earlier, at an international scientific symposium in Geneva, on one of his last visits to the West before taking up the military post. The British scientist had impressed him greatly, with his strong determined face and secretive eyes. It would not be easy to get the better of Peter Joyce, he had concluded. The GRU's incompetence at the start of their operation was certain to have put Joyce on his guard. Getting hold of the Skydancer plans would not be simple now.

Kvitzinsky had been bitingly critical of the GRU at the start of his meeting with the general, angrily accusing his agents of incompetence. The intelligence chief had rounded on him harshly for so readily believing what he heard on the BBC. The plan was proceeding steadily, he insisted. What had happened was only a small hitch which had required minor changes to the schedule. Those adjustments had now been carried out, and the complete plans for Skydancer should be in Moscow within a few days, he had assured him.

'I shall believe that when I see it,' Oleg now muttered to himself pessimistically, savouring the whisky growing warm in his grasp.

Through the forgiving haze of the spirit he looked across the room to where Katrina sat, still pointedly ignoring him. Her freshly coiffured hair and cream dress, patterned with large peach-coloured roses, made her look like a woman dressed for a party but with no party to go to. She was a picture of discontent.

It was not just the prohibition on travel to the West which had created her unhappiness, as Oleg knew only too well. The cause was far more basic than that. Katrina was unsatisfied in the most fundamental way a woman can be.

They had been married now for over ten years, but were childless. Their marriage was barren, and in the Soviet Union, where children symbolise the future and the justification for all the struggles and hardships of the present, being childless was not a happy state.

Oleg insisted to his friends that the fault lay with Katrina. In truth, medical examinations had revealed nothing wrong with Katrina at all. She blamed Oleg for their failure to conceive, but he had refused to undergo medical tests himself.

Her nagging suspicions had seriously undermined his libido, and now that age and excess had taken their toll of her once shapely figure, he found it increasingly difficult to produce a useable erection. When he was totally sober the task had become almost impossible. After an invigorating intake of alcohol, he could usually succeed, yet with one glass too many he would slip back into impotence.

But tonight he had no sexual expectations, and no intention of limiting his intake of comforting liquor.

'Oleg?' Katrina had finally put down her magazine and was trying to smile.

'Mmmm?'

'Why don't you take me out to dinner? I feel like going out. What about the Tsentralny? We haven't been there for months.'

It was a trap, and he knew it. He should have realised that as soon as she had started demanding the impossible – a visit to Geneva. It was a game played many times before, but which never failed to take him by surprise. Dutifully he played the counter-move she expected.

'We'll never get in there this evening. They're always full,' he replied wearily.

'I telephoned this morning,' Katrina smiled triumphantly. 'I booked a table. I thought it would make a nice change.'

He shrugged his inevitable consent. He knew what it meant: the evening had been prearranged, and they would be meeting other couples who were Katrina's friends rather than his. The conversation would revolve around Paris and New York, and he would have nothing to say because he had not been anywhere recently apart from Novosibirsk in Siberia – and he could not even mention that, because his work there was top secret.

It was going to be a dreadful evening. He knew he would get very drunk indeed.

In the kitchen of the old farmhouse in Berkshire, Belinda Joyce held open the door of her deep-freeze, trying to decide what to cook her children for supper. It would have to be fish fingers – she could not concentrate enough on anything more elaborate.

Something had transpired that day which gave her a strange creepy feeling: Helene Venner had disappeared.

She had first met the woman three years earlier, when Belinda was already establishing her skills as a lathe-operator at the craft co-operative. Helene had joined as a potter, producing attractive hand-made jugs and bowls which sold well to American tourists in a souvenir shop in Oxford. They had taken an instant liking to one another, sharing the same jaundiced view of the vested interests of big international companies and of the nuclear arms race.

Belinda had quickly recognised that Helene had lesbian tendencies, and knew that Helene found her desirable. To start with she was mentally quite attracted to the idea of sex with another woman, just as an experiment, but in the end her deep-seated disinclination had proved insurmountable. Even so, their friendship remained firm and intimate.

It had been Helene who encouraged her to join ATSA, or Action To Stop Annihilation, Helene who had helped her co-ordinate her loosely gathered anti-nuclear thoughts into a coherent thread, and Helene who tried to persuade her to steal secret papers from her husband so that they could be leaked to a left-wing newspaper.

Yesterday Helene had not turned up for work. Today she was again absent, and there had been still no phone-call to explain. So Belinda had called round at the terraced cottage she rented in the village, but found no one at home. A neighbour who held a key let her in to the house. Every trace of Helene was gone: the cupboards were bare, the bed stripped of linen; even the fridge had been emptied. The place was spotlessly clean, as if it had been scrubbed to remove any sign that she had ever lived there.

Belinda could not make herself believe Helene would just disappear without a word. She would surely have said something if going away of her own choice. So at first she wondered whether her friend had been kidnapped. But then she reflected on the line of questioning John Black had pursued, and began to consider that his talk of subversive left-wing groups plotting to undermine the fabric of the nation might not be entirely fanciful after all. Had Helene Venner been a spy? Surely not. Yet with growing disquiet Belinda remembered how close she had come to being physically seduced by Helene, and began to wonder whether such an act had been designed to achieve her final mental seduction as well.

The sound of a bicycle bell jerked her thoughts back to the present.

'Oh Christ! Back already,' she cursed, pushing the fish fingers under the grill.

By the time she next had a moment to herself, the early evening news was coming on television. The lead story concerned the Prime Minister's statement that afternoon to the House of Commons that 'following the untimely death of a female employee of the Ministry of Defence, the source of the leak of secret documents from the Ministry seems to have been uncovered. There is no evidence of any loss of secret material to a foreign power.'

'He doesn't know about Helene Venner,' Belinda thought. 'Nobody knows about Helene, except me.' Suddenly she longed for Peter to come home.

At that very moment he walked in. Belinda turned towards him anxiously, and the sight of his ashen face and crushed expression brought her to her feet.

'What's the matter, Peter? What's happened now, for God's sake?'

'I've been suspended,' he croaked. 'I've just spent the afternoon being bollocked by the Defence Secretary, Mr Michael bloody Hawke, and he's suspended me from duty until further notice!'

Chapter Five

Just before sunrise a US Navy tug positioned itself to ease the smooth fat shape of the submarine away from the quayside. The grey, pre-dawn light cast no shadow, and the overall-clad dock-hands looked almost faceless to Commander Carrington as he peered down at them from the top of the fin. The anonymous figures unhooked the mooring lines from the bollards and cast them into the water. The seamen on the narrow casing of HMS *Retribution* hauled the sodden ropes from the sea and stowed them securely under a steel hatch.

Once clear of the dockside, the multi-bladed fan-like propeller began to turn, causing the water behind the rudder to bubble and foam. The tow-line from the tug was released and the submarine's foredeck party hurried below, closing the forward hatch tightly behind them.

'Slow ahead!' Carrington almost whispered the command into the microphone he held close to his lips. His voice was hushed in spontaneous reverence at the sight of the crimson curve of the sun rising smoothly over the edge of the world, separating at last the greyness of the sea from that of the sky.

'Take a good look at it!' he told himself. It might be weeks before any of them on board saw the sun again.

The growing intensity of the light caused Carrington to shade his eyes. They were passing through the harbour entrance and he squinted anxiously along the line of buoys that marked the deep-water channel, to ensure there were no other vessels ahead which could hamper his passage. It would be a while yet before the water would be deep enough for them to dive and return to the secret world which had become his most natural environment.

His orders from Northwood had been at the same time specific and vague. He was to make his boat ready to launch the test missile at twelve hours' notice, but no hint had been given as to when that firing might take place. In the meantime he had been instructed to hide his submarine in the eastern Atlantic and to avoid the attention of any Soviet vessels that might try to track him, but the intelligence reports had been less specific than usual as to what Russian ships might be in the area.

Carrington focused his powerful binoculars on the furthest of the channel buoys which he knew, from his earlier study of the chart, to be three miles ahead. A thin haze covered the sea, and he scanned slowly to the left and then to the right, searching for the support ship which was essential to their success in hiding below the waves. The *Retribution*'s most sensitive listening device was her sonar array, the plastic tube towed hundreds of yards astern which contained hydrophones capable of hearing ships and submarines two hundred miles away. The technology had been invented long after *Retribution* had been built, so the array had to be clipped on by a support ship each time she went to sea.

'Any sign of her, sir?' The officer of the watch had joined Carrington on the bridge. He shivered briefly at the coolness of the morning air.

'Not yet. She can't be far away though. Only left harbour about half an hour ahead of us,' the captain replied, lowering his glasses and scanning the horizon with the naked eye.

'Half ahead! Revolutions for eight knots!' he ordered

into the microphone. Within seconds the water at the stern began to splash and froth more strongly, and a creamy wake spread out behind them.

'Give me a shout when you spot her,' Carrington called, as he gripped the handrails of the ladder and disappeared down the tower into the metallic warmth below. Passing through the control room he paused by the chart table.

'Where is the rendezvous point exactly?' he enquired, looking over the navigator's shoulder.

The young officer pointed to a cross on the chart.

'Three miles inside the territorial limit, sir,' he added smartly. 'Shouldn't have anybody watching while we do the deed.'

Carrington nodded and returned to his cabin.

Lieutenant Robert Simpson sat quietly in the tiny ship's office next to the wardroom. In front of him on the small table was the galley stores register, and he was making a pretence at checking it through. But the task that really concerned him was quite different, one of obsessive importance to him, one he was convinced could save millions of lives. It was to prevent HMS *Retribution*'s nuclear missiles from ever being fired in anger. It was a mission inspired by his conscience.

Bob had been educated at a small, select boarding school, where his housemaster had made a lasting impression on almost every pupil who passed through his care. An old-fashioned crusader, seeking to inspire his pupils to fight for morality and justice in whatever areas their careers might take them, Andrew McGregor had created on his own a sort of secret society perpetuated by annual reunions held at the school.

By the time Bob ended his studies there, he had

become the man's devoted disciple. On his last day at school, 'old Greg', as the teacher was known, had warned him as he had warned others before him, that he might need to 'go underground', to work in secret, if he was to strike his eventual blow for morality.

They were words of advice that Simpson took to heart in the years that followed. An only child, he had decided to follow his father into the Royal Navy eventually, but wanted to take a degree course first. During his three years at Exeter University, he had faithfully returned each summer to his school for the weekend reunion with Old Greg. At that time, he had still had no clear idea what the 'great mission' in his life would be, but felt instinctively that the Navy would one day present him with it.

At university he had fallen in love with Susan Parkinson, who was sweetness itself. Yet even when she had become his closest friend as well as his lover, he had not dared confide in her totally his sense of mission. She was different from him – lively and extrovert, forming firm opinions from first impressions. She had joined a Ban the Bomb group and urged him to accompany her on protest rallies, but he never did, preferring to keep his views private until he had developed them fully.

Susan lived near Newbury now, and worked as a schoolteacher. As they grew closer Bob had become more open about Andrew McGregor and his moral crusade, and when he had been posted to HMS *Retribution* she had understood immediately that he had finally found the role he had been looking for.

It had not been easy trying to decide what was right and what was wrong, when it came to warfare. Simpson could understand the moral rectitude of using military means to destroy a man like Adolf Hitler, and could accept the need for nations to be armed to prevent such tyrants from gaining power again. But those armaments were for use against other military forces, not civilians. 'The bomb' was different. Every missile on *Retribution* was aimed at Moscow. Millions of innocents would die if they were ever launched.

'You've got it, boy,' McGregor had said to him at the last school reunion. 'It's that crucial difference which makes the nukes immoral. You know what you have to do. Don't tell me anything about it – I don't want to know the details, but you'll know what to do when the time comes. It's no accident you are where you are, remember that! You're there for a purpose, boy!'

Simpson devoutly hoped it would never come to that – the weapons were intended as a deterrent after all. But the fact that chance, or the Almighty, in the form of a Naval selection board, had chosen *him* to be on board that particular boat made Simpson fear the worst.

It would be no easy task to stop a launch of the Polaris missiles if war broke out, he concluded. The firing procedures on board the submarine were hedged about with safeguards designed to prevent any individual acting on his own, either in firing the missiles or in sabotaging the launch. Simpson had studied those procedures carefully. As a supply officer he was not closely involved in the war-fighting tasks of the boat, but the policy of the Navy was that every one of the thirteen officers on board had a part to play if the missiles were ever launched. It was a way of spreading the responsibility and making it seem less awesome.

Simpson's war role was to verify the navigation data to be fed into the missile-guidance computers, data which told the missiles precisely where they were on the globe at the moment of firing. He had soon realised that a simple refusal to carry out his task would achieve nothing; the data could easily be verified by any of the other officers. The only way to stop the launch would be through deliberate sabotage.

When he had first joined the boat, the captain had talked to him privately in his cabin to ensure that he had no doubts about the rightness of maintaining a nuclear deterrent and of being prepared to use it. 'If you have any doubts, you shouldn't be here,' Carrington had told him. Simpson had kept his thoughts to himself. He believed this was *precisely* where people with doubts should be if the world was to be saved from destruction.

Bob often worried about his girlfriend. It was hard, his being away at sea for months at a time. Susan had always had a lively social life, and he had a fear in the back of his mind that she would get tired of his frequent absences and find another man.

Opposition to nuclear weapons had become the strongest bond between them. Susan was now actively campaigning for the cancellation of the Skydancer project, and needed all the information she could get. His phone-calls to tell her what was happening on board the submarine did not reveal much, but she always seemed grateful for them, and to Simpson they were a lifeline keeping Susan attached to him.

With a steely hiss the main periscope was raised from its housing in the control room deck. Carrington pressed his face against the binocular eyepiece and rotated the sight through a full 360 degrees.

'Officer of the watch, I have control. Come below. Shut the upper lid!'

Carrington's order triggered a routine on board the boat that was so well practised it was automatic.

'Upper lid shut! And clipped!' the voice of a crewman yelled from inside the top of the tower, as the spring-loaded latches completed the hermetic sealing of the hull. Another voice at the base of the ladder relayed the message to the control room.

'Dive the submarine!' Carrington ordered.

'Open one, two and three main vents,' yelled a strong Glasgow accent from the buoyancy control panel. Hands scrabbled at the stopcock switches above, and there was the roar of air escaping from the main tanks as water rushed in to replace it.

'Diving now!' the helmsman shouted, pressing forward on his joystick controls. The hydroplanes cut into the water and pressed the bulbous nose of the vessel down towards the depths. On a gauge above his control stick, the helmsman watched a miniature silhouette of the boat tilt downwards through five, then ten degrees. It was enough to ensure that HMS *Retribution* would slide cleanly and smoothly beneath the waves.

'Keep periscope depth!' Carrington called, raising the scope again for an all-round look. Satisfied that the only vessel in the area was the support ship that had just helped them with their towed sonar, and that they were leaving it well astern, he lowered the periscope and moved over to the chart table. The navigator pointed out a line indicating the edge of the continental shelf, beyond which they would be able to dive into the comforting deep of the Atlantic.

For a while yet they must stay close to the surface, and every few minutes Carrington raised the periscope for a further all-round scan. Small fishing boats with trawl-nets were a hazard that might be visible only seconds before collision or entanglement.

One hour later Carrington ordered the submarine to two hundred feet, and the periscope was lowered into its seating for the last time. No one knew when they would need to raise it again.

The excitement of their shore leave over, the crew of the Polaris submarine slipped quickly back into their routines, almost as if they were a part of the machinery itself. The task of the boat now was to remain undetected and wait for orders. Trailing horizontally from the stern was the sonar array, several hundred yards behind the rudder, listening intently for the tell-tale sounds of other ships and submarines in the area. A second cable also streamed out from the vessel, stretching upwards at an angle of forty-five degrees towards the surface of the ocean. At the end of it was a float which would remain just below the surface throughout their patrol, a buoy which could pick up radio signals from England while staying hidden beneath the waves.

This was the Very Low Frequency radio antenna, able to hear transmissions which could penetrate the surface to a depth of twenty feet. It kept the submarine in permanent contact with Naval Headquarters, ready to receive at any time the order to go to war. The antenna could not easily be detected by surface ships or aircraft, so did not reveal the existence of the 'bomber' in the depths below.

Although *Retribution* could listen thus for her orders, she could not reply to them; the antenna could receive but not transmit. Normally she did not need to, and only in an emergency would come up to periscope depth and transmit back through a satellite aerial pushed above the waves.

The rumbling in his stomach told Carrington it was close to lunchtime. Breakfast had been very early that morning to accommodate their dawn departure from the Cape. He was naturally a very thin man with sunken cheeks and a tall angular frame. It always surprised his wife that he could be such a healthy eater and remain so skinny. As he walked to the wireless room to reassure himself that the communications link was properly established, he tried to calculate what hour of the day it would be in the Hampshire village of West Meon, which was home. His wife Alice would still be asleep there unless the baby had woken her early.

'All hunky-dory, sir,' his executive officer announced. 'Everything bleeping away nicely.'

To confirm that the radio link was established, a coded message was transmitted constantly from three giant aerials situated in remote parts of Britain.

'Very good, Number One,' Carrington smiled. 'I think it's lunchtime, don't you? I'll just check the sound room, then we can eat. Happen to know what's on the menu?'

'"Babies' Heads", I think, sir,' replied Lt. Commander Smith.

Carrington rubbed his hands. He was very fond of the individual steak-and-kidney puddings so named.

Inside the sonar room, the rating at the towed array control panel was clasping his headphones to his ears, and he looked puzzled. In front of him a green cathode-ray tube displayed the oscillating wave patterns of the multitude of sounds the array was detecting. By selecting switches the operator could direct the inbuilt computer to filter out unwanted noises and concentrate its analytical power on one particular frequency, which was what the rating was now trying to do.

'Got a problem?' Carrington asked, tapping the blue-shirted operator on the shoulder.

The man slipped his earphones off and shook his head.

'Don't understand it, sir. Never heard nothing like it before. Don't even know if it's really there, it's so faint.'

The words sent a shiver up the captain's spine, and all thoughts of food disappeared.

'What sort of thing are you talking about?' he asked. 'And where is it?'

'Well, the array says it's dead astern, sir. But what it is, I don't know. There's no cavitation or anything, no propeller noise. Sounds like something moving through the water, but there's no machine noise or reactor bubbling. No propulsion sound at all.'

'Computer doesn't recognise it?'

'No way, sir. Thinks it's just background. Can't pick it out at all.'

'But *you're* sure it's there?' Carrington pressed anxiously.

The rating hesitated before replying: 'I suppose it could be damage to the array, sir. The Yanks might have knocked it about a bit while we were in the Cape. I'll run a test on it. Shouldn't take more than ten minutes.'

Instinctively Carrington felt sure there was nothing wrong with the sonar. He recalled his orders for this voyage, which had been so specific and yet so vague; the extra warning to be on the alert for Soviet shadows, as if Fleet HQ suspected there was something in the area, yet could not identify what sort of vessel.

'No. Stick with it. I'll reduce speed and we'll go silent – see if that helps clarify things.'

Carrington strode back to the control room and seized the microphone that hung from the roof by the main periscope.

'Assume the ultra-quiet state! Ultra-quiet until further notice!'

His voice was relayed throughout the length of the boat on a network of loudspeakers. At his command, conversation stopped, or was reduced to a whisper, and all inessential domestic or mechanical tasks that could make a noise were brought to a halt.

'Reduce speed to one knot,' he ordered quietly.

'One knot it is, sir.'

He could not stop altogether, or the array would start to sink towards the ocean floor.

The executive officer came out of the wireless room, his eyebrows raised inquiringly.

'Sound room's got something, Mike. Something very faint,' Carrington explained.

The two officers returned to the sonar booth, where the operator was working away at his control panel. Impotently they stood behind him, waiting for him to report.

'Coming closer, sir!' he hissed suddenly. 'There's a doppler shift.' Then he forgot himself in his excitement. '*Must* be a fucking sub!'

The frequency of the sound had risen, shifting up the scale, indicating, like the whistle from an approaching train, that the object creating the sounds was moving towards them.

Behind them the spools of a tape-recorder turned continuously, recording the full spectrum of sounds picked up by the array, for further analysis later. If Carrington's suspicion was correct, what they were recording was history, the first sounds ever heard in the West of a new type of Soviet submarine.

Until five years earlier the Russian nuclear-powered boats, operated from the base at Severomorsk inside the Arctic Circle, had been characteristically noisy. Their loudness was due to a lack of sophistication in sound-proofing, and was largely caused by particularly noisy pumps circulating cooling water in the reactors. When they sailed south towards the Atlantic, they passed over a network of listening devices laid on the floor of the ocean by the US Navy. Those sensors reported their passage to NATO ships and aircraft, which could then follow them with comparative ease.

Details of NATO tracking capabilities had been leaked to the Russians by the Walker family spy-ring, early in the 1980s, and the shock of learning how much the Western navies could hear had led the Soviet navy to institute a crash programme of new design.

The first of the latest type of Soviet submarine had recently been photographed by American satellites as it left Severomorsk on patrol, and again three weeks later when it returned, but no sound trace whatever had been found of it during the intervening period. Code-named Akula by NATO assessors, the submarine was a massive eight thousand tons, similar in size to *Retribution*, but instead of ballistic missiles for threatening Western cities, she carried a stock of torpedoes and anti-ship missiles able to destroy boats like HMS *Retribution* before they could fire their weapons at Moscow.

The silent operation of the Akula class boats had made many of NATO's listening techniques obsolete. It was feared the Soviets could now patrol the Atlantic shipping lanes undetected by the West. No one knew how they had achieved such silence, but there were reports that the Akulas had a secret new motor in addition to their nuclear-powered turbines, a motor that used the revolutionary technique of electro-magnetic thrust, producing a speed of ten knots in almost total silence and without leaving any detectable wake.

'Akula!' Carrington exclaimed hoarsely. 'It has to be. Nothing else could be as quiet as that. The bastard must have been waiting for us!'

'He's still closing on us, sir! Doesn't seem to realise we've slowed down,' the rating whispered excitedly. 'I can definitely hear turbulence round his hull. I don't understand it, sir! Why can't I hear his fucking propeller?'

'Because he's not using one,' Carrington answered softly. 'Right, let's see what he can do!'

He leapt to his feet and strode back to the control room.

'Wind in that VLF antenna, or we'll lose it. Then make maximum revs!' he barked. 'Full speed ahead!'

The helmsman turned from his dials and hydroplane controls in astonishment. Polaris missile patrols were normally conducted at a stately three knots. Now the skipper was ordering a speed of thirty!

An even vibration took the submarine in its grip as the control rods were raised in the nuclear reactor core, producing an instant increase in heat and steam for the turbines. The needle on the dial showing the rotational speed of the propeller shaft rose steadily, until it approached the section marked in red. The chief engineer watched it closely.

'Twenty-eight knots!' the executive officer called, peering fixedly at the log.

Carrington prowled round the control room, glaring at the dials one minute and studying the chart the next. He had taken a calculated gamble. If the Soviet submarine which he believed was sitting on his tail was to keep up with the speeding *Retribution*, it would have to abandon its silent electro-magnetic thrust and resort to the greater power of its nuclear reactor and large propeller. That was bound to be noisier, and they would be forcing the Akula to make a sonar fingerprint, allowing a Western navy to record its noise characteristics for the first time.

Carrington grinned to himself; either way he was going to win something. If the Akula stayed on his tail the Soviets would lose some of their secrets. If the boat stayed quiet, it would rapidly drop behind and *Retribution* would give it the slip.

Confident that all was well in the control room, the captain returned to the sonar booth where the rating was urgently pressing switches on his panel. Their high speed through the water was making so much noise on their own sonar systems that he could no longer tell if the Russian was behind them. Suddenly he cocked his head on one side.

'Cavitation, sir!' he exclaimed. 'Dead astern! Suddenly come on. Nothing there before, but I can hear the bubbles on his propeller now.'

'So! We have a huntsman on our tail! A hunting pinko no less!' Carrington looked at Mike Smith for appreciation of the pun. He glanced across at the spools of the tape-recorder, rotating smoothly, and debated how to make the most of the opportunity that faced him.

'We'll keep up this speed until he's firmly hooked, then cut the power and let him come closer,' he decided.

The sonar operator was busy with his controls again, filtering and processing the signals which were now audible not only to the towed array but also to the hydrophones fixed to the side of the hull. By comparing bearings from the two sets of sensors, he could now calculate that the Soviet submarine was fifty feet above them and about half a mile astern.

The captain returned to the control room and bent his tall frame over the chart, talking urgently with his navigator.

Lieutenant Robert Simpson leaned into the control room, eager to know what had caused the submarine's unaccustomed burst of speed.

'George? What's going on?' he whispered to the assistant Polaris systems officer who was standing to one side with his arms folded.

'Hide and Seek! And we're "it"!'

'Who else is playing? A Russian?'

'Well, it's not one of ours, is it?'

Commander Carrington paced past them, scowling.

'Permission to be in the control room, sir?' Simpson asked smartly, knowing he had no automatic right to be there.

'As long as you keep out of the way,' was the brusque reply.

The commander carefully scanned the dials which showed how the propulsion machinery was performing.

'I want you to cut the power and dive to four hundred feet,' he told the marine engineer quietly. 'Then turn hard to port – that'll keep us in the deep water. What I want is to let the bugger go shooting over our heads, so we can get a good listen to all his noise parameters, and then for us to creep back the way we came in an effort to lose him. Think you can make us quiet enough?'

'Can but try, sir,' the engineer answered stolidly. 'After all that speed, the reactor pumps'll keep churning for a bit, even if everything else is quiet.'

'Right away then,' Carrington ordered.

The depth at which the hunt had been pursued up to now was in the middle of a broad band of water of even temperature, allowing free passage of sound waves. Nervously rubbing his jaw, inadequately shaven in his haste that morning, Carrington judged that by diving steeply the *Retribution* would pass through a thermocline, where the water would become sharply colder. The temperature difference should create a sound barrier, below which the *Retribution* could hide. What an extraordinary medium the sea was; its salinity and temperature variations sometimes allowed sound waves to travel for hundreds of miles, and at others made it impossible to hear another craft just a few feet away.

The men in the control room grasped at the pipework as the large vanes either side of the bulbous nose tilted the submarine steeply downwards.

'Oh, shit!' Simpson whispered at the suddenness of the manoeuvre.

The tension on the faces around him had given him a nightmare vision of what it would be like in war, wrestling in the deep with a Russian submarine: a trial of strength which only one of them could win.

He had been taught that when it began, the Soviet boats would make an all-out attack to try to neutralise the Western missile submarines in a pre-emptive strike. For a split-second he imagined it could actually be happening at that very moment: men in a Russian submarine trying to kill them, kill him even though he was committed to saving the lives of those same men's wives and families.

In sudden confusion he thought about the secret role he had been chosen to play, and realised with a jolt that he was far from ready, far from certain what he would do. The meagre preparations he had made were secreted illegally in the drawer beneath his bunk.

He glanced at the captain. There was a look in Carrington's eye that was not just excitement; it was fear too.

To hide his uncertainty, Carrington quickly turned away and went over to the sonar booth. The Soviet boat was faster and quieter than his own, and its sonar equipment probably at least as good. If the contest was purely technical the Russian would win, he felt sure of that. There was another element, though, which could decide this contest – human skill.

He had never faced the test so directly before. The endless simulations he had practised were supposed to have prepared him for this moment, yet now he felt strangely unready. In the past they had tended to take for granted that British equipment and techniques were so superior that the Soviets would never get close enough to challenge the Polaris boats' mastery of the deep.

'Want to listen on these, sir?' the rating asked, passing him a spare set of headphones. Carrington struggled to separate the different sounds that crowded in on his brain. It took him a few moments, but at last he could pick out the cavitation, the turbulence caused by the Akula's propeller biting into the water.

'Getting closer?' Carrington asked anxiously.

The sonar operator nodded. 'And following us down, sir.'

'Shit!'

He snapped the headphones back on to the table, then swung his long body out of the swivel-chair and through the doorway back into the control room, in one continuous movement.

'Hard a-port now!' he yelled at the helmsman. 'We're going to have to shake the bastard off!'

Bob Simpson felt the shirt sticking to his neck. The submarine manoeuvred with unaccustomed violence. It was not just the motion that made him feel queasy; it was also the claustrophobia created by the tension of the men around him.

He thought of Susan. Was she really with him still? Would she care if he died here at sea, buried alive? The uneven motion of the boat began to affect him seriously, and he hurried back to his bunk.

Carrington hovered over the chart table in a pose that was almost predatory. His hair was ruffled where he had nervously run his fingers through it, and his once-crisp white shirt had dark patches under the arms.

The chart itself was scrawled with lines marking the zig-zag course they had followed in their unavailing efforts to lose the Akula.

He was beginning to despair; the readiness of the Russian captain to reveal the capabilities of his new boat suggested that his orders had been very specific: any price was worth paying in order to observe from close quarters the test launch of the missile that would carry Skydancer aloft for the first time.

'Captain!'

The shout had come from the sound room.

'Got something here you might be interested in, sir,' the rating grinned. He turned up the volume on one of the loudspeakers. The heavy rumbling noise was unmistakeable.

'*QE2*, sir. On her way south from New York to the Caribbean!'

A grin spread across Carrington's tired features. The good old *QE2*. It was the answer to a prayer.

'What's her range?' he asked eagerly.

'About thirty miles, sir.'

'Good! Give me the very best bearing you can! We're going to say hello to her!'

By the time Bob Simpson returned to the control room, he was feeling better and had regained his composure. HMS *Retribution* had settled on to a steady course at a speed of twenty knots. High speed would not shake off their adversary; the Akula was faster than they were and was firmly on their tail. What they needed was a sonar 'smoke screen', and there was none bigger than the *QE2*.

He went over to the chart table and rested an elbow on the edge of it.

'What's the latest?' he asked the navigator casually.

'We're on our way to a rendezvous with a big, fat, red herring!' his young colleague answered, grinning.

Simpson raised his eyebrows.

The navigator pointed to the chart and a small cross where two straight lines met.

'This one's us,' he indicated, 'and the other line is the estimated course of the liner *QE2*. We're on track to intercept her in about two hours' time.'

'And this track here?' Simpson asked, pointing to a third line running parallel and very close to their own course, but a short distance astern. 'That's the Russian?'

''Sright. That's Boris, currently playing the part of the cat. A fat cat at that, at eight thousand tons.'

'About the same size as the mouse,' Simpson commented quietly.

'True,' the navigator conceded, 'and in a couple of hours we'll find out which one's more cunning. My money's on the mouse!'

Back on the American mainland, the FBI's electronic surveillance systems had been carrying out their allotted tasks meticulously. With so many sensitive military installations close to Cape Canaveral, every public phone-box within a fifty-mile radius of the missile-launching centre was monitored by a central computer. Every call was listened to electronically; the bugging was by microprocessor rather than by man.

The computer was programmed to analyse speech. Each call made from those hundreds of telephones was recorded digitally. The computer would listen for the use of certain key words stored in its memory, and would check the callers against a 'voice-print' file, in case they were known to the authorities. Each digital recording would be checked through twice, but if the voices were unknown, and if no keywords were present, then it was automatically erased. If it held something of significance, it was transferred to magnetic tape, together with a record of when and from where the call had been made. Twice a day the tapes were studied by FBI agents at a counter-espionage centre in Miami.

The telephone-call which Lieutenant Robert Simpson had made from outside Millies' disco to his girlfriend in England was now on that tape. His English voice had produced no response from the digitised 'rogues' gallery' in the central memory. However, one particular word that he had used had not gone unnoticed. It was one which had never triggered this particular alerting system before; 'Aldermaston' was not an American establishment after all, and had only been included in the list of FBI keywords as a gesture of transatlantic co-operation. But there it was, in the middle of a conversation from a Florida call-box to a number in the home counties of England.

Because it was an unusual word, not related to any American defence project, 'Aldermaston' had caused the computer's priority coding system to work in Bob Simpson's favour for a while. If he had referred to an American defence establishment, his conversation would have received urgent attention from a human agent. 'Aldermaston' did not mean much to the men from the FBI, so for the time being the tape which could reveal that an informer was on board the British nuclear submarine *Retribution* lay on an American intelligence officer's desk marked 'Low Priority'.

Commander Carrington had returned to his cabin to

think, after instructing the officer of the watch to call him when they were within ten minutes of their rendezvous with the *QE2*.

'What a fucking shambles,' he muttered, as the long-term significance of what was happening began to sink in. The Soviet Navy had managed to sail a hunter-killer submarine right through several lines of Western detection barriers in the Norwegian sea, through the Iceland-Faroes gap which NATO considered almost as a Maginot line, and right across the Atlantic to within a few miles of the American coastline, but had remained utterly undetected until it revealed its presence by giving chase to HMS *Retribution.*

With this new Soviet capability, NATO's chances of defending itself against a Russian submarine attack had been dramatically reduced, as Carrington realised with dread. But more than that, the Royal Navy's confidence in being able to successfully hide its Polaris missile submarines could no longer be justified, particularly when the Skydancer warheads were installed. Carrington had been told that the manoeuvring and decoy equipment in the Skydancer nose-cones made the new warheads heavier than the old ones, and the rockets would have a shorter range as a result. Less range meant that the *Retribution* and her sister vessels would have to patrol closer to the Soviet coast than before, and the closer to Russia they came, the easier it would be for the Soviet navy to find them.

Carrington shuddered. He pulled a signal pad from his locker and began to outline the message that he must send back to his HQ as soon as it was safe to poke the transmitter mast above the surface.

'Control room to Captain!' The voice of the officer of the watch squawked from the communications box on the cabin wall.

Carrington pressed a key. 'Captain!' he called back.

'Three miles to target, sir!'

'Right!'

He opened his wall safe and pushed the signal pad inside. He would finish it later. The message was top secret, so he closed the safe door and spun the combination lock to secure it. Then he headed back to the control room.

At the navigator's table he paused briefly to look at the chart. He was pleased to note there was more than a thousand feet of water beneath them, and it was getting deeper all the time as they headed east.

Then he hurried to the sonar room, where he clamped on the second set of headphones. The throbbing cavitation from the giant screws of the Cunard liner seemed to be drowning out everything else. However, the sonar operator pointed to the green cathode ray tube, and indicated a barely-visible but separate line, below the jagged pattern created by the *QE2*.

'That's our Akula, sir,' he explained. 'Still sitting on our tail about half a mile astern, keeping about three cables off our starboard quarter. He'll be nibbling our array if he comes any closer!'

'What's he expect us to do, that's the big question isn't it?' Carrington asked, half to himself.

'Certainly is, sir. Trouble is, this stuff's pretty good but it can't read minds yet,' the operator joked, patting the top of his screen.

'Damned shame, I call it!' Carrington forced a laugh.

Back in the control room the captain was suddenly conscious of the harsh meaning of the words 'the loneliness of command'. Here he was, surrounded by young enthusiasts who would be only too eager to give him their opinions of what to do, were he to ask them. It was the last thing in the world that he needed at that moment, however; to listen to a host of conflicting views could only hinder the already difficult process of deciding on his tactics when they met the *QE2*.

In his mind he had narrowed the options down to two: they could take up position underneath the liner and follow the same course, knowing that all noises from the submarine would be masked for as long as they stayed there, or he could pass right through the 'noise footprint' of the ship and out the other side, hoping the Soviet boat would think he had stayed beneath the liner and would follow the *QE2* towards the Caribbean.

What if their positions were reversed, Carrington thought to himself? What would the Soviet captain do if he was 'driving' *Retribution*? There was an obvious answer to that, based on years of study of Soviet submarine tactics. A Russian captain would hide his vessel under a surface ship for days, if necessary. They did it regularly, particularly when sailing their northern fleet round into the Mediterranean for annual exercises. A submarine would invariably try to make the journey undetected by sailing beneath the keel of an aircraft carrier or a cruiser.

But even if the Soviet captain's own instinct would be to hide himself under the liner, would he expect Carrington to think in the same way? There was no answer to that.

'Rendezvous point now half a mile distant, sir!' the navigator shouted across the control room.

'What speed the Cunarder?' he snapped back.

'Twenty-four knots sir!'

'Chief, give us maximum revs! I want twenty-eight knots on the clock!'

'Aye, aye, sir!'

All round the control room, men stiffened at their

posts. Eyes focused hard on charts and dials, hands hovered over levers, ready to respond instantly to the orders which were about to come thick and fast.

'Where's Boris?' Carrington barked into the intercom linking him with the sound room.

'Still on our starboard quarter, sir!'

'Cunarder's dead ahead, three hundred yards, sir!'

'Course?'

'One-nine-five, sir.'

'Coxswain! Steer one-nine-zero! Maintain one hundred and fifty feet!'

The chief engineer glanced uneasily at the captain. Getting close to a fast-moving liner was a dangerous business. Unexpected suctions and vortices could suddenly drag the two vessels together. The Cunarder would draw about forty feet, so that only gave them about a hundred feet clearance, not much when travelling so fast.

Suddenly, as one man, the control-room crew all looked up to the curved roof. The sound of the *QE2*'s propellers was pounding through the hull. The coxswain wiped the sweat from his brow.

'Cunarder overhead now, sir!' the voice barked from the sound room intercom.

'Steer one-nine-five! Drop back to twenty-four knots! Stay under her!'

They were now on exactly the same course as the massive cruise liner above them, where three thousand passengers and crew continued their afternoon activities, blissfully unaware that two gigantic submarines were playing hide-and-seek in the dark waters beneath them.

'Can you still hear Boris with all this din?' Carrington shouted into the microphone.

'Fallen behind to one mile, sir! Still on the quarter!'

What was he doing, that Soviet captain? What was he thinking? Carrington was sure the Russian was now 'deaf', unable to hear the British submarine any more because of the noise from the liner. The *Retribution* was not quite so 'deaf', however, because her listening array was towing well behind the liner and between herself and the Soviet boat. They could still hear the Akula, but she could no longer hear them. It was the best situation possible.

What the Russian did next would dictate which tactics Carrington would choose.

'Sound room!'

'Captain here!' Carrington came back.

'Burst of speed, sir! He's gone up to thirty knots! Just crossed our track, coming up fast to port!'

At last! He had made his move! Carrington grinned. The Soviet skipper had gambled that the *Retribution* had maintained a speed faster than the liner overhead and was hoping to disappear through the noise screen. The Akula was racing ahead on the port side of the ship, hoping to recapture a trace of *Retribution* as she came out ahead of her.

But the bastard's got it wrong, Carrington chuckled gleefully. He's not going to find us where he's going.

'Coxswain! Hard-a-starboard!'

In the control room, men hung on to tables and supports as the submarine began to heel over and turn sharply to the right. The thudding of the *QE2*'s propellers began to fade away to port, but they were keeping the noise firmly between themselves and the Soviet vessel. Carrington calculated that as the Akula pulled steadily ahead of the liner on the port side, the *Retribution* would fall back further and further to starboard, and the liner's noise shadow would continue to hide them.

'Lost him, sir! Sound room here! The Russian's the other side of the liner. Still making thirty knots at last trace.'

'Reduce speed to ten knots and take her down to five hundred feet, Coxswain,' Carrington ordered quietly. They needed to go deep rapidly, but had to cut their noise dramatically, too. At twenty-four knots the *Retribution* sounded like a steam train, but at ten she was a lot quieter.

'Well, gentlemen? Do you think we've done it?' the captain smiled round the control room.

'I think you may well have done, sir!' the navigator grinned back.

'Better not count the chickens just yet, though,' Carrington continued, hooking his hands together and stretching the tension out of his shoulder muscles. 'I'll be in the sound room.'

Weaving his tall frame round the periscope housings, he headed for the sonar booth.

Two thousand miles south-east of the submarines' position, Kapitan Karpov was finding the almost equatorial heat of the mid-Atlantic increasingly uncomfortable. The giant *Akademik Sergey Korolev* was now steaming slowly in circles, waiting for information from Moscow that would tell her precisely where to position herself to observe the British missile test. The British could launch their Polaris from anywhere within an area of several thousand square kilometres. Where the missile was fired from would dictate the part of the ocean in which it would come down, and it was within fifty kilometres of there that the *Korolev* had to be.

For the time being her massive radar and telemetry dishes were at rest, but when the time came they would be pointing upwards, carefully recording the responses from the Skydancer warheads as they re-entered the earth's atmosphere, trying to crack the code for the data being transmitted to earth, and to learn something from the outlines and reflections recorded by the radar.

'I suppose we do have something following that British submarine,' Karpov grumbled to his first officer. His headquarters had told him no more about the operation than he needed to know. 'We'll probably find our submarine is still in harbour with engine trouble!'

'Perhaps we should ask Comrade Smirnov!' the other said sarcastically. They had managed to escape the overbearing company of the ship's political officer for a few minutes. Colonel Smirnov had his own communications equipment on board which kept him in direct touch with KGB headquarters in Moscow. Hence he was often better informed about the ship's plans than the captain himself.

'To do that, I'd have to like the smell of his arse,' Karpov growled. 'And I don't.'

That morning a Nimrod reconnaissance plane from the Royal Air Force had flown out from Ascension Island to take a look at them. Kapitan Karpov had never expected to be able to hide a ship as large as his, but he was nonetheless annoyed that the British should have pinpointed his location so easily. He felt certain they had had help from their American allies, who could have used an intelligence satellite to fix the Soviet ship's position by detecting one of the political officer's radio transmissions. Even when Soviet naval rules dictated radio silence, the KGB man could not be stopped from calling up his headquarters, much to Karpov's annoyance.

The RAF Nimrod had made several low passes over the ship, taking photographs of all the antennae mounted on the upper deck. Karpov hadn't minded that so much; the most sensitive pieces of equipment were safely covered up.

It was late afternoon; there would be no more activity that day. Karpov looked at his watch. The KGB man was bound to inflict his presence on them again before long, and there was something very important to do before he did. Comrade Smirnov was a very youthful political officer, who had done his KGB training at the height of First Secretary Gorbachev's anti-alcohol campaign. And Comrade Smirnov was not a very understanding man.

The captain pulled open a drawer in his desk and took out a bottle of vodka. With a conspiratorial wink, he passed it to his first officer.

Chapter Six

Peter Joyce had spent much of that Friday pacing round his house in frustration. He was still smarting from the ignominy of being suspended by the Defence Secretary, pending completion of the investigation into the affair of the Skydancer papers.

Shortly before lunchtime an official car had arrived from the Ministry of Defence, and the driver had handed him a letter from Sir Marcus Beckett formally confirming his suspension on full pay. There had been no other communication and, with Belinda working at the craft co-operative and the children at school, he had been left alone with his thoughts all day.

He knew he had been careless, knew he had broken several security regulations, and that the department had every right to dismiss him if they chose to. But he was certain too that the crisis over the Skydancer secrets was not the result of anything he had done, and had nothing to do with his affair with Mary Maclean.

The night before, his wife had told him about Helene Venner's strange disappearance, and her consequent suspicion that the woman might have been something other than she seemed. He had telephoned John Black first thing that morning to inform him about it, but the MI5 man had been almost dismissive.

'You'd be surprised, Mr Joyce,' he had purred, 'but in almost every investigation I've ever run, there's always been at least one unnoticed little predator that has felt the heat and decided to break cover and run. We know about Ms Venner . . . and about her dubious relationship with your wife. But it wasn't she who left your secret documents on Hampstead Heath, I can assure you of that.'

Peter had felt so soiled by that conversation that he had vented his anger on a pile of logs that needed splitting. Later he had taken a walk in the beech woods, unable to shake from his mind the picture of the bloodstains in Mary's flat. Guilt gnawed at his soul; perhaps it had been suicide after all. Perhaps he was just trying to avoid acceptance of his own responsibility for her death – as Black and Field-Marshal Buxton seemed to believe.

'No, dammit!' he thought. 'They're wrong, but how the hell do I prove it?'

Something or somebody was being overlooked in the official investigation, deliberately or otherwise. There seemed no other explanation for MI5's unquestioning acceptance of Mary's death as suicide. Who or what had they missed? One name kept coming back to him; he *knew* it was significant. One name . . .

In his house in Hampstead, Alec Anderson took off his spectacles and put them on his father's old desk. In the last few days it seemed he had spent every waking moment sitting in this library when he was not at work at the Strategic Nuclear Secretariat in the Defence Ministry, with Mary Maclean's unattended desk outside his office door as a constant reminder of his dilemma.

Pressing down on the leather-upholstered arms of the lovingly restored swivel-chair, he lifted himself up and rubbed the small of his back. He took little regular exercise apart from an early-morning walk, and his joints were stiff. His normally ruddy cheeks had grown visibly paler in the last few days, and dark shadows under his eyes reflected his difficulty in sleeping. Every evening when he came home with another worry-line etched into his face, he took shelter in this room in an effort to avoid Janet's mostly unspoken questions.

When Mary's suicide had been reported on the television news – with the Prime Minister's reassurance that the Skydancer leak had not affected national security – Janet could simply not understand why her husband seemed more distressed at the news rather than relieved that the crisis appeared to be over. When she had probed him about it, he had mumbled something about the situation being a 'tragedy', but that it was impossible for him to explain the real reason. How could he tell her that he *wanted* the crisis to continue, wanted the Ministry to keep its guard up, all in the interests of protecting his wife and the children?

He now looked at his watch: nearly time to go down to the Maid's Head pub. Every Friday he would go there to meet a small group of friends for beer and billiards. This particular evening it was the last thing he wanted. But Karl had insisted.

Karl Metzger had first joined their drinking circle one evening about a year ago. He had introduced himself as a West German working in the travel business, with an agency in Hampstead High Street specialising in Rhineland cultural tours. He had stood up patiently to their schoolboy jokes about 'Krauts', and had quickly shown himself a master with the billiards cue. Soon he had become a regular member of the Friday group, and Alec discovered their shared interest in nineteenth-century painting, which led to a more personal friendship between them.

Anderson sat on the edge of the desk and polished his glasses with a handkerchief. The fruits of that year's friendship now hung on the walls of his library: some of the finest works in his collection of Victorian miniatures had been acquired thanks to Karl.

Setting his glasses firmly in place again, he peered at the exquisite craftsmanship contained within these small gilded frames. The intricacy of brushwork depicting Swiss and Italian landscapes was the closest thing to perfection that he knew. Yet now he wished to God that he had never clapped eyes on them. Those exquisite little masterpieces had brought him to this present situation which threatened with destruction both his career and his family's happiness.

Joyce had decided against telephoning before he arrived in Hampstead. He was determined to talk to Alec Anderson that evening, and was worried that Anderson might find some excuse to avoid a meeting. He had never visited the house before, but knew the address from a Christmas card Anderson had sent him the previous year. Belinda had a habit of hoarding old cards which he had never had cause to be thankful for before.

It was nearly ten o'clock as he drove down the quiet side-road, peering at the numbers, till he found the house. A reproduction brass coach-lamp glowed in the porch. Somehow the style of it seemed wrong for Anderson.

The doorbell chimed a melody. Through the bottle-glass panel he could see the outline of a figure moving down the hall towards him, hesitating and leaning to one side as if trying to recognise his shape through the glass.

There was the rattle of the lock and the door opened a few inches, secured by a chain.

'Yes?' came a timid female voice from inside. Peter could see one dark eye blinking at him through the gap.

'Mrs Anderson?' Peter enquired gently.

'Yes?'

'I'm so sorry to trouble you. My name is Joyce, Peter Joyce. I'm a colleague of your husband's from work. Is he . . . is he at home?'

There was silence as Janet pondered what to do next.

'Do you have some identification?' she demanded, talking in a louder voice to project a braveness she did not feel.

For a moment Peter was thrown by the request. It was hardly what he had anticipated.

'Oh, er, yes, of course.'

He fumbled for his wallet, wondering what sort of document would satisfy her.

'If Alec is here, he would . . .'

'He's not,' she replied sharply.

'Well, look, here's my security pass from Aldermaston. That's where I work. The atomic weapons place.'

He slipped the card through the crack in the door and she snatched it from his fingers. She seemed to study it for ages, then suddenly the chain was slipped free and the door swung open.

'I'm terribly sorry, Mr Joyce,' she fluttered. 'You must think me very foolish. It's just that some truly dreadful things have happened in this area to people opening their doors to strangers. And I'm on my own, you see, with two little *girls* upstairs . . .'

The way she stressed the word *girls* conjured a vision of rapists prowling for victims. Perhaps he *should* have telephoned beforehand.

'I quite understand, Mrs Anderson. You're absolutely right to be careful, and I suppose it is rather late for me to turn up on your doorstep. It's just that I need to talk to your husband right away. Do you expect him back soon?'

'Oh yes, I should think so,' she replied resignedly. 'When the pub shuts. It depends on Karl really, and you know what he's like.'

Janet Anderson was one of those women who tend to assume that even complete strangers know all the friends and personalities who feature in their lives.

'I'm sorry, Mrs Anderson, but I don't know Karl,' Peter explained patiently.

'Oh, good heavens! But how silly! Why should you! Well, he's a great friend of Alec's. They meet at the pub every Friday. You see, this is Alec's night for getting away from me and the children!' She laughed awkwardly.

'I have my night off on Mondays, though I don't always take advantage of it. Anyway, Karl rang this evening to check that Alec was going to be drinking. Sounded terribly keen to see him, and Alec went rushing off hot foot. I wish *I* could say something to Alec that would have the same effect!'

She laughed shrilly at her own cattiness. She was a short, bird-like woman, forever touching her hair to ensure it was in place.

'What would you like to do? You could wait for him,' she suggested eagerly. The thought had suddenly occurred to her that if her own husband would not talk to her about that suicide girl, perhaps this man would.

'Well, if he's not going to be very long . . .' Peter answered hesitantly.

'Why don't you come into the library, Mr Joyce?'

She opened the door to the front room and led him in.

'This is Alec's favourite room. All his pictures and things are here.'

Peter was immediately struck by its style. An antique glass-fronted mahogany cabinet was packed with leather-bound volumes, and the floor was covered with a Persian rug. At least a dozen small paintings lined the walls.

'Lovely room,' he began, crossing to the far wall to examine one of the pictures more closely. 'These are nice. Have they been in your family a long time?'

'Oh, no. Alec's bought them all. It's his hobby. They're sweet, aren't they?'

'Mmmm, delightful.'

'Karl knows a dealer who specialises in that type of art, so Alec's bought quite a few of them in the last six months.'

She could have added that there were plenty of other things they needed which he could have spent his money on, but she restrained herself. Instead she was silent for a moment, wondering how to raise the subject that was concerning her.

'Are you . . . are you involved in this secrets business?' she blurted out eventually.

Peter was surprised by the directness of her question.

'Well, yes. I suppose I am.'

'What . . . on the investigating side? Police? Security, that sort of thing?'

'No,' he replied carefully. 'No, I'm not the police. I'm a scientist. I helped design the weapon that all the fuss is about.'

'Oh. Oh, I see.'

Her eyes seemed to lose their concentration and she gazed vaguely into the corner of the room, puzzling whether he might be able to answer her questions.

'Have you been under suspicion, too, then?' she went on. 'I mean Alec, he . . . he's been so nervous lately. As if he was going to get blamed for everything. He said they were investigating *everybody* involved. You . . . you too, I suppose?'

'Oh yes. None of us has escaped the suspicion of MI5,' Peter said bitterly.

'Then I suppose you must have been upset about this woman who killed herself. His secretary, Mary something or other. Alec is devastated. I heard him crying last night, and I've never known him do that before.'

Peter did not want to talk about Mary, but he was startled by what the woman had just said. Why should Anderson have been so affected? Mary Maclean may have been his secretary, but he had never shown any particular interest in her. Why should he be so distressed?

'Did he talk to you about what happened?' he asked cautiously.

'No. He's said nothing. But he was so upset I . . . I began to wonder if there'd been something between them!' The corners of her mouth turned down involuntarily, betraying her unhappiness.

'No, definitely not. I can promise you that,' Peter reassured her. But then what *was* the reason for his grief?

'And then there was something they said on the television news, about the crisis being over. That seemed to upset him even more.'

She looked at him expectantly, hoping that he might explain. But suddenly Peter had the uneasy feeling there was no time to lose: he had to get to Anderson right away.

'I've just had a thought, Mrs Anderson. If the pub is not too far away, I might go and find him there. If I wait here until he gets back, it could make it a rather late night for all of us, don't you think?'

Janet Anderson was disappointed: she had learned

nothing from him. Her face took on a look of resignation.

'Well, you can try,' she conceded, staring at the floor. 'The pub's called the Maid's Head. It's just down the bottom of the road. Turn right out of the house and keep going. You can't miss it.'

'All right, I'll try there. Thank you,' Peter smiled. 'If I don't find him, I'm afraid I'll have to come back and disturb you again. I hope you won't think me a dreadful nuisance.'

'No,' she shrugged, 'I shall be here.'

She stood on the doorstep watching him as he headed down the road.

The pub was crowded and smoky. Amid such a sea of faces he began to doubt whether he would ever spot Anderson. However, being tall and stocky, he managed to ease his way through to the bar, and looked about him uneasily. But what exactly would he say to Anderson if he did find him? He still did not know.

'Yes?' the barman asked.

'Er, a half of bitter, thanks.'

A shout of jubilation caused him to focus on the far corner of the bar-room. A burly youth was waving a billiard-cue in the air.

'That's sixty-five pence.'

Momentarily the barman drew back his attention.

'Thank you.'

He sipped at the glass and peered through the fog of cigarette smoke. The men at the billiard table looked too young to be company for Anderson. He scanned them carefully to be certain, but Alec was not there.

Damn!

Drinkers eager to refill their glasses before closing-time were elbowing him away from the bar. He eased back through the crowd, searching faces, searching looks. Suddenly he stopped.

Alec Anderson was sitting at a small table just six feet away.

He was not alone and he looked like death. Peter backed away so as not to be seen. He found a shelf by the wall where he could rest his glass, and from where he had a clear view.

The man sitting opposite him must be Karl, Peter thought. He had thin, straight hair, a pointed nose, and metal-framed spectacles, and seemed to be issuing instructions. His eyes never left Anderson's face, which was pale and slack-jawed, as if from shock.

Peter sipped his beer, and kept his eye on the two men. It was ten to eleven and the landlord was calling for last orders.

Anderson had an almost full pint in front of him, but was making no effort to drink it. The other man had been drinking spirits, and his glass was empty.

Suddenly Anderson shook his head as if in violent disagreement. The other man eyed him threateningly and reached down to the floor. His hand came up clutching a brown-paper parcel the size of a small book.

Anderson looked thunderstruck as the parcel was pushed across the table. He clearly did not want to take it, but Karl thrust it into his hands.

A group of people sitting at a large table in front of Peter stood up suddenly, and began to pull coats over their shoulders, obscuring his view.

'Hurry up, for God's sake!' he hissed under his breath.

They took their time, though, discussing whose house they would return to for a nightcap. Finally Peter took his glass from the shelf and pushed his way round them, desperate not to lose sight of Anderson. But he saw with annoyance that the two chairs were now empty, Anderson's full glass still standing on the table unconsumed. He looked desperately round the exits and caught sight of the back of Karl's head disappearing through a door into the street.

He dumped his glass and hurried after them, but ran into the group who had been blocking his view. They were still debating where to go as he tried to push through them.

'I'm so sorry. I'm in a terrible rush,' he mumbled.

'Careful!' a woman shouted, as he trod on her foot.

Outside he heard car engines being started in the small car-park. But surely Anderson would have come on foot?

Then he saw them, on the pavement. Anderson was still being forcefully urged to take the parcel. Harsh words were clearly raised between them. Suddenly Karl turned and crossed the road to a large Mercedes. He opened the door, slipped inside, and drove off at speed. Anderson stared after him.

Slowly Anderson turned and began to walk up the hill towards his house. Peter strode briskly after him.

'Alec! I thought it was you. I've been looking for you,' he announced breathlessly as he came up to him.

Anderson swung round, not recognising the voice at first.

'What the hell . . .? Peter? What are you doing here, for God's sake?' he stammered.

'I was looking for you. Wanted to talk to you. Your wife said you might be down at the pub.'

The astonishment on Anderson's face turned rapidly to bewilderment and then to fear as he began to suspect what Peter might have witnessed.

'I was having a drink with someone,' he explained lamely.

'So I saw.'

'What . . . what is it you want?' His voice seemed flat with dread.

'I wanted to talk to you about Mary.'

Anderson's face crumpled. He looked like a schoolboy faced with a caning.

'I don't see there's anything to discuss,' he said abruptly, starting up the road again.

'What is it that man Karl wants from you, Alec?'

Anderson's head spun round like a snake's. His eyes were wild and desperate, searching Peter's face for a clue to what he knew. Joyce sensed he was on the verge of finding out everything he wanted to know.

'You've got a choice,' he needled. 'You can either tell *me* about it or tell John Black. If I call him, he'll be round like a shot.'

'Oh Christ!' Anderson's words came in a strangled gasp. 'Look, why don't you p-piss off! It's none of your business!'

'Yes, it bloody well is!' Peter snapped back. 'Mary was murdered, and you know all about it!'

He peered at the package under Anderson's arm. It had a broad, hard edge, like a frame.

'What *is* in that parcel, Alec? Another picture?'

Anderson seemed paralysed, unable to respond. The brown package clamped under his arm felt like a ticking bomb.

'Oh Jesus!' He said at last, his words hardly audible. 'Look, Peter, I need time to think. That's not too much to ask, is it?' His eyes begged. 'Please? Look . . . I admit I'm in some trouble, but I'm sure I can find a way out if only I have time to think.'

Peter grabbed him by the arm and began to hurry him up the hill.

'I can ring from your house. It's down to MI5 now.'

'Peter, Peter!' Alec croaked. 'I'll get life! Do you understand? *Life!* And for Janet that'll mean death!'

For a moment Peter was silenced.

'Do you mean . . . are you telling me that *you* killed Mary?' he asked aghast.

'No, no! God no! Not me . . . Oh, Christ!'

Anderson had become a pathetic, desolate figure.

'I think you'd better explain, Alec. Then we'll see if there's a way to avoid bringing in the police. Come on, now.'

The brass coach-lamp in the porch had been switched off. Anderson fumbled with his key, still hugging the parcel tightly. He opened the door and led the way inside.

'You can leave your coat round here, Peter.' He indicated a small cloakroom. Peter hung his raincoat on a hanger, next to a remarkably shabby brown overcoat. Anderson must use it for gardening, he guessed.

'Alec?' Janet called from upstairs. 'Oh, I see you found each other,' she continued, as Peter was led across the hall towards the library.

'Yes, it's all right, darling,' Alec reassured her. 'You go to bed. I'll be a little while yet.'

'I was in bed already,' Janet grumbled, before disappearing.

Alec closed the library door firmly behind them. At last he released his grip on the parcel, placing it on the desk. For a while he stood there, staring down at it, without a word. Peter sat in an upright Victorian armchair and waited. Anderson would start talking in his own good time.

Alec expelled a deep sigh, then he pulled out a handkerchief and blew his nose.

'You've seen these, have you?' he asked, indicating the paintings on the walls. 'Janet showed you in here?'

'Yes, she did. They're very fine.'

'Well, they're the reason I'm in this mess!' he began to explain as he lowered himself into the swivel-chair. 'Karl got most of them for me. Karl Metzger, that's what he calls himself. I don't know what his real name is.'

Anderson put his hand to his mouth and tugged at his lower lip. His eyes seemed to beg for Peter's sympathy.

'Karl Metzger is a colonel in the East German intelligence service – the HVA. He's a spy!'

'Good God!' Peter murmured.

He had suspected something like that, but it was still a shock.

Anderson's face showed the helplessness of a child.

'I only learned this two weeks ago. They set me up, Peter. They just set me up; it was the oldest trap in the book, and I fell right into it. But it really wasn't my fault – I . . .' His voice tailed away.

'Go on,' Peter urged grimly.

Alec pushed his fingers underneath the rims of his spectacles and rubbed his eyes.

'I've known Karl for about a year,' he went on awkwardly. 'He joined our Friday group at the pub. Beer, billiards, dirty jokes – you know the sort of thing. All harmless fun and gets us away from our women-folk. Well, I must admit I *liked* the man when he joined us.' He seemed pained at having to make this small confession.

'He was funny – made jokes about the Germans, and there aren't many Krauts who'll do that. He said he was from West Germany, of course. I had no reason to doubt that. He said Hamburg was his home town. He's in the travel business, sells German culture to tourists, or that's what he said. Well, er, he and I became . . . sort of chums. We had plenty to talk about . . . specially the paintings. You see, we shared an interest in Victorian miniatures.'

Anderson shook his head.

'Shared an interest, huh! He was just setting me up, of course. But he was good, oh, he was good! He really knew his stuff. Must have taught himself the lot just to get me on his hook!' He laughed bitterly.

'Well . . . he knew what I collected. I only had three or four of them at that time, but he said he knew a dealer who specialised in them and who would look out for some for me at a reasonable price. They can be pricey, you see. And suddenly, one day in the pub, he appeared with a picture wrapped up in brown paper. That one there.'

He pointed to the small gilded frame nearest to the door.

'The thing was so elaborate – that's what I can't get over. I mean, in my sort of job you're on your guard. Spies and so on. It never occurred to me that they would go to such lengths, just to make me feel everything was all right. That's what the pictures were for – just to lull me into a false sense of security.'

'But what *happened* exactly? I still don't understand,' Peter sighed with exasperation.

'There were photographs,' he whispered.

He seemed reluctant to continue.

'It was one weekend,' he began sheepishly. 'Karl said he and I had been invited to spend a couple of days at a house in Suffolk which belonged to the dealer who'd found the paintings for me. He claimed the man was keen to meet me, and it would be just Karl and me – no wives. It sounded interesting – a weekend talking with a real expert, and no women to be kept occupied.

'And so it was . . . initially. The man said he was from

Eastern Europe originally and had come to this country as a child, just after the war. He lived in a lovely old farmhouse with enormous gardens. The house was *full* of paintings . . .'

Beads of sweat were breaking out on his brow.

'He lived there on his own, but he had a . . . sort of servant. A . . . a young man.'

Anderson's face began to turn grey.

'I . . . I . . .' He shook his head, faltering.

'What *happened*?' Peter could guess the answer.

'It's difficult to explain it . . . *cold* like this,' he stammered, wiping the sweat from his lip.

'I mean . . . I'm not gay, I'm really not. But, it was just one of those occasions when the atmosphere made one think of doing things that one would never normally consider . . .'

'I see.'

'Please . . . *please* try to understand.' Anderson picked up a paper-knife from the desk and fiddled with it.

'It was just the atmosphere. We were all very relaxed. We'd all eaten well and drunk plenty, and it was . . . bohemian, I suppose. The dealer and his servant were obviously homosexuals. It was the atmosphere – they might even have put something in my drink. And . . .'

He was searching for the right words.

'And I suppose there are plenty of normal men who think about having that sort of sex – *think* about it but never *do* it, because of the social conventions. But . . . but there *weren't* any conventions that weekend, and so I . . . I did it!'

He completed the sentence in a rush of acute embarrassment.

'But there was a camera,' he added in a whisper.

'I never saw it, but there was a camera taking pictures of everything that happened.'

He swallowed hard.

'Karl said he would send the photographs to Janet, to the Prime Minister, to the Defence Secretary, to everyone necessary to ruin my career and my personal life. Janet – God! If Janet ever saw them! – it would kill her. She could never understand. She worships me, you know,' he whispered pityingly. 'Karl can destroy me and destroy everything dear to me. He's got me where he wants me.'

'And what exactly does he want?'

'Skydancer! The full technical blueprints for the warheads!'

'And you've given them to him?'

'No!' Anderson shouted defiantly. 'No, I've given him nothing. Nothing at all. Not yet. But . . .'

'Yes?'

'But I did agree to do it! I had to tell him that, Peter, I had no choice, don't you understand?

'I arranged to leave them under some leaves by a tree on Hampstead Heath, where he could collect them. Only I had a plan, you see. A trick so that he wouldn't actually get any of the secrets.'

He leaned forward, eager for Peter to accept his good intentions.

'I reckoned that if I could make the handover go wrong in a very public way, I might be able to persuade him that the sudden security hoo-ha would make it impossible for me to get the stuff for him at that time, and that we should delay everything. That way I thought I could buy time to think. To try to work out a way of saving both the secrets and my own . . . situation.

'So I pretended I had made a mistake about the place where I was to leave the papers, and I put the folder with just one sheet from the Skydancer plans inside a litter bin close to the real dead-letter box. You see, I knew that General Twining walked along that path every morning early, regular as clockwork. I occasionally go for early morning walks myself, and I'd passed the time of day with him there in the past.

'So after I left the folder, I rushed back to some bushes where I'd hidden some old clothes, and dressed up as a tramp . . . wore an old overcoat –'

'The one I saw hanging up in your cloakroom?' Peter interrupted.

'Yes. That one,' Anderson answered, obviously put out that he had not thought to dispose of it.

'Yes. You see, I reckoned that if I got back to the litter bin right away and pretended to be rustling through it I could stop Karl's men collecting the folder, and could also see that it was conspicuous when the general came by. I knew he was a meticulous sort of man and was bound to pick up the mess.'

'My God, Alec! You were taking one hell of a risk, weren't you? Suppose the East Germans had got there first?'

'Well, there was only one page from the set, remember. They wouldn't have learned much from that.'

'Don't be so sure.' Peter frowned.

'Anyway, it worked. The general delivered the folder to the Defence Ministry just as I thought he would, but there was a hitch after that. I desperately needed a great public hue-and-cry to convince Karl that the hullabaloo would make it impossible to get the rest of the plans for the time being. Only, Sir Marcus Beckett decided to try to keep the whole business secret so as not to stir up the politicians. That was a potential disaster for me, so I did the only thing I could think of: I leaked the story to the press.'

'So that was you, was it? But what was your friend Karl's reaction to all this?'

'He went wild, of course. He had copies made of those dreadful photographs, and had the envelopes already addressed to send off. He didn't send them, though. I swore to him that it had all been an honest mistake, and said I would do what he wanted eventually – but that they had to give me more time. Well, that promise kept him quiet for a couple of days, but then . . . it was like a bombshell.

'Mary Maclean was dead! Killed herself, they said, confessing to something she hadn't done! I was terribly upset. I couldn't believe it. But then suddenly I realised what it meant. The hue-and-cry was over. The pressure was off, and Karl could now demand that I get him the papers immediately. My excuse was removed by the death of one carefully selected victim!'

Alec caught Peter's look of anger.

'Yes. Karl Metzger killed Mary. He admitted it this evening. He doped her with some hypnotic drug untraceable by forensic tests, then dumped her in her bath and cut her wrists.'

Peter recoiled at this abrupt summary of her end.

'He gave me this.'

Anderson reached his shaking hand across the desk and lightly touched the brown-paper parcel he had brought back from the pub.

'He said it was to remind me. I don't dare . . . Here, *you* open it, would you?'

Peter shook his head, struggling to control the bitter emotions welling up inside him. He had felt certain that Mary was murdered, but this confirmation was devastating. He felt his whole body begin to tremble. Just a short while ago he had stood within feet of the man who had killed her.

'What the . . .?' Alec started in surprise. He had now opened the parcel himself. It contained a picture, and he passed it across.

It was the photograph of Mary with her nephew and niece, the one that Peter had not been able to find in her flat.

Anderson stood up and crossed to the sideboard. He poured whisky into two glasses.

'Here.' He passed one across, and Peter swallowed a mouthful.

'The bastard!' Peter exploded. 'The evil little bastard! He's got to be caught. Come on! Call the police now! You've no choice! Mary died because of you – you and your efforts to save your own skin!'

'It's not just *my* skin! There are three people upstairs, two of them small children, who matter more than I do. Their lives will be ruined if those photographs get out!'

'Look, if you co-operate fully with John Black, he'll probably be able to grab Karl before he has a chance to do anything,' Peter insisted, knowing he did not sound convincing.

'John Black! You trust that man, do you? Have you ever asked yourself who he's *really* working for?' Anderson leaned forward intensely. 'Karl has got someone in MI5! At the top. An informer,' he whispered.

'What?'

Anderson nodded meaningfully.

'How many people know that you went over to the United States to make alterations to the test missile, Peter? I didn't, and I'm head of the Nuclear Secretariat. It was my business to know, and I didn't – until Karl told me!'

'Christ! Karl told you about that? Bloody hell! That was classified top secret! Only the most senior military men, some ministers and security chiefs, and a handful of blokes at Aldermaston knew about it. Did Karl say his source was in MI5? Was he specific?'

'Well, yes, the hint was pretty heavy.'

Peter's thoughts were racing. If the Soviets knew that he had made changes to the Skydancer warheads, then what was to be done about the test launch? The weapons had been reprogrammed specifically to make the Russians doubt the genuineness of the plans they might have stolen – though it was now clear that they did not have the plans at all. If he turned Anderson in and got Metzger arrested, it still would not be the end of the affair for the Soviets. They would try some other way to get hold of the blueprints, he was sure of that. They would only stop trying once they had obtained what they thought were the real Skydancer plans.

Anderson, he suddenly realised, had a unique value.

'What were Karl's last instructions to you?'

Alec shivered. 'He's given me until midday Monday. I have to phone a number at twelve noon on that day to confirm I have the Skydancer papers, and to arrange a handover point. If I don't do this, he'll put the photographs in the afternoon post.'

'So we have the weekend in which to think,' Peter murmured to himself. 'Alec, if you want me to help you, you've got to do precisely what I ask you. I have the beginnings of an idea which might save you *and* save Skydancer at the same time.'

The snow that had fallen in the past few days in Moscow had melted in a sudden thaw. The winter had receded for a while, and it felt like autumn again. Even the grey clouds that covered the city almost continually at this time of year had parted sufficiently that morning to let rays of watery sunshine cast shadows in the road.

Oleg Kvitzinsky was loading suitcases into his car. He had not expected to be able to leave the city that weekend. The GRU had told him repeatedly that the British missile secrets would be in his hands any day, and he had believed them. Suddenly, however, on the previous afternoon he had decided to ignore General Novikov's unfulfilled promises and try to forget about the problem for a couple of days. The pressure of waiting was making him dangerously irritable.

'Where can we put this? It mustn't get damaged,' Katrina called out, struggling towards him with a large pot-plant.

'What are we taking that for?' he demanded in exasperation.

'For my mother. A present for my mother. It's her anniversary, you know!'

Oleg shrugged, and wedged the pot safely in the corner of the rear seat. His wife's family was aggravatingly conscientious about celebrating. Katrina's father had died four years earlier, but she still insisted on marking the date of her parents' wedding every year.

The traffic flowed steadily on the ring-road as he headed for the turning that would take them north-east towards the town of Zagorsk. Their dacha belonged to Katrina's family, and was a large timber house with enough bedrooms to accommodate her brother's family and her mother as well as themselves. Oleg knew it was going to be a weekend of tears mixed with happiness. It always was when Katrina's family got together.

As they drove away from the city and into the birchwoods, the sun broke through the clouds again, gilding the white bark of the trees. He opened the window to smell the air, and patted the steering-wheel with spontaneous enthusiasm.

'Katya, this was a good idea!' he exclaimed.

She smiled at him and stroked his knee. She wanted him to relax this weekend, to forget the secret work about which he would never talk, and to remember the fun they used to have when he was just a computer specialist in the civilian sector, travelling all over the world. She was determined to persuade him to return to that way of life somehow.

'Bella promised to do lunch,' she commented, 'and I shall cook this evening. Will you be going to see the priest?' There was a certain frost in her voice. She had no time for religion, and it annoyed her that her husband found such solace in communicating with clerics.

'I might,' he stated firmly. 'If there's time.'

But he had every intention of finding time to drive into Zagorsk during the next two days to visit a small house with a hand-decorated doorway, close to the Trinity-Saint Sergei monastery. For the man who lived there was not only a priest in that town celebrated as the spiritual centre of the Russian Orthodox church; he had also been Oleg Kvitzinsky's confidant for many years.

It took them a little over an hour to reach the dacha, seven kilometres outside Zagorsk on the Moscow road.

'Look, Oleg! The children!' Katrina suddenly pointed ahead.

As they neared the dacha, her brother's two daughters could be seen walking by the roadside, carrying baskets full of mushrooms.

Oleg pressed his foot on the brake pedal and smiled. He would give them a lift back to the house.

Peter Joyce looked at his watch for the fifth time in as many minutes. It was after 8 a.m. He would try the number the Chief of Defence Staff had given him; the man was bound to be awake by now.

Lady Buxton answered the phone of their Pimlico townhouse, only to tell him that her husband had gone out for a walk. Peter silently cursed the way military men seemed to be obsessed with early-morning exercise. However, the field-marshal's wife promised to get her husband to call back the moment he returned home.

'Hiya, Dad!'

Peter's eleven-year-old son bounced into the kitchen in his pyjamas.

'You won't forget I'm playing in the first eleven this afternoon, Dad? You will watch, won't you?'

'Oh, Mark,' Peter groaned, smacking himself on the forehead. 'It's not that I've forgotten . . .'

'It's just that it slipped your memory,' Mark cut in sarcastically.

Shoulders stiff with resentment, the boy walked past his father and began to search for some breakfast.

'Look, it's not that. I *will* try to come and see you play, but it just may not be possible in the end, that's all. I'm sorry, old chap. You know what's been going on the last few days,' he explained. 'Well, it's not over yet.'

'But I've never played in the first eleven before,' Mark insisted, sulkily shaking corn-flakes into a bowl.

'I'm sure Mum will come and watch you.'

'Yeah . . .'

'I *do* promise I'll come if I can.'

Belinda was awake and sitting up in bed as he brought in the tray. The strain of the past few days had deepened the lines on her face. Peter thought she suddenly looked old.

'Was that you on the phone?' she asked.

'Yes, I need to get hold of someone urgently.'

She took the mug he offered her and murmured her thanks.

'You were very late last night,' she ventured, sipping

slowly. 'I don't even know what time you got back. Where did you go?'

Peter sat down on the bed.

'I went to see the person who is at the bottom of this whole spying business. I think I know the entire story now.'

'But you're not going to tell me.'

'Not yet. I can't.'

Belinda raised an eyebrow disdainfully, and drank more tea.

'You're still suspended?'

'Yes. That's not changed.'

'Wouldn't this be a good time to resign?' she suggested quietly. 'I mean, they suspended you because they thought it was your fault the secrets went missing. Now if you have evidence that someone else was to blame, your good name will be restored. So you could resign in protest at the way you have been treated, and everybody would support you.'

'God! That's a bit tortuous, isn't it? Why should I want to resign, anyway?'

'So that you could take up a new job that didn't involve building weapons of mass-destruction,' she explained gently, as if addressing someone of lower-than-average intelligence.

Peter snorted with laughter. 'You never give up, do you?'

'Peter, I'm serious!' she pleaded. 'You're a highly qualified electronics specialist. British industry must be crying out for people like you! Why not get out of this nuclear business while you can?'

Her dark eyes implored him to listen.

'And, frankly, all this cloak-and-dagger stuff is frightening the life out of me.'

There was the hint of a tremor in her voice. Peter

reached across to where her knees made a mound in the bedclothes.

'Even if I wanted to change jobs, it's not that easy. My knowledge of electronics has been related to nothing but nuclear weapons for the past fifteen years. It's not the sort of knowledge needed by many companies in Britain.'

'Where there's a will . . .' she murmured wistfully.

Peter turned away from her again. He did not want to have to cope with an argument that morning.

'Look, I expect to be out most of the day. I've got to see the Chief of the Defence Staff, if I can get hold of him . . . It's Mark: his football match this afternoon. I don't think I can get there. I'm going to have to disappoint him. Can you go and watch?'

'Of course. I was going anyway,' she said dismissively.

The telephone rang on the bedside table, and Peter leaned across to answer it.

Field-Marshal Buxton suggested they meet in his office at the Defence Ministry. He had warned security staff on duty that Saturday to expect Peter.

'Not sure this is quite proper, with you being suspended from duty and all that,' the CDS stated with some discomfort when they were alone together. 'Not sure I'm allowed to speak to you officially. Still, if necessary we can pretend this conversation never took place!'

'I don't think you'll have any objections when you've heard what I've got to say.'

As Peter began to describe his visit to Alec Anderson the previous evening, the old soldier's face was fixed in an expression of unyielding concentration. Peter talked for nearly ten minutes.

For a moment Buxton seemed to be searching for words.

'Dammit! That's one of the most appalling stories I've ever heard!' he exclaimed at last. 'But what have you done about it, apart from telling me? You've put the security people on to him, I hope?'

Peter shook his head.

'Why not, for God's sake? The man's a menace, and that East German – he needs to be locked up right away.'

'It's not as simple as that,' Peter urged. 'Anderson is convinced that the East Germans have an agent in MI5! Somehow this man Karl knew that I had been over to Florida to adjust the warheads on HMS *Retribution*!'

'Oh? Buxton looked startled. He well remembered how highly classified that visit had been. 'And Anderson thinks the source was in MI5?'

Peter nodded.

'You had your own suspicions about Mr John Black, didn't you?'

'I'm sure he tried to deliberately conceal the fact that photograph was missing from Mary's flat. Perhaps it was because he knew who'd really got it.'

Buxton looked doubtful. 'But we can't disregard the entire security service just because of a vague suspicion over one individual!' he exploded. 'I mean, for God's sake, these men have got to be apprehended right away, before they can do more damage. They might skip the country any minute. There must be plenty more information inside Anderson's head that could be useful to the other side.'

'Well, I had another idea,' Peter ventured, not sure how Buxton would take it.

'Anderson's control is expecting him to deliver the complete Skydancer plans on Monday. Why don't we let him think he's doing that?'

'Go on,' Buxton frowned.

'Only it won't be the real papers that he hands over. Instead I'll provide him with a set that'll match the changes I made to the warheads; so when they are fired off in a few days' time, our deception will be complete. With any luck the Soviets'll think they have the real plans, with the warheads' performance confirmed before their own eyes, and no matter how much they spend on devising counter-measures, they'll all be totally irrelevant.'

'And the man who killed that wretched girl will get off scot-free?' Buxton spluttered.

Peter remembered what he had seen in Chiswick. Yes, he wanted revenge on the man who had done it.

'Perhaps he won't,' he replied noncommittally.

'It'll be a political decision,' the field-marshal said eventually. 'Have to be. Too much at stake. Too much that could go wrong. I'll have to talk to the PM.'

He looked at his watch. It was after midday.

'When are you due to contact Anderson again?'

'Sometime later today. I didn't fix a time.'

'Hmmmm. Best thing you can do, Peter, is to go for a walk. Let me sort things for a bit. Find a nice pub, have some lunch, and come back here at about half-past two. Perhaps I'll have an answer by then.'

To have two hours to kill was agonising for Peter, and left him feeling uncomfortably impotent.

Following the defence chief's suggestion, he took a walk along the Embankment to Westminster Bridge and crossed to the other side of the river. Heading east along the South Bank towards the City, he put the traffic behind him and felt invigorated by the brisk breeze and the sight of the thick, brown Thames water swirling seawards in a full ebb-tide. Pleasure boats, now unused in the winter months, strained at their moorings in the middle of the stream, and a police patrol launch nosed its way curiously amongst them.

Pulling up the collar of his fawn raincoat against the wind, he sat down on a bench overlooking the river. The South Bank walkway was deserted except for one solitary figure who had found a seat some fifty yards away. The man wearing a thick anorak pulled a folded newspaper from his pocket and began to read it.

Events had moved so rapidly in the past few days that Peter had had little chance to consider where they were leading. Now the idea of enacting a complete deception of the Soviet Union in the immediate future preoccupied him fully. But assuming the plan succeeded, what then? He assumed success would result in his suspension being rescinded, but it worried him that the Government was not committed to any nuclear weapons developments beyond the Skydancer project. Even if they wanted general research at Aldermaston to continue in the years ahead, how satisfying would his own job be without a specific advanced technology project to work on? For the first time he began to wonder whether Belinda's urging him to quit might be worth considering.

Peter breathed in deeply and stood up, his chin thrust forward. The wind blew his hair into his eyes and he pushed it back with his hand. The man in the anorak noted the gesture. He had seen him do the same several times in the last ten minutes.

Changing career at his age was risky, and surely even to think of it at that time was being defeatist, wasn't it? Peter turned towards Waterloo Bridge and set off down the pavement. The man in the anorak stood up casually, stuffed the newspaper back in his pocket, and ambled after him.

'Do sit down,' Field-Marshal Buxton gestured to a chair.

It was nearly four o'clock, and Peter had been waiting over an hour for the Chief of Defence Staff to return from Downing Street.

'They've agreed,' the old man declared conspiratorially. 'They want you to draw up some dummy plans, good enough to fool the Russians, but which don't reveal any sensitive information. Think you can do it?'

'Hmmm. There'll have to be *some* sensitive bits in it just to make it convincing. They must realise that, for heaven's sake!'

Buxton's intense grey eyes peered over his gold-framed half-moon glasses. He was wondering how frank to be.

'I've been discussing this business for the best part of an hour at Number 10. The Prime Minister called in the Defence Secretary and the heads of MI5 and MI6. Their initial reaction was far from favourable, I can tell you. Michael Hawke seemed to want you locked up in the Tower, along with Anderson and that East German fellow! He's very bitter about your disregard for security procedures; says he's going to ensure you are fully disciplined – thrown out of the Civil Service and all that!'

Peter groaned.

'Shouldn't worry. I don't suppose it will come to that,' Buxton soothed. 'Just trying to give you an idea of the atmosphere at this meeting! Well, I eventually managed to persuade them to give serious thought to your proposal, and interestingly enough it was the MI6 man who came to your aid. Liked the idea. Said it reminded him of the 1960s when they fed a doctored version of the plans for Concorde to the Russians – and you know what happened to Concordski!

'I, er, told them about your suspicion of a spy inside MI5. Dick Sproat said it was rubbish, of course! Couldn't really say anything else. He, er, he said that they knew about Anderson and Metzger. They've been keeping a watch on Anderson apparently. They suspected Metzger was an intelligence man, though they hadn't been able to confirm it yet.'

Peter's eyebrows arched with interest. If Anderson had been under observation, then presumably he must have been too!

'In the end they agreed, but they want strict safeguards. You're to have the plans ready for Monday morning, and then there will be a vetting committee here to check it out. Just a small select group; we've got to keep this utterly secret.'

'I hope Anderson will agree to all this,' Peter cautioned.

'He'll bloody well have to! He's got no alternative!' Buxton snorted.

'But what will happen to him when it's over? Does he get immunity from prosecution?'

Buxton's eyes twinkled for a moment.

'I'm sure the Ministry of Agriculture can be persuaded to find a job for him,' he mused.

It was six in the morning when Peter parked outside Anderson's house. This time he had telephoned in advance.

Alec opened the door within seconds of his ringing the bell – as if he had been waiting behind it. There was no sign of Janet or the children as Peter was ushered hurriedly into the library.

'What's happening? Who've you told?' Anderson demanded nervously.

He was dressed in bottle-green corduroy trousers and a navy-blue pullover. A small twist of cotton wool was stuck to the underside of his jaw where he had cut himself shaving. The corners of his mouth were tight with anxiety.

'Look, Alec, people are sympathetic, really they are,' Peter reassured him, hoping he sounded convincing. 'They'll do all they can to help you, and to ensure that Janet and the children are safe. But they want you to do something in return.'

'What exactly?' Alec asked tremulously. 'And who *are* these people?'

'People at the top. The *very* top. And they want you to help turn the tables on the Russians. To get our own back.'

He paused, noting the look of apprehension on Alec's face.

'On Monday morning I shall meet you in the Defence Ministry and give you a set of plans for the Skydancer warheads. They'll look convincing but they'll be deliberately misleading. Now, you are to pass these to Karl Metzger, insisting of course that they're the genuine ones. And in return you should demand from him the negatives of the photographs he's been using to blackmail you. It's that simple.'

Alec shook his head.

'Nothing is that simple, and you know it. Supposing he can tell they're false?'

'He won't,' Peter insisted. 'You'll have to trust me on that.'

Anderson stared at him silently for a moment.

'And if it all works like you say, what then? What

happens to me – at the Ministry?'

'They'll find something suitable for you,' Peter answered irritably. 'For God's sake, Alec! You're on the floor! You're being offered a hand up!' He suppressed an urge to take the man by the throat and shake him.

He glanced down at the desk, with its top rolled back. The photograph of Mary still lay there, half-wrapped in brown paper. He took it in his hand and held it under Anderson's nose.

'Yes. Yes, of course I'll do what you say,' Alec whispered. 'What else can I do?'

Peter stood up, the photo-frame still in his hand.

'I'll take this with me, if you don't mind,' he said.

Alec looked up questioningly.

'Sentimental reasons,' Peter explained.

On Sunday morning Oleg Kvitzinsky did not wake early. It had been a difficult night.

Saturday had been a relaxing day for him, immersing himself in the inconsequential issues that preoccupied the lives of Katrina's family.

Katrina herself had passed most of the day hovering around her little nieces, remarking to anyone who would listen that they were the most perfectly delightful children she had ever known. Oleg had cast the occasional anxious glance in her direction, knowing what this was leading to. His wife always became obsessive about her childlessness when they came to the dacha. The fecundity of the countryside and the ease with which her brother's wife produced babies made her reason inwardly that it must be possible for her to conceive here, at the dacha.

At supper she had frowned at Oleg and scolded him as glass after glass of vodka had passed his lips. Then, when her brother-in-law produced two bottles of Georgian wine for them to taste, she could feel tears of despair welling up in her eyes. Her husband would be no use to her drunk.

Before they finally fell into bed, Katrina had sprayed her body lightly with the Dior perfume carefully preserved from their last visit to the West. At first Oleg had shown all the signs of falling into instant slumber, but she had quickly unbuttoned his pyjamas and began to caress the soft, furry dome of his stomach. Slowly but surely she sensed his arousal.

Oleg himself had been surprised at the liveliness of his feelings after so much alcohol, and he had begun to believe that a rare degree of mutual satisfaction might be achievable that night. But then the noise had started in the next room. Katrina's brother and sister-in-law slept on the other side of the wall. The rhythmic creaking started softly and unevenly, but built up steadily to a persistent tempo.

'Oh, this is a farmyard!' Oleg groaned, feeling the vitality draining from him.

They had both lain awake after their failure, back to back, their bodies not quite touching. Oleg told himself he should have had more to drink, so not even the mirage of sexual potency could have arisen. On the other side of the bed Katrina let her tears of frustration soak into the pillow.

In the morning she had risen early to help her mother and busy herself around the house, trying to project an image of contentment. She found it impossible to discuss her personal difficulties with her family.

The intermittent sunshine of the previous day persisted, and Oleg took the children for a walk in the birch woods while the women prepared lunch. Katrina's brother spent the morning asleep. The freshness of the air, away from the pollution of Moscow, had a sweet taste to it which he savoured.

From a distant village the wind blew the sound of bells tolling the faithful to church. In this part of the atheist state the Orthodox Church was at its strongest. Congregations were growing as a result of the tentative liberalisation of the Gorbachev government.

But for Oleg the value of priests did not lie in their performance of ceremony and ritual for the masses, but in the unfettered communication of ideas which a select few were prepared to encourage.

It had been while walking in woods like these just outside Zagorsk that Oleg had first come across Father Yuri, one bitter winter about five years ago when twenty degrees of frost had given a crisp skin to the deep layer of snow. The priest's dog had fallen into a drift and the cleric had been struggling to free it.

Father Yuri had a small parish in Zagorsk, and led a necessarily simple life. The size of a parish was important to a priest, because his salary depended on donations made by his congregation. What Father Yuri lacked in funds, however, was compensated by gifts of food and drink from his parishioners. Whenever Oleg went to visit him, he would be pressed to help himself from the quantities of cakes and sweetmeats that seemed permanently to adorn the priest's table.

That Sunday, Oleg waited until four in the afternoon before making his visit. Lunch at the dacha was a necessarily lengthy affair, starting with borscht, and cucumbers in soured cream, followed by local wild duck and fried cheese cakes with plum jam. The side dishes alone had taken the women most of the morning to prepare.

Zagorsk was dominated by the onion domes of the Cathedral of the Assumption and the Trinity-Saint

Sergius monastery. Oleg parked his car just outside the fortress walls, and walked through the narrow streets with their doorways and pillars decorated in blue and gold until he came to the house which had almost become his confessional.

The door was opened by Yuri's wife, who beamed with pleasure to see Oleg again. It had been several months since his last visit.

She led him through the hallway with its faded green and gold wallpaper. On the floor the bare boards were covered by a threadbare length of carpet whose oriental pattern was scarcely discernible now. A single light-bulb, under a shade of etched glass, hung from the ceiling to illuminate their way.

She opened the door at the end of the passage.

'Look who it is who has come to visit you, Yuri,' she announced with delight.

'Oleg Ivanovich!' the priest bellowed, rising from a small wooden armchair in the corner of his study, and bustling towards the door with his arms outstretched. He was a large man, in his fifties, with a square face and widely-spaced eyes. The thick beard that completely concealed his chin had been jet-black in younger days, but was now flecked with grey. His strong, straight hair was brushed sharply backwards, revealing a baldness at the temples.

The two men embraced each other fondly, as the woman left them on their own together.

'Come, my friend! Sit down and be warm.' The priest beckoned him towards the two chairs on each side of the tiled stove. He opened its door and pushed inside small pieces of wood he had collected while out walking. His dog lay curled up in front of the heat, observing the arrival of the visitor with one eye.

'I expected to see you out walking this morning,'

Oleg exclaimed. 'The weather was so fine. But then when I heard the bells I remembered you had more pressing duties!'

The priest's bellow of laughter seemed to shake the brass chandelier whose electric candles cast a soft light into the room. They continued in flippant, jocular terms for several minutes while Yuri prepared the samovar. The priest did not touch alcohol but made an elegant ritual out of serving tea.

'And how are things at the centre?' he asked over his shoulder. 'It's so long since you visited that I imagine life must be very busy for you.'

The charcoal was well alight now and the water began to sing. Oleg stretched out his legs and hooked his hands behind his head.

'Things move in their own way,' he answered enigmatically, his eyebrows arched almost derisively. 'If what passes for life in Moscow is reality, Yuri, then this life of yours is pure fantasy,' he mocked. 'But on the other hand, if this is real, then . . .'

He didn't complete his sentence but his meaning was clear.

'Well, if you don't know which is the real life, it is too long since you last came to Zagorsk!' Yuri retorted, and bellowed with laughter again.

The samovar boiled, and the priest turned his attention to it.

'But, my friend,' he continued with concern. 'If you are serious, then you have a problem. For the truth is that it is all real. There – and here.'

There was a knock at the door and the priest's wife entered with two plates of cakes.

'Oleg Ivanovich must be hungry after his journey,' she fussed, placing the plates on the table by the window.

'Ravenous!' Kvitzinsky joked, reaching across to take a pastry.

She beamed at him and bustled out of the room again.

A silence fell between them for a moment.

'But you are troubled, my friend,' the priest prompted eventually. 'Troubled by doubts about the purpose and reality of your life? It's a common condition, you know.'

'Perhaps it is more a question of rightness than of reality,' Oleg explained. 'Morality even . . .' His voice tailed away.

'That's a subject I'm supposed to know something about,' the priest said gently, knowing for sure that Oleg had an overwhelming need to unburden his soul.

'You know I work for the military now?' Oleg looked up at his friend uncertainly. He was strictly forbidden to talk to anyone about his job, but in this house it was customary for such rules to be ignored.

Yuri handed Oleg an elegant porcelain cup and saucer. 'Is it still about computers?'

'Yes, it's still computers,' Oleg confirmed, sipping the pale green tea whose smoky perfume seemed to complement the scent of the charcoal in the samovar. 'Computer technology can free man from industrial slavery, so that his talents for craftsmanship can be liberated and developed. I really believe that.

'But it can do other things too, unfortunately. It can delude men into believing they can achieve almost anything . . . even total security against enemy attack. It's what the Russian people have dreamed of for centuries! Now there are those who believe it is a dream that can come true!'

'And that is why they moved you into military work, my friend?'

'Exactly,' Kvitzinsky whispered in reply. 'They believe that I . . . and my computers can achieve the ultimate for them. To build a shield which will be directed electronically and automatically to fend off every type of attack. It was an honour to be given this duty. I was deeply flattered. And a challenge – there is none greater. But . . .'

'But anything so perfect – it is of course impossible!' The priest completed his sentence for him.

'The funds are unlimited . . . everything can be sacrificed for this aim, it seems to me. The arthritis of Katrina's mother can go untreated . . . Katrina herself can remain childless – but nothing must hinder my work, so they say.'

The priest shivered. The window was not firmly latched, and he stood up to attend to it.

'You talked of morality. You know, of course,' he explained as he readjusted the curtains, 'that when it comes to morality, your masters and mine are in conflict. In my house, right and wrong are decided by a higher order than the Party. And it is for each and every man to decide for himself in whose house he is going to live. There is no other way, my friend.'

'Yes,' Oleg answered unhappily. 'I know. Sometimes, though, the circumstances make it too difficult to take a decision like that, don't they?'

For some time the priest let his hand rest on Oleg's shoulder. Then slowly he moved away and lowered himself back into the chair by the stove.

'I don't know,' he answered kindly. 'That's a question you will have to put to yourself.'

John Black lived alone in a three-roomed South London flat, surrounded by the few possessions he had accrued during his life. He had been married once, a long time ago, but it had been an unsatisfactory experience and he never talked about it.

He had felt certain that his Sunday at home would be disturbed before long. Indeed, he would have been worried if it had not. The plan to supply false versions of the Skydancer documents to the Russians was fraught with dangers, and he had ordered a tightening of the surveillance on all those involved.

After lunching on a frozen chicken pie hurriedly cooked in his microwave oven, he had settled down to watch an old Bette Davis film on television.

The interruption to his viewing came from a source he had not anticipated. Indeed he had not realised until then that the FBI worked on Sundays. The message from the signals analysis office in Miami had him kicking off his carpet-slippers and pulling on his thick-soled shoes within seconds.

His own office had rapidly found an address for the telephone number the Americans had supplied. It was the Berkshire area again. With a quick phone-call to Reading police station, so that they could alert his friend in the Special Branch that he was on his way, he slipped behind the wheel of his car and headed for the motorway.

On the passenger seat next to him he had placed a facsimile printer, and plugged it into a socket on the dashboard. Then he picked up the handset of his car-phone and dialled a number which would connect the printer directly with his office. While he sped on his way to Reading, the entire text of the intercepted telephone conversation between an unknown Englishman in Florida and a Miss Susan Parkinson in a Berkshire town would be transcribed for him to study.

It took him three-quarters of an hour to reach the

police station. Tom McQuade was waiting for him, still wearing the mud-caked shoes in which he had been doing his weekend gardening.

'Taking your disguise a bit seriously today, aren't you?' Black mocked, looking down at them.

The policeman scraped his shoes against the front wheel of the MI5 man's car. 'We know Susan Parkinson,' he announced as he slid on to the passenger seat from which he had removed the facsimile printer.

'She's in that same mob as the wife of the Aldermaston man; you know, Action to Stop Annihilation; the organisation our WPC got inside. Interestingly enough, our Jenny was at one of their committee meetings on Friday night. None of them seemed to know why the Venner woman had done a bunk. There was a lot of talk about it. Big mystery apparently.'

John Black handed him the facsimile sheet and lit up a cigarette. The policeman wound down the window to let the smoke out, and began to read the page.

'Who is he?' he asked when he had finished.

'We don't know, but he's obviously one of the officers on board HMS *Retribution*, and he shouldn't have been talking like that to *anyone*!'

'Too bloody right!' McQuade replied.

The address they had been given was in a street of small semi-detached houses on the outskirts of Newbury. The policeman had discovered that the woman was a schoolteacher.

Black stopped the car just short of the house so that they would not be seen too readily from the windows.

'There's a passageway at the side,' he murmured, stubbing out his cigarette. 'You pop round to the back while I do the front door, just in case any little bunny rabbits come running out of the stubble!'

The two men hoped they would be mistaken for

Jehovah's Witnesses if anyone saw them approaching the house. John Black waited until McQuade had slipped round the side, before pressing the doorbell. There was the faint sound of music from inside, which he recognised as Tchaikovsky, but it stopped abruptly.

After a minute with no response, he pressed the button again and held it pressed. He could hear the bell shrilling at the back of the house. Suddenly he saw through the patterned-glass door panel that someone was coming.

'What the hell are you doing with that doorbell?' a woman shouted at him as she wrenched open the door.

She was quite attractive, he thought to himself. Better than most of her type. The look in her eyes, though, reminded him suddenly of the woman to whom he had once been married, many years before. It set his teeth on edge.

'Ms Parkinson?' he enquired softly.

'Yes?' she answered nervously. 'What do you want?'

'I'm from the Ministry of Defence. I'm afraid I have some bad news about your boyfriend. May I . . . may I come in for a moment?'

For a split second her eyes registered shock, but she quickly hid it. Black put one foot on the sill. She pushed the door towards him to block his path. Suddenly Black saw a shadow move behind her at the far end of the hallway.

'I . . . I don't know what you're talking about!' she shouted. 'I don't have a boyfriend.'

'It's a security matter, Ms Parkinson. You'd be well advised to invite me in.'

He pushed hard on the door and she stumbled backwards. Then she began to scream. He hated this type; they were the worst, the screamers. His wife had screamed at him when she did not get her way. With these 'peace women', though, he knew it was a tactic to provoke arresting officers to resort to physical violence, which could then be held against them in court. In his case it often came close to succeeding.

Suddenly the screaming stopped. She had heard a noise behind her and turned to see Tom McQuade emerging from her kitchen with his large hands firmly clamped round the arms of another woman.

'Got someone here I think you'd like to meet, John,' he announced with a wry smile. 'This lady is Helene Venner!'

Chapter Seven

Shortly before midday on Monday an audio tape of the intercepted phone-call arrived in London. The flight from Miami had been delayed by a technical fault, and at Heathrow airport a police squad-car was waiting to rush the cassette to the Royal Naval headquarters at Northwood. There, a lieutenant-commander formerly with HMS *Retribution* had been briefed to listen to it carefully in an effort to identify the speaker. Ms Susan Parkinson had remained stubbornly silent about the name of her caller. Meanwhile preparations at the Ministry of Defence had been almost finalised.

Peter Joyce had spent his Sunday in the chief draughtsman's office at Aldermaston, doctoring the drawings and descriptions on the Skydancer blueprints so that a new version could be prepared to meet the criteria set by the security chiefs. At the front of his mind hung his mental picture of 'the Russian', to guide his thoughts.

At eight o'clock on Monday morning the documents were being pored over in Field-Marshal Buxton's office by intelligence experts and scientists. They had to be convincing without jeopardising national security.

Now that it seemed certain Karl Metzger had learned about the changes to the Skydancer warheads from a source on board the submarine, Peter's suspicions about the reliability of MI5 had diminished. He was not entirely satisfied however, still wanting to know why John Black had lied about the photograph in Mary's flat.

When the blueprints were finally approved, Peter was left on his own with the field-marshal and Sir Marcus Beckett.

'Is Anderson happy about what he's got to do?' Buxton inquired.

'*Happy* isn't the word for it,' Peter replied. 'But he realises he has no choice.'

'Shall we get him in, then?' Sir Marcus suggested, eager to start things moving.

Buxton pressed a key on the intercom.

'I wish to God I could be sure we're doing the right thing,' Sir Marcus mused uncomfortably. 'The Soviets have put a hell of an effort into getting hold of the Skydancer secrets. We may have found out about the East German and the spy on the boat . . . but I'm bloody sure they've got more tricks up their sleeves.'

'A spy on board one of our Polaris submarines!' Buxton exploded. 'How did the Navy let *that* happen? What on earth are they doing with their vetting procedures? I can tell you there are going to be some damned hard questions asked when we find out who the man is.'

There was a tap at the door, and Anderson came in.

'Good morning, Anderson. Sit down.'

Sir Marcus had taken charge. Anderson was a civil servant, answerable to him rather than the Chief of the Defence Staff.

'I think I should make it clear, Anderson,' Beckett began, 'that this is being seen as a salvage operation rather than an opportunity any of us would have sought. It would have been much better for the Skydancer project to remain under wraps instead of gaining such public exposure, and indeed the politicians look upon your activities with the deepest concern. Only by doing what you are about to do, will you earn *any* chance of favourable treatment. I'm not authorised to make promises about the likelihood or not of any prosecution against you. No decisions have been taken yet. Suffice to say, if what you are about to do proves successful, it can only count in your favour. Do I make myself clear?'

'Perfectly, Sir Marcus,' Anderson answered nervously.

'Now, what are your orders from the other side?'

Anderson cleared his throat.

'They haven't told me much yet. I . . . I have to be in a certain telephone-box at exactly twelve noon. Someone will ring me there and give me further instructions.'

'You will be under surveillance . . .'

'No!' Anderson almost shouted.

'For your own protection as much as anything else.'

'I don't want it! If they get the slightest inkling that this is a put-up job, I'm finished,' Anderson pleaded. 'Don't you see? It could ruin everything. Karl is already highly suspicious. He said he wouldn't hesitate. First sign of any trickery and he's going to send off those photographs.' Anderson coloured at this.

Buxton looked contemptuous and patted the envelope which contained the blueprints.

'No! I won't do it if you're going to have people tailing me!' Anderson insisted.

'Won't do it? I'm *ordering* you to!' Sir Marcus cut in.

'Perhaps . . .' Buxton intervened, 'perhaps the answer would be for you to discuss that little detail with John Black, since it's his department.'

Anderson cast a glance of alarm at Peter.

'It's all right,' Joyce nodded. 'They've found out who leaked the information about my visit to Florida – and it wasn't Black.'

Anderson seemed far from reassured. Nevertheless he took the envelope from the table and stood up.

'Then I'd better talk to him now. There's not much time.'

He looked at the carriage clock on Buxton's desk. He had just thirty minutes before his telephone rendezvous with the East German agent.

Peter decided to accompany Alec down to the security office where John Black had taken up residence for the day. Anderson led the way through the grid of corridors which Peter still found confusing, even after dozens of visits to the Ministry.

'They're pretty good, those plans,' Peter reassured him, when there was no one close to them. 'I don't think the comrades will guess.'

'Don't be too sure,' Anderson grunted. 'You're not dealing with children, you know.'

As they neared the security office, Peter took the other man by the arm.

'I'll leave you to talk to Black on your own,' he said. 'And . . . you'll ring us later? To tell us how things went with Metzger.'

Anderson's expression was blank.

'Yes, I'll call you.'

He turned and pushed open the door in front of him.

'Take a seat, Mr Anderson.' John Black was replacing the receiver of his telephone.

'Is there something that worries you about our arrangements?'

'Yes!' Alec almost shouted. 'It's imperative you don't have anybody following me today!'

'Could ruin things, you mean?'

'It might even be fatal if they get wind of this being a counter-intelligence operation,' Anderson insisted.

'Too much at stake, you think?'

'There certainly is! And if you have somebody tailing me, I'm not going through with it!'

John Black smiled benignly, and inhaled deeply from his half-smoked cigarette.

'I quite understand.'

Alec was startled by the other's conciliatory tone.

'You mean you agree?'

'Utterly. Nothing must be allowed to compromise the success of this operation.' Black oozed sincerity.

'But upstairs they were *insisting* . . .'

'Just a little misunderstanding. There'll be no surveillance, I promise you.'

John Black stood up and extended his hand.

'Good-bye Mr Anderson, and good luck!'

Reluctantly Alec shook the offered hand, but had no idea whether the security man had been telling the truth.

Black took a last lungful of smoke, crushed the cigarette on to the lid of his ashtray, and shredded the stub between his fingers.

Buxton and Beckett were waiting for Peter Joyce when he returned to the sixth floor. Both looked worried.

'Did Black manage to sort that out?' Sir Marcus asked.

'I didn't stay to see,' Peter responded.

'He'll let us know if he's got any problems, I'm sure,' the field-marshal soothed.

'Now, look here, Joyce,' Sir Marcus said hurriedly. 'I think we'd better clarify *your* position a bit. Officially, you're still suspended on full pay pending a security enquiry, but that's pretty impractical in the circumstances. You're right in the middle of this business and . . . well, your uncovering of Anderson was pretty sharp, let's face it.

'So, the Defence Secretary has authorised me to lift

your suspension as of this morning, and the fact that it occurred will be struck from the record. That's not the end of the matter, however. There will still be an enquiry into your disregard of security procedures, and your reinstatement today will not prejudice the outcome of that. But you can forget about the suspension.'

'Thank you,' Peter answered non-committally.

'Right. Well, I'll leave you to it.' Beckett rubbed his hands, and left the room.

Field-Marshal Buxton lowered himself into the large chair behind his desk.

'Now, Peter. About the missile test. I've decided it'll take place this afternoon,' he announced, '*if* they can get their act together down in the Atlantic. But they've got a spy to deal with first.'

Carrying a brown leather briefcase marked with his monogram, Alec Anderson walked along the Embankment until he came to the pair of telephone boxes described to him by Karl Metzger. The briefcase had been a rather ostentatious present from Janet several Christmasses ago. He did not normally take it to work, preferring the more anonymous black variety supplied by the MOD; but he had chosen the brown bag today because it did not immediately identify him as a civil servant.

He looked at his wristwatch again, even though he had already studied it just seconds ago. It was still only five to twelve.

The closest of the two kiosks was the one where he had been told to expect the midday call. He cursed silently: it was occupied. Of course, it would be! A large, fat black woman seemed in no hurry to finish her conversation.

Alec slackened his pace and tried to look relaxed. Pretending to have lost his way, he turned his head as if looking for street names. He was searching for faces, though, for any sign of anyone deliberately watching him. A shiver ran down his spine; he felt so exposed.

In the distance Big Ben began to chime the preamble to the hour. Still there was no sign of the black woman ending her chat. She saw him waiting and pointed to the other box.

'Doesn't work,' Alec mouthed.

What would they do? What would happen if they could not get through to him at noon? A harsh wind off the Thames chilled the sweat gathering under his armpits.

'Arl right now,' the black woman smiled at him, exposing broad gaps in her teeth. 'Sahry now to be so long.' She squeezed her way out of the phone-box, pulled her coat tight, and bustled away towards an underground station.

Alec hurried into the kiosk, recoiling from the smell of potato chips. A greasy paper bag lay on the floor. Opening the door again with his shoulder, he kicked it into the street. Almost immediately a man in an anorak occupied the booth next to him; a woman with a small child waited outside. He lifted the receiver, trying to conceal the fact that his fingers were holding down the rest.

His heart pounded and the sound of his anxious breathing seemed amplified by the confines of the booth.

At the first hint of a ring, he lifted his finger, and recited the number of the telephone.

The voice that answered him was not one he recognised.

'Is that the Stock Exchange?' a man asked. He had the hint of an accent.

'No. It's the Maid's Head public house and we're closed,' Alec answered, reciting the code that Metzger had instructed him to use.

'Listen carefully,' the voice continued. 'Walk to Charing Cross Station. Go in from the Strand. Just inside on the left is a row of phone booths. Use the third from the right. I'll call you there in ten minutes. Got that?'

'Yes. I . . .'

There was a click, then the dialling tone. Frantically Alec tried to remember exactly what he had been told.

He looked at his watch again. He had ten minutes.

It took less than five to walk to Charing Cross, but he stopped at several shop windows and looked round furtively to see if he was being followed.

He located the row of telephone boxes without difficulty. Third from the right – that was what the man had said. It was unoccupied. Lucky this time!

He quickly stepped into the booth and studied the directories while waiting for the call. At precisely twelve-fifteen the phone rang.

'Stock Exchange?' the voice asked again.

'Still the Maid's Head,' Alec replied.

'What's your name?'

'Anderson. What's yours?' he demanded with sudden boldness.

There was a snort of laughter at the other end.

'In front of you there is a shelf,' the voice continued. 'Put your hand under it. Do you feel something?'

'There's something stuck here. Something metal.'

'Correct. It's the key to a left-luggage locker. Do you have it now?'

Anderson peeled the sellotape from under the shelf and held the key in his hand.

'Yes. It's here.'

'Pick up a small suitcase from the locker. Take it to the gents' toilet. Go into a cubicle and look inside the case. There will be instructions to tell you what to do next.'

'But when do I . . .?'

The line went dead.

Anderson backed away from the phone. Sudden panic set his stomach churning. Perhaps the suitcase was a bomb? Were they trying to kill him?

Calm down, he told himself. Where were the left-luggage lockers anyway? Breathe slowly.

The station looked enormous. One or two people in the lunchtime crowd were staring at him – or was it his imagination? Suddenly he felt certain: someone *was* watching him.

The man on the phone, could he be here at the station? Was he being controlled by someone he could actually see?

Quiet, he told himself. Keep cool! Find that bloody luggage locker and get on to the next clue in this paper-chase!

It was twenty yards away, clearly marked with a sign. He started to walk, stifling an instinct to run.

The key slid stiffly into the lock, and the door sprang open. Inside was a maroon overnight bag.

Alec selected a cubicle at the far end of the row in the gents'. He flushed the lavatory in case anyone was listening, then sat on the seat.

The case had a zip-fastener which he undid slowly, covering the sound by clearing his throat.

Inside were a shirt, a pair of pyjamas, a washbag and shaving kit, and a large brown envelope. What the hell . . .?

With shaking hands he slit open the envelope and

emptied out a British passport in the name of W.J. Allenby. He opened it and saw that the photograph inside was of himself.

There was a British Airways ticket issued in the same name, for a flight to West Berlin leaving Heathrow at three-fifteen that afternoon.

Berlin! The handover was to be in Berlin! Oh God! He would be entirely at their mercy there! A sense of dread began to overwhelm him.

A typewritten list of instructions told him to travel to Heathrow airport on the underground immediately. He must make no attempt to inform anyone where he was going. When he reached Berlin he should take a taxi to Friedrichstrasse, and cross over into the East. He would be expected.

Oh God, oh God, oh God! Suppose they held him there until they checked the Skydancer plans? Suppose they decided the blueprints were fakes? They'd kill him, wouldn't they? Torture him first perhaps?

Anderson gulped. He had to control himself, get a grip!

He opened the passport again. It looked a perfect forgery. There was money in the envelope too, pounds sterling and West German marks. There was even an underground ticket to the airport. They had thought of everything.

The man in the anorak watched Anderson come out of the gents' toilets, and walk towards the underground station. He watched him pause by a tube-map to check his route. His own instructions had been very strict, to follow at a good distance at all times. Anderson must never guess that he was being watched. Any moment, though, things could get very tricky.

He flashed a pass, and followed Anderson through the barrier towards the escalators, keeping fifty yards behind. Right behind Anderson, he noticed a man in a dark blue overcoat glance over his shoulder and look around with professional thoroughness. Anderson had collected a minder, though he did not know it yet. The next part would be a matter of luck.

A thundering in the tunnel as he reached the bottom of the escalator told him that luck was on Anderson's side that day. He walked as fast as he dared, but was well behind the two men, who were already on the platform as the train came in.

The doors hissed open and shut again. Shit! He had blown it! From inside the carriage the figure in the blue coat looked out with ice-cold eyes. The edge of his mouth turned up slightly in a mocking smile.

The MI5 man cursed. John Black was not going to be happy.

When the signaller came hurrying to his cabin, clutching a sheet from his note-pad, Commander Carrington breathed a sigh of relief. They had spent the weekend idling in the depths, successfully avoiding their Soviet shadow, and waiting with growing impatience for orders to proceed with the missile launch.

The signal received on the VLF circuit from England consisted of just three words in code. Carrington dismissed the signaller, then spun the combination lock on the wall-safe and opened it to pull out his manual for codes of the day.

It took just a minute to translate the message, and he stared at it in surprise. This was *not* what he expected. What he had hoped for was a command giving the time and place of launch and the co-ordinates of the target area. Instead Northwood was instructing him to push his satellite terminal above the waves to receive a lengthy message from HQ. Carrington cursed. This could give away his position to the Russians.

By using burst-transmissions at predetermined times, large amounts of data could be transmitted in a few seconds, but even that could be long enough for a Soviet radar satellite over the Atlantic to pick up a minute reflection from their mast, and to report back the location of the sighting to Moscow and to any Soviet ships in the vicinity.

Carrington looked at his watch. They would have to close with the surface and push their antenna above it in just fifteen minutes.

In the control room, he checked with the navigator and the sonar operator to make sure the *Retribution* would be well away from other shipping when the satellite link-up took place. Then he ordered the long, trailing VLF aerial to be wound in, to prevent it fouling the propeller when they were just below the surface.

In the navigation centre next to the control room, he checked the time with the atomic clock whose accuracy ensured that the submarine and HQ could synchronise their actions perfectly. He made a small adjustment to his own watch.

'Right, officer of the watch! Bring her up to periscope depth,' he ordered when the moment came.

At the engineering control panel, hands reached up to open valves. Pumps began to hum and hiss as the buoyancy was adjusted to keep the boat just below the surface.

'Periscope depth, sir!' the coxswain reported.

'Up periscope!' Carrington called, and the shiny tube slid upwards from the floor of the control room.

He pressed his eyes to the rubber cups, gripped the

focusing handles, and carefully scanned the horizon.

There was a light swell, but not another vessel to be seen anywhere.

The periscope hissed back into the floor.

Carrington watched the second-hand.

'Up satcom!' he ordered. There were thirty seconds to go to their deadline.

Just two minutes later the antenna was lowered again and Carrington instructed the officer of the watch to return the submarine to the depths and to head away from the area, back towards the sector from where they expected to launch the missile.

The radio operator ripped the long sheet of paper from the teleprinter. The message was in full code.

'For your eyes only, sir.'

Back in his cabin, Carrington set to work again with his code books. This time he knew it would take him a good quarter of an hour.

But within minutes he realised he was translating the most staggering message he had ever received.

'Regret to inform you that enemy agent is aboard your boat. Lieutenant Robert Simpson must be put under close arrest immediately . . .'

So it began. Carrington stared in disbelief at the words and ripped a page of the code-book in his eagerness to translate the full signal.

At last it was done. It revealed that Simpson had telephoned England and talked about the secret visit to *Retribution* by the Aldermaston scientists, information which had subsequently found its way into the hands of Soviet intelligence. It was incredible!

'God almighty!' It felt like a personal blow. A member of *his* crew! It was like being told one of his family was a spy.

Also in the signal were included the orders for the test

firing. It was to be that afternoon, in three hours' time. They would have to get a move on to reach the firing zone by then.

Carrington returned to the control room grim-faced. He took the officer of the watch and the navigator to one side, and told them of the launch plans. He made them responsible for seeing that the submarine was in the right place at the right time. Then he asked his executive officer to come with him to his cabin.

With the door closed firmly behind him, Carrington gestured for his deputy to sit down.

'What I'm going to say will stun you!' he announced quietly.

Since the signal had been marked for his eyes only, he paraphrased its contents.

'I don't believe it!' Lt Commander Mike Smith exploded after listening open-mouthed. 'I could kill him, with my bare hands!'

'That's just the point, Mike. That's just what mustn't happen. But if it becomes known on board that Simpson is a spy, someone else might try to do that.'

'Unbelievable!' Smith exclaimed, shaking his head. 'Simpson? He's just a kid, hardly the stuff spies are made of. I suppose there can be no doubt? I assume they know what they're talking about in London?'

'We'll have to pull him in here and ask him. But it'd be better if you and I did it on our own. If we get the Chief to form an arrest squad, then word of it'll get round in no time. Let's try to keep it quiet. We'd better find out where Simpson is.'

That was not difficult. The supply officer was sitting in his cabin, checking his dry stores manifest.

'Lieutenant Simpson,' the executive officer began formally. 'The captain would like to see you immediately.'

Simpson frowned in surprise. He would normally expect to be addressed by his first name. Something was wrong.

'Right, sir,' he answered, rising to his feet. 'I'll come along then.'

He preceded Mike Smith down the short corridor to the captain's cabin. Carrington's face looked gaunt and drawn as Simpson walked in. Smith closed the door behind them and stood next to it.

'Lieutenant Simpson,' Carrington spoke softly, 'the Commander-in-Chief has instructed me to place you under arrest. You are to face charges under the Official Secrets Act and under Queen's Regulations, and I am to caution you that anything you say may be used in evidence against you.'

Simpson gasped. He shot a glance over his shoulder and saw that the executive officer was holding pen and notebook, ready to take notes.

'Wh . . . what do you mean, sir?' Simpson stammered. 'What's this all about?'

'Does the name Susan Parkinson mean something to you, perhaps?'

Any colour that was left in Bob Simpson's face drained away.

'Well . . . yes. Of course.' A look of pained confusion spread across his youthful features.

'You telephoned her from Miami, I believe.' Carrington's voice was cold.

'She . . . she's my girlfriend, sir. That's all,' he answered weakly.

'*All?* Just your girlfriend? That's not the impression they have back home.'

Simpson glanced around nervously and saw the hostility on the executive officer's face.

'Could you . . . could you explain to me, sir, just what

it is I am accused of?' he asked in a meek voice.

'I am informed by Northwood that you passed information to Miss Parkinson about work being done to the test missile on board this boat, and that the information subsequently arrived in the hands of an enemy power,' Carrington announced.

Simpson's face reddened. But then he frowned.

'Eh? Enemy power, sir? What enemy power?'

The thin lines to the left of Carrington's mouth began to twitch. He was fighting to control his anger.

'It's not my job to try you, Simpson,' his voice grated. 'You can fight your corner in court. But from what I've been told by Northwood they've got the evidence they need. My orders are simply to detain you until we hand you over to the authorities ashore. You will be locked in your cabin twenty-four hours a day. Meals will be brought to you, and you will be allowed to use the heads only under escort. Do you have anything to say?'

Simpson shook his head. He wanted to tell them that they had got it wrong: he'd not been passing secrets to an enemy. What he had told Susan would not have gone any further. But in view of the mission he *had* been planning, the less he said the better.

'Prisoner! Stand to attention!' ordered Lt Commander Smith.

Simpson was visibly shaking. The room seemed to be spinning in a blur.

'That will be all,' Carrington snapped.

The executive officer took him firmly by the arm and led him out. They stopped at an empty cabin and Simpson was guided inside.

'You'll stay in here for a while. You can go back to your own cabin, after I've searched it,' the Lt Commander told him, and locked the door.

Simpson's cabin was no more than eight feet square.

Smith looked around it, searching for anything out of the ordinary. The small desk was covered with routine paperwork. On the shelf above were two snapshots: one of a middle-aged couple, Simpson's parents he presumed; the other of an attractive dark-haired girl, warmly wrapped up in woolly scarf and gloves against the bright chill of an English winter's day. Written on it in ink were the words '*Love you. Sue*'

'So that's the girlfriend,' he thought to himself. 'Not bad! Quite a little Mata Hari!'

He then went through the lockers under the bunk. From Simpson's wash kit, he removed the razor and spare blades, but left an aerosol of shaving foam. Scissors and a pen-knife he put with the razor to take away for safe-keeping.

He could find nothing to connect Simpson with espionage, no diary or personal notebooks, and the volumes on the shelf were all standard textbooks or novels. Nothing subversive amongst them. He was disappointed.

'Right, Simpson, you can go back now,' he announced after unlocking the door to the spare cabin.

'Thanks very much!' Simpson grumbled. He was over the initial shock and had begun to resent this treatment. 'You're making a big mistake. I'm not a spy.'

'It's no good telling *me* that. Save it for the interrogators when you get back to England.'

Interrogators! The words struck a chill into Simpson's heart. Those sinister men with their black arts of mind-bending, what would they have done to his girlfriend?

'Do you know what's happened to her, sir?' he asked with sudden concern.

'No, I don't. Now sit here quietly and behave yourself. I'm going to lock you in. You'll get some food later.'

The sound of the lock turning seemed to echo inside

the small cabin. Left on his own, Simpson began to panic. 'Enemy power'? What were they talking about? If only he could talk to Susan!

Suddenly he began to fear she had told them everything, all about his real reasons for being on board HMS *Retribution.* That did not involve any enemy power. But what had the captain said? It was his words to Susan on the telephone that they were complaining about. Could she have passed the information to . . . He was wide-eyed with alarm. Surely not . . .

One thing seemed quite clear; the security men back home would treat him as a spy, a traitor. He had been incautious on the phone, and he *had* been planning sabotage on the boat. He could get thirty years, he realised – for trying to stop people being killed!

With dazzling clarity he suddenly knew that returning to the UK was something he could not afford to do.

Hanging from a hook on the wall was a dark blue canvas bag, standard equipment for every member of the submarine's crew. Its contents were going to be vital to him in the next few hours.

'Shouldn't we have someone on guard outside his cabin?' Smith suggested to the captain.

'It would have to be an officer if we're going to keep this business away from the crew,' Carrington answered thoughtfully, 'and with a missile-firing coming up we won't have anyone to spare. He can't get out, can he?'

'Not without breaking the door down.'

The two men returned to the control room. Preparations for the launch were well under way. The executive officer reverted to his normal duties and began to check that the submarine was on course and on time to meet its deadline. In the navigation centre he ascertained that the twin inertial navigation systems were performing perfectly. At the moment of firing, they would feed into the rocket the precise coordinates of the launch point so that the missile's computer could calculate the trajectory needed to reach the target with accuracy.

In the missile chamber he noted with satisfaction that the countdown procedure was moving ahead smoothly. Finally he descended the companionway to the missile control centre, where the Polaris systems officers were running test programmes on the electronic firing panel.

In due course all these men would have to be told about Robert Simpson, but now was not the moment. There should be no distraction from the work they had in hand.

Back in the control room he was told that the captain had returned to his cabin and wanted Smith to join him there. He set off immediately.

'Simpson's been hammering on his door. Says he's got the shits and needs to go to the heads,' Carrington explained. 'Bit difficult really; it was the chief steward who heard him. He was a bit puzzled to find the supply officer locked in. I had to explain, but swore him to secrecy. God knows how long we can keep this bottled up! The sooner we get Simpson off the boat the better. Anyway, would you deal with it, Mike? Take him to the heads?'

The executive officer grimaced at the prospect of having to watch the prisoner relieving himself.

'Of course, sir. I'll do it now.'

When he pushed open the door to the supply officer's cabin, Simpson had his back to him. There seemed to be something odd about his hair. It took Smith a split-second to realise what was wrong, but he was already too late to save himself. The prisoner spun round, his face encased in a gas-mask.

Simpson's arm reached out like a ramrod, clutching the aerosol of shaving foam Smith had left in his locker. He jammed his thumb down on the button, and the canister emitted a loud hiss.

Smith reeled back as the pain shot through his eyes! It was like needles piercing his eyeballs, from behind as well as in front. Instinctively he clawed at his eyes, thinking he could wipe away the foam, but there was none there!

He gasped at the pain, and the CN gas caught the back of his throat. He began to cough and choke. The muscles of his chest went into spasm. He felt he was going to die!

Beginning to twitch convulsively, he fought for clean air to sooth the burning of his nose and throat, but Simpson kept his finger firmly pressed on the aerosol button. Smith then tried to hold his breath, but an uncontrollable coughing overtook him. His head began to spin through lack of oxygen, and slowly blackness overtook him.

Simpson stepped over the body and went out into the corridor.

Startled by the noise, the chief steward came bustling out of the wardroom. He stopped dead in his tracks at the sight of the officer in the gas-mask, and within seconds he too was reeling backwards in pain and confusion.

The door to Carrington's cabin was at the end of the corridor and slightly ajar. Simpson ran for it, slamming the door open with his shoulder.

The captain's wall-safe was wide open, just as Simpson had hoped.

'What the hell . . .?'

The stream of gas hit Carrington right in the face. Eyes screwed up with pain, he reached out to try to close the safe, but Simpson lunged forward and punched him on the head with his free hand, knocking him off his chair and on to the floor.

Carrington had held his breath in an instinctive reaction to seeing the gas-mask on Simpson's face. So far the pain only burned his eyes. His own mask hung on the wall. Without breathing, he crawled across the floor and began to grope his way up towards it, expecting at any second to receive another blow on the head.

But Simpson was scrabbling amongst the papers in the open safe for the leather holster which he knew would be there. There it was!

Smiling grimly under the mask, he unbuttoned the retaining strap.

'That's enough, Captain!' his muffled voice threatened as he pressed the muzzle of the automatic pistol into the back of Carrington's neck. 'This is your gun, and I'm ready to use it! Now just get back to your chair and sit down.'

Simpson quickly closed the cabin door and locked it.

Carrington had staggered to the chair and was dabbing a handkerchief to his eyes and nose. His lungs were inflamed and burning though he had only received a small dose of CN.

Suddenly the tannoy on the ceiling crackled into life.

'Gas, gas, gas!' the voice of the officer of the watch bellowed from it. His message was being relayed throughout the submarine. 'Gas, gas, gas! This is no drill! Repeat, no drill! Gas-masks on immediately!'

The air-conditioning system of the boat had carried some of the tear-gas into the control room. Simpson heard heavy feet pounding the metal decks as men raced for their bunks to retrieve their masks. Outside the captain's door there were shouts as someone found the chief steward slumped against the wall, coughing uncontrollably – and then the feet of the executive officer poking out into the corridor from the supply officer's cabin.

There was a sharp rap on the door.

'Tell them to go away,' Simpson ordered in a whisper.

But Carrington could only cough.

'This is Lieutenant Simpson,' the supply officer shouted towards the door. 'I'm holding the captain prisoner. I've got his gun and I'll shoot him unless you do as I say!'

There was complete silence from outside. Then someone tried the doorknob and swore.

'Go back to your posts!' Simpson yelled.

After a moment, he heard footsteps moving away. So far, so good! But this was as far as he had planned. The next part would not be so easy.

'Captain, sir? Control room here!' A voice came from the intercom on the table.

Carrington was still wheezing and gasping for breath. Simpson leaned forward and pressed the key on the communications box.

'This is Lieutenant Simpson. The Captain is my prisoner. I have a gun. If you do what I say he won't be harmed.'

'What do you want, Simpson?' the voice answered angrily. At first he could not identify it; the man must be wearing a mask, too. Then he realised it was the PSO, Phil Dunkley. As a lieutenant-commander he would be the most senior man left, since the executive officer was out of action. For a moment he was fearful of what he had done to Mike Smith. He had given him a hell of a dose of gas; perhaps he'd killed him.

'The test launch is cancelled,' Simpson called back. 'There must be no missile firing, do you hear?'

There was a pause, with only static on the circuit.

'Anything else?' the PSO asked icily.

'Yes . . . there's a lot else. But I'm not going to tell you yet. I want you to send the surgeon in here, with some handcuffs for the captain. But no tricks! I don't trust any of you, and I'll use this gun if I have to!'

There was a longer pause this time.

'Very well,' Dunkley said eventually.

Five minutes passed before there was a tap at the door. Carrington's breathing had become easier.

Simpson tightened his grip on the pistol and trained it at the captain's head. Slowly he stood up and edged towards the door, turning back the bolt in the lock.

The surgeon-lieutenant stood outside nervously, wearing a gas-mask and carrying a set of nylon wrist-restraints. Simpson had selected him as the intermediary because of a vague feeling that a doctor should seem less of a threat than the other officers.

'Come in. Stand over there,' Simpson ordered, pointing towards the captain. He locked the door again.

'What do you want me to do, Bob?' the doctor asked in a quiet voice.

'Put those on the captain and loop them round the leg of his chair.'

The doctor fumbled with the restraints, unsure how they worked.

'Sorry about this, sir,' he whispered.

'Don't worry,' Carrington replied hoarsely. 'Just do as he says.'

The task completed, the doctor stood up again. Through the lenses of the mask, his eyes looked frightened.

Simpson stared, uncertain how much to trust him.

'Have they told you what I'm being accused of?' he began.

The doctor shook his head. 'Didn't know you were accused of anything.'

'They're saying I passed secrets to the Russians!'

'What?' The doctor turned towards Carrington. The captain nodded in confirmation.

'But it's not true! I just wanted to save millions of people from being killed . . . that's all,' Simpson insisted.

The doctor shifted uneasily. He still did not understand what this was about, but it looked as if Simpson had gone off his head.

'Well, we're all in the same boat there,' the doctor replied calmly. 'None of us want to see people killed, so why don't you just put that gun down, Bob?'

Simpson glared angrily at the surgeon-lieutenant, the pistol wavering between the doctor and the captain.

'Well, what exactly do you want?' the doctor pressed. 'It looks as if you're in command of the boat, at the moment. They want to know what to do.'

He gestured over his shoulder in the direction of the control room.

'I've got to get off,' Simpson explained, removing his mask. Carrington seemed to be recovering, which suggested the air had cleared. The doctor followed suit.

'I've got to get off this boat. Somewhere where I can be free,' he continued, holding the gun firmly in both hands. The gas canister was stuffed into his trouser pocket. 'I'm not going back to Britain!'

'But we're in the middle of the Atlantic, Bob,' the doctor explained reasonably, keeping his voice as smooth and even as he could.

'Yes, I know *that*!' Simpson snapped, 'but we're not too far from America, and there are islands. Cuba. What about Cuba? If we got near there, I'd get ashore in a Gemini. The captain'll come with me – as a hostage.'

'Well, what shall I do? Shall I tell the control room that you want to go to Cuba?' the doctor asked mildly.

Simpson hesitated. Cuba was some way away, and he was not sure what sort of reception he would get there.

'I want to see some charts. Bring me some charts so that I can see where there is that's closer.'

Simpson edged to the door, keeping the gun trained on the doctor.

'And no tricks!' he growled as he unlocked the door, and the doctor went out. He locked the door again and turned to look at the captain.

Carrington's breathing was easier now, though his eyes remained red and moist.

'What were you keeping that gas for, Simpson?' he rasped curiously. 'When were you planning to use it?'

Simpson laughed awkwardly.

'Well, sir, I'll tell you this. You'd never have launched the missiles if the order came. Somehow I'd have stopped you from genocide – that's what I planned.'

'On the orders of Moscow? So that the Russians would be free to commit genocide against the British people, when they had no means of retaliation?' Carrington snapped back.

'This has nothing to do with Moscow! It's to do with conscience, something you don't know anything about.' Simpson sneered.

There was a tap at the door. 'It's me,' came the doctor's voice.

Simpson turned the key, then strode back across the cabin and pressed the gun against the captain's head.

'Come in!'

The door opened gingerly, and the doctor entered, clutching a roll of charts under his left arm. His gas-mask was in his right hand.

'Lock the door!' Simpson ordered.

That done, the doctor stood waiting for the next instruction.

Reassured that the surgeon-lieutenant had returned alone, Simpson lowered the pistol.

'Bring them over here,' he said, indicating the captain's bed. 'We can sit here and spread them out.'

The doctor obliged, handing him the roll with a smile.

'They're all here, Bob. I'm sure we can sort something out.'

Simpson took the charts in his left hand, but still clutched the gun in his right. He paused for a moment, realising he would need both hands to study the charts properly.

He shot a glance at the captain to see that he was securely fastened to his chair. The doctor was still smiling benignly.

He hesitated, then slowly and carefully Simpson put the gun down on the bed beside him.

'Let me help you spread those out,' the doctor suggested.

He leaned forward as if to take hold of the first chart with his left hand. But suddenly his right arm lunged forward, jamming the gas-mask hard against Simpson's thigh! Bob felt the needle of the concealed hypodermic jab into him.

'You bastard!' he screamed, scrabbling frantically for the gun.

The doctor threw himself forward, punching with his left hand, and knocked the weapon to the floor. Carrington's foot reached out and kicked the gun into the far corner of the cabin.

Simpson struggled frenziedly, but the surgeon was a deadweight across his body.

'Five, six, seven, eight,' the doctor counted the seconds in his head, praying for the knockout drug to work. He had reached eleven before Simpson slumped across the bed.

Slowly, waiting to be sure the drug had taken full effect, the surgeon-lieutenant eased himself up, shaking from the shock of what he had just done. He carefully extracted the syringe from Simpson's leg, then pulled the lieutenant's head straight and checked his breathing. The man who had terrorised the submarine a moment ago was now his patient.

'Well done!' Carrington shouted hoarsely. 'Bloody brilliant!'

There was a hammering at the door and the doctor unlocked it. The chief petty officer burst in with two of the heaviest members of the crew, carrying clubs. He stared down at the supply officer, unconscious on the bed.

'Fuck me! You done it all on your own!' he exclaimed.

On the Caribbean island of Antigua, one thousand miles south of HMS *Retribution*'s position, the giant telemetry dishes of the US Navy Space Tracking Center rotated their bearings slowly and in unison, so that they were all pointing north, ready for the test firing of the British missile.

A further two thousand miles to the south-east, on the British island of Ascension, a further set of antennae lined up on the part of outer space where the Skydancer warheads would begin their dive into the atmosphere, obscured amongst clusters of decoys and behind a barrage of electronic deception techniques.

Both monitoring stations had been sent signals in

unbreakable code, giving the time and position of the Polaris launching.

Halfway between Antigua and Ascension, the 21,000 tons of the Soviet vessel *Akademik Sergey Korolev* wallowed in a long, slow, mid-Atlantic swell. The crew had been on stand-by for over forty-eight hours already. The Akula had signalled three days ago that it had lost the trail of the *Retribution*, and had warned that the missile test could take place at any time. The heat and the lack of sleep had made Kapitan Karpov extremely irritable.

On board HMS *Retribution* Simpson's abortive mutiny had jolted the entire crew and had created a greater than usual tension on board.

Carrington was again in command in the control room, his eyes red and swollen and his voice still hoarse. His executive officer was recovering in the sick bay.

Inside the missile control centre the dials on the launch control panel certified that the guidance gyros of the missiles were up to speed. The final countdown could begin.

They had had to sprint at nearly thirty knots to reach the launch position at the appointed time, but now they were in the right place, with a few minutes to spare. Carrington paced between the sonar operator's booth and the navigator's table. The signal from Northwood three hours earlier had predicted the ocean here would be empty, and the sonar equipment seemed to confirm it. If this had been war, he would have launched the missile without further checks, but in peacetime the demand for absolute safety was such that he needed to put up his periscope for a visual crosscheck.

'Better be sure there are no Atlantic oarsmen bobbing about above us!' he joked, as the officer of the watch peered through the eyepiece. After Simpson's attack Carrington did not trust his own eyes to be clear enough to see.

'Not a soul, sir,' the officer confirmed, sliding the scope down into its housing.

'Right! Descend to launch depth and zero knots!'

The rating at the helm pushed his control column gently forward, his eye fixed on the depth gauge.

On the engineering panel, the dial registering the rotation of the propeller shaft slipped back to zero.

The captain stood at the back of the control room and inserted a key into the switch with which he would give the final authority to launch the missile.

'Prepare to fire!' he called into the intercom.

On the deck below in the missile control centre, the Polaris Systems Officer opened the combination lock of a small safe on the floor below his control panel, and pulled out the pistol-grip with its red 'fire' button, which in war could execute millions of people at a single touch.

'Open missile hatch! Flood the tube!'

Dunkley dabbed on the buttons in the sequence prescribed in the control manual.

Behind him the computers had verified the co-ordinates of the target area, and had beamed the data into the missile itself.

'Ten, nine, eight . . .' he began.

In the control room above, Commander Carrington turned his key in the switch that activated the firing button below.

A green light appeared on the panel in the launch centre.

'One away!' the PSO yelled, clamping his finger round the pistol-grip.

With an explosive roar, the gas generator at the base

of the missile tube burst into life, pouring gas into the space below the rocket, propelling it upwards, out of the submarine and up to the surface in a cocoon of bubbles. As the tip of the missile appeared above the waves, the rocket motor ignited and with a brilliant flash the Polaris hurtled towards the sky.

'Up periscope!' the captain yelled.

The officer of the watch trained the lens upwards to see the missile arcing away towards the sun.

Carrington grabbed the microphone and pressed it to his lips.

'Your attention, please! This is the captain. I should like to inform you all that we have just enacted a perfect launch of one of our Polaris missiles. In the extraordinary circumstances of this day, to achieve our aim in any form would have been worthwhile; but to do it at the right time, in the right place, with such perfection, amounts to nothing less than brilliance on the part of everyone on board. Congratulations, and thank you very much.'

He hung the microphone back on its hook. There was an urgent radio signal to be sent but once he had completed that, he could at last get stuck into a long-delayed lunch.

The first inkling Kapitan Karpov had of the impending launch was the appearance of an aircraft on the *Korolev*'s radar. It soon became clear that the RAF Nimrod which had taken photographs of them a few days earlier was paying another visit. This time it was flying much higher.

Suddenly the giant radar dish that scanned the horizon over which the Polaris missile was due to rise detected its first blip. There was no mistaking the echo, rising fast into the sky overhead: it could only be a rocket.

At that very moment, six miles above the decks of the Soviet ship the RAF Nimrod began to scatter millions of tiny strips of aluminium foil which fanned out into an enormous reflective umbrella. Deep in the bowels of the *Korolev*, the radar screens suddenly became a blur of false echoes.

The operators knew instantly what had happened, and cursed the British. For days they had sat in sweltering darkness, waiting for the test launch, and now it looked as if they were going to be cheated of their ability to track it. Frantically they flicked switches and spun control knobs in an effort to filter out the unwanted echoes from the 'chaff' that had been scattered above them. The missile seemed to be aiming unerringly for the part of the sky that had now been obscured.

But their fury turned to delighted astonishment when they realised that the RAF had scattered its confusion in the wrong place. High-altitude winds were blowing the 'chaff' away from the line drawn by the trajectory of the rocket. The radar operators turned to one another and laughed at the incompetence of the British.

The missile's path had flattened out and they had seen the rocket section fall away from the 'space bus'. Suddenly the echo from it multiplied into a score of blips, as the decoys were released and the warheads ejected in that vital but indecipherable pattern which would dictate where they would strike the earth.

In the radar control room, giant data-recorders spun their spools to soak up everything that could be detected. The full analysis of the results would take weeks to accomplish, though preliminary data samples would be transmitted to Moscow that very day.

As the cloud of echoes from space began to descend towards the atmosphere, the aluminium-coated balloons used as decoys began to fall back and burst on contact with the air. Then a new pattern of blips began to confuse the screens as electronic jammers projected echoes forward, giving the Soviet observers the impression that the warheads were much closer to the ground than they were in reality.

On the foredeck of the *Korolev*, a robot-like structure studded with ruby lenses had been uncovered at the last minute. This was an infra-red scanner, whose capabilities were highly secret and which Kapitan Karpov had been instructed to keep hidden from Western eyes.

The scanner searched for tiny pinpoints of heat in the sky, heat generated by the friction of objects falling from space at great speed. It locked on to the first target detected, while continuing to search for others. Soon it was tracking a second and a third, and every few moments another, until thirty or forty 'targets' had been identified. The electronics specialists monitoring their computer screens sucked their teeth as they realised their equipment could not tell the difference between the warheads and the flares being released every few seconds to confuse them.

Two minutes later it was all over. The screens were blank; Skydancer had splashed into the sea.

Suddenly the Nimrod appeared from behind the stern of the Soviet ship, flying serenely at two hundred feet. It banked sharply across the bows of the *Korolev*, snapping a stream of pictures of the infra-red detector before the ship's crew had time to cover it up again.

Kapitan Karpov laughed as he watched the plane turn away and head back to Ascension Island. He nudged his first officer in the ribs.

'One crumb! One crumb of comfort for those

British, that's what their pictures will produce!' he sneered, pulling a Cuban cigar from his shirt pocket and clamping it between his teeth.

'They came here to stop us seeing what their missile could do, but they bungled it! What they've done – it's like losing the football match and then stealing the winner's champagne!'

The laughter that rang round the bridge was partly to humour the captain, but largely for a simpler reason: their work was over now and they could go home.

Chapter Eight

The telephone broke the edgy silence in the Defence Chief's office. The field-marshal snatched at the receiver. His eyebrows shot up as he listened to the message.

'Well, I'll be damned!' he exclaimed. 'At Heathrow Airport you say? Berlin! My God! Yes. Yes, he's here. I'll send him down right away.'

He slammed down the telephone.

'Well, that's buggered it. Absolute bloody disaster! You'll never guess where your sodding blueprints have turned up now!'

Peter's heart sank. 'Did you say Berlin?'

'Berlin be buggered! No! In another bloody rubbish bin, that's where!'

'What?'

'That was John Black. A Special Branch chap at Heathrow found an envelope with what looked like your doctored Skydancer plans, in a rubbish basket in one of the departure lounges. Straight after a load of passengers had departed for Berlin. Black wants you to go down to the security office to identify them.'

Peter snatched up his briefcase and hurried from the room. Heading down the corridors, he looked at his watch. It was seven in the evening. Anderson had promised to contact them long before this.

John Black's face expressed no emotion as he pushed a folder of papers across the table towards Peter.

'Recognise these?'

Sick with apprehension, Peter turned the pages. They were the same ones he had spent Sunday preparing.

'Yes. They're mine,' he sighed. 'But what does all this mean?'

'Don't know,' John Black answered flatly. 'But Anderson boarded a flight to Berlin four hours ago. We sent a picture of him to the airport and one of the British Airways check-in staff identified him. He must have crossed over to the East as soon as he got to his destination.

'We also know that he dumped these papers before he left. Now why? He must have been scared of something, scared that his people in East Berlin would recognise them as fakes, and carry out their threat to use the blackmail pictures. But he would hardly go off to Berlin empty-handed, would he now?'

'Christ! You don't mean . . .'

'Perhaps he didn't need your fake plans at all, Mr Joyce. Perhaps he still had a copy of the real ones . . .'

'Oh, no . . .' Peter groaned.

'Oh *yes*, Mr Joyce. Don't forget that because of this scheme of yours – a scheme which I never agreed with by the way – because of this scheme of using Anderson as a double agent, I was never authorised to set my boys on him. I never had the chance to do even something as basic as searching his house in case it alarmed his friend Metzger.

'So we have no idea if it was just one page of the real Skydancer plans that he originally photocopied, or the whole lot. My guess is that he had them all, and in the end the fear of those dirty pictures being seen by his wife made him decide to betray his country after all!'

Peter stared, horrified. 'I have to admit I can't think of any other explanation,' he answered. The strain of the past week suddenly began to crush him unbearably. 'It looks as if we've just given the Kremlin the complete secrets of Skydancer!'

John Black could not resist twisting the knife.

'The trouble is you lot just wouldn't leave security to the professionals! Insisted on plotting and planning all by yourselves, didn't you?'

His taunt stung Peter painfully.

'The security service hasn't exactly earned itself a reputation for loyalty and reliability in recent years, has it?' he snapped back. 'And if you *had* behaved like a professional, Mr Black, we might have had more confidence in you!'

The investigator's face hardened.

'I take exception to that remark,' he murmured ominously.

Peter reached down to his briefcase and pulled out the photograph of Mary Maclean which Karl Metzger had taken from her flat. He pushed it across the table.

'Remember this?' he asked sharply.

Black flicked the lid of his zippo lighter and took his time lighting a cigarette.

'Ah! Now where did that come from?'

'This was the picture you said never existed,' Peter pressed firmly. 'But you recognise it, don't you? Only a few days ago you assured me that it hadn't been in Mary's flat on the evening she was murdered. You knew perfectly well it had, though, and that the murderer had taken it. Lying about that wasn't very *professional*, was it?'

The investigator took hold of the photo-frame and turned it over in his hands.

'You'll have to put that down to foolish pride, Mr Joyce. Not very professional, I'll agree. To be honest, I hadn't noticed the photo was gone after she was found dead, and I should have done. When you remarked on it the other day, I just didn't feel like owning up. That's all there is to it.

'Tell me though,' he went on, skating over the awkwardness. 'How did you come by this?'

'Metzger gave it to Anderson as a warning of what he could expect if he didn't do as he was told,' Peter explained, 'and I got it from Anderson.'

Black fingered the photograph, pressing the glass against the backing to test the thickness. His forehead creased into a frown, and he placed the frame face-down on his desk.

'When did you say Metzger gave it to Anderson?'

'Last Friday evening,' Peter answered, irritated that his case against Black had been explained away so easily.

The investigator took out a razor-blade and carefully slit round the gummed brown paper holding the backing in place.

'And when did you get it from Anderson?'

'Saturday evening.'

'Ah,' Black murmured softly, lifting the rectangle of card from the frame. 'Look at this now!'

He tilted the frame towards Peter; a small electronic circuit had been sandwiched between the photograph and the backing.

'Good grief!'

Black touched a finger to his lips, and opened the desk drawer again to take out a soft leather pouch containing a radio mechanic's toolkit. He lifted the circuitry from the photo-frame, examined it cautiously, then snipped free the connections to a small flat battery.

'Microphone, transmitter, and battery. Standard issue East German bugging device,' he explained. 'Very clever.'

He slipped a miniature test meter from the pouch, and touched its probes to the wires still connected to the battery.

'Dead as a dodo now. Probably only lasted forty-eight hours, if that. But for two days or so this little device was listening in to everything within earshot. The transmitter's only short-range. Anderson's friend Karl probably had someone parked outside his house with a receiver.'

Peter was lost for words.

'Now let's see how good your memory is, Mr Joyce. See if you can remember everything you said to Anderson in the presence of this picture.'

Peter sighed, daunted by the prospect, but he realised the importance of what Black was asking him.

'Well, that first day, the Friday, he told me everything. It was like a confession! So Karl would have known immediately that Anderson had given him away.'

The MI5 man listened with pursed lips.

'Then on Saturday, I saw Anderson again, and told him he was to hand over the doctored blueprints to the East Germans; I told him he had to help us deceive the Soviets if he was going to save himself! I said all that while this bug was sitting on his desk.'

'So the Comrades were *expecting* to be given fake plans for Skydancer,' Black mused.

'But Anderson is giving them the real ones!'

'Now there's a turn-up for the books!' the MI5 man said facetiously. 'But will they believe him, that's the question?'

Peter's thoughts raced ahead. He closed his eyes to concentrate. Now more than ever he needed to think himself into the mind of 'the Russian', but it was like trying to break through an impenetrable wall.

'If only I knew exactly who was running the Soviet BMD improvement programme, it might make it easier to gauge their reaction.'

'Does the name Oleg Kvitzinsky mean anything to you?' the MI5 man enquired casually.

Peter was surprised.

'Oh, yes. He's pretty well known. A very clever man. He's been pushing the use of computers and robotics in their consumer industries. Making better washing-machines for the domestic market, that sort of thing.'

'He's not doing that any more. I had a note from MI6 this afternoon. Their men in Moscow have been doing a little overtime. Apparently Kvitzinsky switched to a secret military project over a year ago. They'd been having trouble integrating their radars with the new anti-missile missiles, and drafted him in to sort it out.'

'I met him once,' Peter said, his spirits reviving. 'At an international computer conference in Geneva. Can't say I got to know him well – we talked a couple of times, but at least I can put a face to him. Sadly it doesn't mean I can read his mind, though!'

The phone on the desk rang, and Black picked it up. Peter could hear Field-Marshal Buxton bellowing at the other end.

'Yes. Yes, he's confirmed it, sir. We'll come up right away, then,' Black replaced the receiver.

'CDS wants a conference – just the three of us – to put everything we know on the table. Looks as if we're all going to co-operate for once. Make a nice change, won't it?'

The field-marshal had set a cut-glass decanter on the table in his office, along with three glasses.

'Sorry there's no ice,' he said briskly, 'but I thought we could do with a drink while we sort out our differences. The past week has been marred by excessive secrecy between departments and even suspicion about each other's loyalty. Well, we now face a bigger crisis than ever before, so we've got to put our differences aside and pool information. All agreed?'

His bluntness took them both by surprise.

'Well, of course,' Peter acknowledged.

'Better late than never,' Black added, considering himself the aggrieved party.

'Right. Let's get on with it, then,' Buxton continued, pouring large measures of whisky into the glasses and nodding towards a low table.

'Now, what conclusions have you two drawn?'

Black raised his eyebrows questioningly, and Peter nodded that he should begin.

He explained how they believed Anderson had now delivered the real Skydancer documents to Berlin. Buxton looked unsurprised; he had already divined as much for himself. He seemed shaken, though, by the revelation of the bugging operation by Metzger's men. It added a new twist of uncertainty to their planning. John Black then also told him they had identified the scientist behind the Soviet plot.

'Kvitzinsky's going to be thoroughly confused, that's for sure,' Peter took over. 'The Russians will have two completely different concepts of how Skydancer works; one from observing the test firing this afternoon, and the other from the blueprints. He may choose to believe the test, or the plans, or neither.'

'Which is just the sort of confusion we set out to create when this whole business started a week ago,' Buxton chipped in. 'We seem to have come full-circle. Oh, you'll be glad to hear the test firing went well. I've just had a signal from Northwood confirming it. The RAF did their bit too, appearing to block the Soviet's view, but in fact dropping their "chaff" downwind to ensure the Russians had an unobstructed look.

'But they had trouble with that bloody traitor, Simpson. Tried to hijack the flaming submarine! The fellow definitely seems to be some kind of a nutter!'

'We've just started looking into his background,' Black replied. 'There seem to be some rather disturbing elements in it. Religious fanaticism, secret societies, that sort of thing. God knows how he ever passed the vetting.'

'Somebody should be shot for that!' Buxton growled.

'Well, we've got his girlfriend in custody,' Black continued. 'But so far we're not sure she was working for the Russians. It's just possible she was more into anti-nuclear campaigning and civil disobedience than espionage. The other woman we arrested, Helene Venner, she's a definite Soviet agent – photographed her last week meeting the KGB resident from the Russian Embassy. We think her real name is Ilena Petrova. But Susan Parkinson probably didn't know that. She may simply have been conned by Venner.

'And there's one more thing,' he went on. 'Karl Metzger left the country this afternoon on the Harwich-Hook of Holland ferry. We've been keeping a close eye on him since Friday night, when one of my men spotted him meeting Anderson.'

'What? You had someone in that pub?' Peter exclaimed.

'Oh, yes, we were there. We'd been tailing both Anderson and you for days. You were both suspects, you know.'

'I see.' He shifted uncomfortably. 'But Metzger's gone, has he?' he snapped suddenly. 'He's the man who murdered Mary Maclean, and you let him leave the country?'

'What else could he do, Peter,' the field-marshal interrupted. 'Deceiving the Soviets depended on Metzger thinking he still had the upper hand.'

Peter laughed bitterly.

'The trouble is, it turns out Karl knew all along that he was being tricked. God what a mess!' He turned to the MI5 man. 'Can you still get Metzger now he's left the country?'

John Black shrugged.

'Maybe. We've got our Dutch friends keeping a lookout for him, but we can't make any sort of move until we know what's happened in Berlin.'

The three men sat back in thoughtful silence and drank their whisky. It was clear to all of them that it all depended on Anderson now, and the mental machinations of Oleg Kvitzinsky.

'Right, that's it, gentlemen,' Buxton suddenly declared, rising to his feet. 'I don't think we can get any further this evening, and the Prime Minister is insisting on a report tonight. So I suggest we meet again in the morning. Peter, we'll need you here again, rather than at Aldermaston.'

Alec Anderson had been left on his own for over two hours. The walls of the small room were drab, and a single neon tube shed a harsh, dull pink light. Occasionally footsteps could be heard outside, approaching, stopping and moving away again.

Anderson was petrified, sweating profusely; his stomach churned remorselessly. The room was quite bare; just a scratched, unpolished wooden table and two chairs. There were no decorations on the wall except an old calendar from the previous year, which heightened his growing sense of having been forgotten and abandoned.

His mind kept returning to the departure lounge at Heathrow. He had had to leave it until the last minute to get rid of the dummy blueprints that Peter Joyce had given him. All the way out to the airport, he had been conscious of a man in a blue overcoat watching his every move. It was only when he had passed through into the departure zone of the terminal that the man had stopped tailing him, and he had felt free to get rid of the plans.

The warning on Sunday night had been specific; Karl Metzger had said that his 'source' in MI5 had tipped him off about the false documents. If there was the slightest hint that the Skydancer papers were not genuine, one of his children would be 'executed'. There had only been one choice: to deliver the real plans, while convincing his colleagues in Whitehall that he had handed over the false ones.

At the airport he had watched a cleaning woman shuffling around all the litter bins, emptying them into a large plastic sack. There had been no scrutiny, no interest in what the bins contained. It had seemed a sure and simple way of disposing of the blueprints without anyone knowing.

It was early evening when Anderson had landed at West Berlin's Tegel airport, and his taxi had had to struggle through rush-hour traffic to the Friedrichstrasse crossing-point, better known as Checkpoint Charlie.

He had been to Berlin once before, accompanying an army minister on a tour of the wall. He had hated the place for its atmosphere of threat and conflict, made permanent by the concrete monstrosity that divided the city.

That evening he had passed almost unnoticed through the American control point; tourists crossing into the East were two-a-penny these days. He had felt sick with fear on the walk to the Volkspolizei guard-house, with its dim lights and suspicious-eyed sentries.

Inside the immigration hall, he had looked around

for a sign of someone waiting to take him through, but there had been no one visible. He had carefully filled in his visa form and currency declaration, and changed his regulation twenty-five West German marks into twenty-five Eastern ones, an exchange designed specifically to benefit the economy of the communist half of Germany.

His passport had been taken from him by a border guard who displayed an overt loathing of Westerners. Anderson suspected it was his primary qualification for the job. The document had been slipped through a flap in the wall, and examined by unseen officials. A few moments later a small hatch had opened up and two pairs of eyes studied him carefully. Then the passport had been returned to him and he was through.

East Berlin. As he had looked back at the concrete wall, trying to imagine the desperation of those who had died trying to escape it, a man in a smart raincoat had tapped him on the arm. A car had been waiting to take him to the headquarters of the HVA, the East German Intelligence Service.

The Skydancer blueprints had been taken from him as soon as they arrived at the slab-sided grey building, and since then he had been alone in this bare room with nothing to look at but last year's calendar.

Why on earth had they bothered to put it there? It seemed a pointless decoration. Unless there was something behind it . . .

His heart began to pound and a shiver ran through him. He realised with horror that for the past two hours every bead of sweat, every flicker of his eyelids had been minutely studied from another room.

*

In Moscow, General Novikov had just returned to his GRU headquarters from a gruelling meeting with his KGB counterpart at the half-moon-shaped offices on the Moscow ring-road. Novikov's operation to get the Skydancer plans was beginning to cost the KGB dearly.

Already one of their key 'illegals' had been arrested, the woman responsible for co-ordinating the manipulation of the anti-nuclear militants in Britain. It had taken years to put Ilena Petrova into place, years of work that was now wasted.

Above all, there was now a threat to one of their longest-serving agents of all time, a man recruited at Oxford University in the 1940s. He had been the subtlest of the academic recruits, gently influencing young men to look kindly on the Soviet Union in their lives ahead.

But now, with the arrest of that young submariner, the British investigators would begin to probe, to delve into the past. It would only be a matter of time before they found the trail leading back to that small, select boarding-school attended by so many boys whose lives had later led them to positions of authority.

General Novikov had promised the KGB that his operation was nearing its end. Just a few more hours and it would all be over – successfully. The sacrifices would have been worth it; Kvitzinsky would have the blueprints he wanted, and Moscow's leaders could again feel that their future safety was as assured as was humanly possible.

Belinda Joyce had just finished watching the Nine O'Clock News when her husband arrived home. She was sitting on her own in the kitchen, looking at a small portable television. The children were watching another programme in the living-room.

After hanging his coat in the hall, Peter walked through to the kitchen and pulled a chair over beside her.

'I was watching the news,' she began nervously. 'They said two women were arrested at Newbury yesterday, and that a senior scientist at Aldermaston had been suspended!'

'They're a bit behind the times,' he replied. 'I was reinstated this morning and the suspension's been struck from the record. They didn't name me, did they? If they did, I'll sue them!'

Belinda saw that the lines around his mouth had deepened and his eyes had lost their brightness. He looked so defeated; she'd never seen him quite like that before. Standing up, she took down a glass from the dresser behind her.

'Would you like a drink?' she asked, indicating the wine bottle on the table.

'Love one.'

He sipped thoughtfully at the cheap burgundy before answering her unspoken question.

'Yes, one of those women they arrested was Helene, if that's what you're wondering,' he told her gently. 'Apparently her real name is Ilena Petrova. She's a Russian spy.'

The look on Belinda's face was one of pain rather than surprise, which made Peter think she had expected the news.

'Can they *really* be so sure?' she asked in the vain hope there might be some doubt.

'They're quite sure. They've photographed her with a KGB man.'

Belinda burst into tears.

'You don't know how hard she tried to persuade me to spy on your work – even steal some of your papers!' she sobbed. 'It all seemed . . . innocent at the time, like a – a game. But it wasn't. God, you must think me so stupid!'

Peter put his arms round her.

'We've both been pretty bloody foolish.'

For a few moments they were silent. They both sensed that the wounds caused by his love affair with Mary Maclean were healing. A permanent scar might remain, but it was one they would be able to live with.

Suddenly Belinda asked, 'Who was the other woman? The other one they arrested?'

'Someone called Susan Parkinson,' Peter replied. 'Know her? She's supposed to be a member of ATSA.'

'No. She must be from another branch. Are they saying she was a spy, too?'

'They think she may just have been a protester who went too far . . .'

'What'll happen next?' she asked anxiously. 'Perhaps they'll arrest me, too.'

'You shouldn't have anything to fear,' he smiled, and poured them some more wine.

'How much longer will this nightmare last?' she asked.

Her face creased with anxiety. Suddenly Peter felt a great fondness for her. He thought of Anderson and his frantic, disastrous efforts to preserve the happiness and integrity of his family. Love, affection, security, call it what you will – it was what they were all motivated by in one way or another.

'I don't know,' he replied eventually. 'But I think it's all about to come to a head.'

*

At eleven the following morning a dark-green saloon car drew up in the courtyard of the British Military Mission in Berlin. A small red and gold plaque on its bumper designated it as belonging to the Soviet Army. Officers from the forces of the four nations that had controlled the city since the death of Adolf Hitler had the right of access to each other's areas. Every day Soviet officers would drive into the West, and every day British, French and American officers would visit the East. However, for a Soviet officer to pay a call at the British headquarters was far from usual.

The Russian army captain walked into the building carrying a small brown envelope. The British major on duty looked surprised as the Soviet soldier slapped it down on his desk, stood back and saluted.

'Captain Borodin of the Military Mission of the Union of Soviet Socialist Republics,' he introduced himself. His voice was thin and nasal.

'Major Howlett,' the British officer replied coolly.

'You see, there is, mmmm . . . a British person in our section, who has been behaving unacceptably,' the Russian continued in a thick accent.

He tapped the envelope with his index finger.

'His papers,' he explained. 'You see . . . his passport has one name, but his driving licence has another.'

'I see,' the major answered non-committally, slitting open the envelope and tipping the contents on to the desk. He picked up the driving licence first, which was in the name of Alec Anderson.

'I *see*,' he said again. The name on the passport was Allenby.

'Tell me, Captain Borodin, do you have this man under arrest?'

The Russian officer shifted awkwardly. He was only a messenger, unable to answer such questions.

'He will be returned to you,' he began again, 'but there is someone special who must collect him.'

He pointed to a folded sheet of paper that had fallen from the envelope.

Puzzled, the major spread it open. It was a short letter.

'But . . . but this is addressed to the Chief of the Defence Staff!' he exclaimed. 'I'm not sure I should read it.'

'You must transmit it now!' Borodin insisted. 'It is very urgent.'

With increasing astonishment the major cast his eye down the page, scanning the conditions set for Anderson's release from the East.

'Well . . . I shall deal with it right away, Captain. We'll communicate with you in due course. Where, er . . . where should we address our reply?'

'I am at our mission. I shall wait for you to come.'

'Very well.'

The major stood up. The Russian saluted again, turned on his heel and strode out.

When Peter entered the field-marshal's office, following an urgent summons, he found the defence chief grim-faced.

'I've been talking with our security people,' Buxton began. 'We've had a message from Berlin about Anderson, to which we have to respond. Everything I say to you has been cleared with both MI5 and MI6, so there are no dissenters. We're all agreed as to the action we have to take.'

Alarmed, Peter said nothing.

Buxton took a deep breath.

'We want you to go to Berlin.'

'What?'

'The Soviets seem to be holding Anderson as some sort of prisoner, but say they will hand him over tonight, but only to you. Don't ask me why, I just don't know. We received a signal from our mission there this morning, relaying the contents of a letter signed by Oleg Kvitzinsky!'

'Good Lord!'

'Yes. It's all quite mystifying. He says the handover will be at a small crossing-point in the wall sometime after midnight, but it can only take place if you're there.'

'Why on earth would they insist on that?' Peter frowned. 'Do you think they're planning to grab me as well?'

'We thought of that, of course. They won't get the chance, though. You can be sure of that. You'll have an armed escort from our garrison, and there's no way the Soviets are going to start a shooting incident over this business. They're showing all the signs of wanting to keep it very quiet and discreet.'

'But what about the Skydancer plans?' Peter was thinking on his feet. 'Presumably this means that the Soviets think they are calling our bluff, that they believe the plans Anderson gave them are fakes and they want to rub our noses in it! Or does it?'

'God knows!' Buxton sighed. 'The big question is why Kvitzinsky should be involved? Presumably they got him to Berlin to cast his expert eye over the blueprints, but why he insists on seeing you is far from clear. My guess is that he is going to demand some further information as a final price for Anderson's release! You'll tell him nothing, of course – I hardly need say that. Our colleagues in the secret service have a different idea. They're quite excited! They seem to think he's going to defect!'

Peter whistled softly. That would be a remarkable bonus if it happened.

'Well, are you saying we've little to lose by doing what they want, and there's no real alternative anyway?'

'That's about it. You'll go, then?'

The same flight that had conveyed Alec Anderson to Berlin the previous day took Peter Joyce to the divided city. With him went a somewhat monosyllabic representative from MI6, to be present if Kvitzinsky did indeed defect, and who would also escort Anderson back to Britain. The two men sat in different sections of the aircraft; the intelligence man wanted to smoke, and Peter did not.

The sky was clear throughout the flight, but darkness had descended as they neared their destination. With twenty minutes to go before they landed, Peter looked out of the left-hand window and saw a line of lights stretching north as far as the eye could see. Suddenly he realised it was the inner-German border dividing East from West, capitalism from communism. He could imagine the lines of fencing and barbed wire that marked that border with its watchtowers and guard dogs, designed to keep the population of the East where it was.

The engine note changed and the Boeing began its descent towards West Berlin.

They were met at Tegel Airport by the major from the British military mission.

'Alan Howlett,' he introduced himself briskly. He had a pointed face with a receding chin, and looked both nervous and excited at the prospect of being involved in what looked like his first real spy drama.

'I've got my car here, so we'll go straight to my HQ for a briefing, and take it from there.'

The MI6 man snorted quietly to himself at the army's preoccupation with 'briefings'.

Peter had never been to Berlin before. It was raining; a steady downpour flowed off the car's windscreen like a river. The wipers made little impression on the blur of water; the garish neon lights of the city were magnified and distorted by the wet glass.

As they set off from the airport, Major Howlett tried to make conversation with the two men, but their lack of response discouraged him from further efforts.

Once inside the Military Mission they were taken straight to a conference room, where a young captain, introduced as 'the briefing officer', gave them an illustrated lecture on the divided city of Berlin. From time to time the MI6 man yawned loudly, to show his own familiarity with the subject, but to Peter much of what he was being told was new.

Then the major took over.

'So much for the general picture,' he began, looking down at his notes, 'which we thought we'd give you just in case you weren't too familiar with the city. But, now, on to tonight.

'The Soviets have named Kirchenallee as the place where Mr Anderson is to be released. It's not normally in use as a crossing-point. The boundary between the Russian and the British zones runs along the western edge of a railway track which is down in a sort of cutting. Because of lack of space on the western side, the Vopos built their wall on the east of the track at that point, even though the railway line is actually theirs. Here . . .'

Major Howlett clicked on the light of an epidiascope, which projected a vu-foil map on to the screen. He indicated the area involved with a billiard cue.

'As you can see, Kirchenallee crosses the railway line here over a narrow bridge. The wall is at the eastern end, with a solid iron gate across the road, and at our western end there is a chain-link fence, with another gate in it, padlocked from their side.

'Now, I've not done one of these before, but looking at the records of past handovers, the procedure seems to be this: we turn up and wait in our cars on our side of the bridge. They give us the once-over through their binoculars from one of the two watchtowers on the other side; then they open the iron gate in the wall, walk across the bridge and undo the padlock on the chain-link gate on the western side.

'They check our papers, then let us walk with them to the middle of the bridge. It's their territory officially, but for events like this the bridge is considered no-man's land. Then, in theory, they bring across the man in question and hand him over. Bob's your uncle!'

'What are your security plans tonight?' the MI6 man demanded suddenly.

'Ah, yes. There should be no problem there. We'll have a platoon with us who will take up firing positions just in case it turns nasty, and a couple of military policemen will escort you on to the bridge as well. We're not expecting any trouble, though.'

'Why are they going to such lengths?' Peter asked. 'Why all the cloak-and-dagger stuff? Why not just shove him across Checkpoint Charlie if they want to get rid of him?'

The major looked at him in surprise.

'I have no idea, sir. I rather assumed you knew the answer to that question.'

Peter felt the MI6 man was laughing at him inwardly. The bastard had seen it all before.

'Well, if there are no more questions,' Howlett continued, conscious of the awkward silence, 'then I'll take you to the mess. We've got rooms for you for the night, and after you've had a wash and so on, we could gather for a drink and some dinner. Our rendezvous with the Russians isn't until two o'clock in the morning, I'm afraid.'

Oleg Kvitzinsky hated Berlin. The Germans might be Soviet allies, but they despised the men from Moscow and did not mind showing it.

He had flown to the city, accompanied by two burly 'specialists' from the GRU, to examine the blueprints of the new British nuclear weapon system which the HVA claimed to have captured.

He had spent most of his time there sitting in the Soviet embassy, exhaustively examining the documents that Alec Anderson had delivered, and comparing them with the preliminary analysis of the Skydancer warhead test in the Atlantic, which had been telexed to him from Moscow.

From the top floor of the embassy building, he could see the endlessly-flashing neon lights on the other side of the wall, set up in prominent positions as a deliberate lure to those in the East. To Oleg it was a cheap capitalist trick – distasteful even – to try to tempt people with bright lights and baubles into a society that was attractive on the surface but which was rotten and crippled by unemployment underneath.

He had been shocked at what he had learned about Skydancer, shocked and dismayed. His decision to use Anderson as a bait to lure the designer of the weapon to Berlin had been an act of desperation. He was taking a considerable risk, but this was an opportunity he could not afford to ignore.

He dreaded that meeting, now; there had been a catastrophe that afternoon. It had made his goal virtually unattainable.

The door swung open. One of the GRU men stood there, pointing at his watch. It was after one o'clock in the morning, and time to go.

They had driven well clear of that section of the city that keeps humming throughout the night with its countless bars and brothels. Peter Joyce peered through the car window down the deserted side-streets, catching occasional glimpses of the wall, which was thrown into stark silhouette by the brightness of the observation lights on the other side. They seemed to be driving parallel with it, the side-streets cut short by its graffiti-covered bulk. The emptiness of the streets was almost eerie, as if no one lived so close to this frontier; as if the contrast between east and west was too painful to bear when seen so close.

'Not far now,' the major commented, trying to sound reassuring.

In front of them three Land-Rovers led the way, their thick tyres humming on the wet road. The red tail-lights of the last one sparkled in their rain-spattered windscreen.

'They could have chosen a better night for it,' Howlett muttered. 'It's ten to two now. We'll probably have a few minutes wait when we get there.'

'I shall stay in the car, out of sight,' the MI6 man growled. 'It'd have to be Gorbachev himself coming across to get me to stand outside on a night like this!'

The brake-lights of the Land-Rovers came on in

dazzling unison, and an orange flashing indicated a turn to the left.

'Kirchenallee,' Major Howlett announced as they rounded the corner.

Ahead of them stood the chain-link fence, with the wall a little way beyond it, just as it had been described in the briefing.

Peter swallowed hard. He felt suddenly unprepared. He had no idea what the Russian scientist would say to him, nor what he would say in reply.

'We're here,' the major said unnecessarily.

The car halted close to the wire gate. Its headlights briefly illuminated the road which ran beyond it, across the iron bridge, and the cold grey wall which finally blocked progress into the eastern half of the city. The drivers switched their headlamps off, plunging the road into blackness. Suddenly they became conscious of the two stark watchtowers on the other side, visible against the glow of the illuminations for the 'dead' zone behind. Shadowy figures looked down on them.

Soldiers were jumping out of the Land-Rovers and spreading out. Rifles in hand, some entered what looked like a derelict building at the end of the row of houses, others crouched in doorways, the rain glistening on their waterproof capes.

'Now we just have to wait,' Howlett explained quietly. The rain drummed on the roof of the car.

The major pulled out an electronic night-sight, and switched it on. After giving it a few seconds to warm up, he put it to his eyes.

'Nothing yet,' he reported, focusing on the edge of the iron gate through which the Soviets would have to emerge.

Peter imagined the unseen soldiers around them lining up the same view on the night-sights of their rifles, ready to kill with accuracy in the blackness, if ordered to do so.

There was a tap at the window, and the major wound it down a crack. 'All in position, sir.'

Peter recognised the voice of the young captain who had given the briefing earlier. Peering through the window he could make out the shapes of two men, one of them carrying a radio-set on his back.

'Right,' the major replied. 'Oh, standby! We've got some movement. Gate's opening!'

The captain hurried off to take up his command position, ready to direct his platoon, if action were needed.

'Vopo coming across the bridge. East German police. Better go and say hello. Stay here for the moment, if you don't mind, gentlemen.'

The major handed his night-glasses to the driver and cursed as he stepped out into the downpour.

A faint light from distant street-lamps made the wire-mesh gate just visible to the naked eye. Peter saw the German guard looming out of the darkness. With the aid of a small torch, he inserted a key into the padlock and struggled to turn it.

'Fookin' rusty, I reckon!' the driver exclaimed in a thick Birmingham accent.

The MI6 man sniffed.

'Last time they used this crossing was three years ago,' he commented disdainfully.

Half the gate swung open. Then the Vopo pulled at the bolt on the second one and opened that, too. The way on to the bridge was now clear.

The two officers stood in the middle of the road, talking. The British major seemed to be struggling to understand what he was being told. Repeatedly he appeared to be asking for clarification.

Eventually he hurried back to the car, his shoulders hunched against the rain.

Howlett threw himself inside, splashing water everywhere. He left the door half open. Peter noticed that he looked both shocked and puzzled.

'Well, I don't know . . . I think I understood him right, but they never mentioned this before. He said he wants us to back a Land-Rover on to the bridge. Something about a box. He kept saying "*eine Kiste, eine Kiste*". I don't know . . .'

'He means a coffin,' the MI6 man concluded sharply.

'Christ!' Peter breathed.

'Yes . . . I think you're right. I'd better get that organised,' the major stammered, and disappeared into the rain again.

'He couldn't have misunderstood, could he?' Peter hoped.

'Doubt it,' the MI6 man answered. 'Sounds bad.'

'Anderson?'

The man nodded.

Two minutes later the major was back. The engine of one of the Land-Rovers could be heard revving behind them.

'If you would come with me now, Mr Joyce . . .' said Howlett tensely, poking his head through the doorway.

Peter felt heavy with dread. He fumbled for the handle. The driver leaned back and opened the door for him.

The rain splattering on to his hair was ice-cold. He was glad of the umbrella that Howlett held ready for him to take.

'This way.'

A heavy gust of exhaust fumes swirled warmly around him, as the Land-Rover backed past and began to edge its way towards the middle of the bridge. An East German policeman waved it on with his torch, the sharply upturned brim of his cap standing out against the lights behind.

A pair of headlights began to approach from the far end of the bridge, the beams see-sawing up and down as the vehicle bumped across the uneven and seldom-used surface of the road.

The two vehicles stopped within ten feet of each other. Howlett grabbed Peter by the arm to prevent him going beyond the tail of their Land-Rover. The headlamps from the other side dazzled them. For a moment nothing seemed to be happening.

'Peter Joyce?'

The voice was high-pitched and tremulous.

Peter cleared his throat.

'Yes, that's me.'

'*Vorwärts bitte!* Please come forvords,' a different voice called this time, with a German accent.

'It's okay. Go ahead,' Major Howlett reassured him.

Peter stepped forward six paces, and stopped.

'Oleg Kvitzinsky?' he called. 'Your turn!'

The lights of the East German vehicle were off to one side now, and had ceased to dazzle him. He could see three men ahead. Hesitantly one of them began to move.

The man was tall and burly, wearing a heavy raincoat and a felt hat. He came right up to Peter and stopped. The spill of light reflecting off the wet tarmac gave a dull illumination to his face. It had been several years since they had met in Geneva, but Peter recollected the arched brows and the eyes that looked poised halfway between laughter and tears. They looked sadder than he had remembered.

'This was not what I planned,' Kvitzinsky stated,

only a slight accent tainting his words.

Beyond him Peter could see four men in uniform sliding something heavy from the back of the vehicle, which he could now see was a hearse.

'This afternoon your Mr Anderson was still alive,' Kvitzinsky continued slowly. 'It was intended that he would walk across here with me. But . . .'

Speechless with shock and anger, Peter watched as the policemen carried the coffin past. Two British soldiers helped them ease the plain wooden box into the back of the Land Rover.

'Who killed him?' Peter rasped.

'The *Polizei* have some papers. They will give them to your soldiers. It explains . . .' Kvitzinsky hesitated. His face was pained. 'It explains that there was an accident, that he was out looking at the city this afternoon when there was a traffic accident . . .'

Peter felt fury boiling up inside him. With his free hand he grasped the Russian by the lapels.

'You have the bloody nerve to just stand there and tell me . . .'

'Don't touch me, please,' Kvitzinsky whispered. 'They might shoot. Please. They are very nervous!'

Over the Russian's shoulder Peter could see that two of the guards had levelled their submachine-guns at him. Slowly he released his grip.

'You are right to be angry,' Kvitzinsky went on hurriedly. 'And of course it is not true about the traffic accident . . . but it was not our intention that he should die! You must believe . . .' he implored. 'He took his own life . . . from a window of the HVA, the police building. I don't know why. It was after he learned that he was to be handed back to you like this. It's the truth, Joyce, but the Germans didn't think you would believe . . . so they have written the other story.'

Peter stared blankly at the Russian, unable to decide whether Kvitzinsky himself believed what he was saying. Would Anderson have killed himself? It was not impossible.

'What do you want, Kvitzinsky? Why did you insist I came here to meet you?'

A gust of wind caught the underside of his umbrella and threatened to wrench it away. Kvitzinsky clutched at his hat to prevent it being blown off.

'I had a proposition to put,' he said, trying to keep his voice to a whisper. 'Now . . .' He shrugged and looked unhappily at the coffin. 'Now you would be right not even to listen to me, but I hope you will.'

His eyes were those of a man struggling under a terrible burden.

'You are a brilliant man, Peter Joyce, and you have a technology already which I am still dreaming of! Yes, I pay you a compliment! Your Skydancer is a very clever weapon. Of course,' he sighed, 'I now know how I can beat it. I know how to build a defence against it, but . . .'

His lips sealed into a thin line.

In the half-light of the car headlights Peter tried to read the Russian's face, to see what new vein of trickery was being mined.

Kvitzinsky had leaned forward so that his head was under the edge of Peter's umbrella. He spoke in a soft whisper, inaudible to anyone more than a few inches away.

'The people at the top in my country want it to be done. If I tell them it is possible, they will spend the money, buy me everything I need, steal me anything that money cannot buy. But if that money is spent on such military equipment, what will happen? Where will that money come from? You know the answer; it is the same in your country, the same everywhere. That money will come from the people. To pay for a defence against a weapon designed never to be used, hospitals will stay crowded and short of drugs; food supplies will run out and schools will close in the bitter days of winter because there is no fuel to heat them.'

Peter steeled himself against Kvitzinsky's outpourings. He smelled trickery. There had to be a catch, and he held himself in wait for it.

'Mr Peter Joyce,' the Russian began to plead with him, 'you and I, we are scientists, not gunsmiths. We are here on this planet to extend mankind's knowledge for his own benefit. For his protection, yes, but . . . if we build him an impregnable fortress and then keep him inside it with nothing to eat, what do we achieve?

'You . . . and me, I want us to try to reach an understanding. I know . . . I know from when we talked before in Geneva, in better times, I know that you are a serious and sensible man. If I build a defence against Skydancer, you will build a new weapon that can beat it, and then I . . . and so on and so on. There is no end to that. No security or peace for our families. Only fear. Joyce, listen to me. We must stop this, and now is the time to do it! No new defences, no new missiles!'

Peter stood back suddenly. He began to believe that Kvitzinsky was serious, that he was earnestly proposing a halt to one small part of the arms race, not a halt negotiated by politicians, but one unofficially agreed by scientists.

'You can't deliver that sort of deal,' Peter answered gently. 'Nor can I. You know that. We . . . people like us, we don't take decisions of that kind.'

The Russian's eyes narrowed.

'We can try.'

There was the sound of footsteps. Kvitzinsky shot a glance over his shoulder; the officers from the GRU were coming up one on each side of him.

He reached into the inside pocket of his coat, and pulled out a thick brown envelope.

'Useless!' he exclaimed in a loud voice, thrusting the envelope into Peter's hands. 'Your attempt to trick me into thinking these were the real plans – a waste of time! You do not fool us so easily, Mr Joyce! That is what I want to tell you. We have not been taken in!'

With that, he turned abruptly on his heel and walked back towards the wall, flanked by the Soviet security men.

For a moment Peter stood stunned and confused by what he had just heard. The hearse began to roll quietly backwards, its engine purring softly. The guards in their watchtowers seemed to relax now that the confrontation on the bridge was over.

'I think we should get moving,' Major Howlett muttered by his ear.

Peter stood for a moment longer, watching the vehicle that had delivered Anderson's corpse slip back behind the wall, Oleg Kvitzinsky walking beside it. The heavy iron gate began to close. For a few minutes there had been a contact on this bridge, a hope voiced, and then stifled.

He looked at the wall stretching away in each direction, with its wire and its searchlights, and the distant barking of its guard dogs. It was mistrust itself, cast in concrete.

Peter turned and walked beside the Land-Rover as it carried Alec Anderson's coffin slowly back into the West. Once they were off the bridge, the East German guard closed the wire-mesh gate behind them and secured the padlock.

'I think we have to assume it was all designed to trick us,' Field-Marshal Buxton stated. Sir Marcus Beckett nodded in agreement.

'It's a pretty standard Soviet ploy, disinformation and all that,' Beckett added.

They had gathered at the Defence Ministry the following afternoon.

'I think he meant it,' Peter answered, half to himself. 'I think he was genuinely trying to make a point. I wasn't sure at the time, but I believe it now. He's not a military man remember. Kvitzinsky got roped into the weapons business because of his achievements in the civilian sector. He's an idealist – still believes in communism as a force to benefit the masses. Naive perhaps, but I'm sure he was genuinely trying to stop one little piece of the arms race.

'He was scared to death of those security men, I'm sure of that. Covered his tracks in a hurry, in case they overheard him. That farce about giving back the plans that Alec had delivered, saying they were fakes. It wasn't for my benefit that he did that, but for the GRU men who were guarding him. It was his own goons he was trying to convince.'

Buxton and Beckett smiled knowingly at one another.

'You mustn't underestimate the deviousness of the Russians, Peter,' the CDS warned. 'We've accumulated quite a lot of experience of them over the years, you know. My guess is that at this very moment he's going through a copy of those plans of yours with a fine-toothed comb!'

Peter shook his head.

'I'm sure he was going to tell his own people that building a defence against Skydancer was impossible – that was the message I got,' he insisted.

'Well . . .' Buxton concluded, 'time will tell.'

'And what about Anderson?' Sir Marcus interjected. 'You don't seriously believe that story about suicide do you? The HVA bumped him off, just the same as they did poor Mary Maclean!'

Peter nodded. They could be right about that. He thought again of those bloodstains at Mary's flat and shuddered.

'And do they get away with it?' he asked bitterly. 'Two people murdered, and we can do nothing about it?'

The field-marshal frowned.

'If Metzger turns up in the West again, you can rest assured it won't be long before he's sent home in a box, too,' Buxton stated grimly.

'There's an emergency debate in the House tomorrow,' Sir Marcus cut in. 'The opposition have demanded it. The PM's going to say something about Alec. Berlin won't be mentioned – but he's going to say that Anderson died in a counter-intelligence operation, details of which can never be revealed, in the interests of national security.'

Peter thought of Janet Anderson. At least she could now believe that her husband died a hero. She would never know that he had been led into blackmail and into betraying his country.

It was the face of 'the Russian' which dominated his mind, a face which was no longer just imaginary. Kvitzinsky. *Was* he just another Soviet official, saying one thing and meaning another? Or had he been pleading with him from the heart?

Supposing Kvitzinsky did keep his word? Supposing

he made no effort to counter Skydancer? Could that be the end of it? The end of one small part of the arms race?

He shook his head. How could they ever be sure what Kvitzinsky would do, or whether some other Russian would soon take his place, some scientist with an altogether different view? Maybe Buxton was right; maybe the only way to predict the future was to remember the mistrust of the past.

The following afternoon, Peter Joyce returned home from Aldermaston soon after lunch, to listen to the radio broadcast of the emergency debate in the House of Commons.

The Prime Minister made a rousing statement about the wickedness of the foreign agents who had tried to steal British missile secrets, and declared that they had failed ignominiously, thanks to the heroic actions of a number of British personnel, including Mr Alec Anderson from the Ministry of Defence.

Pressed by the opposition to state categorically whether British defence interests had been damaged or not, he declared:

'This house may rest assured that Her Majesty's Government will preserve the effectiveness of the British independent nuclear deterrent, whatever measures the Soviet Union and her allies may take in an effort to undermine it. It is and will remain a weapon against which there is no effective defence, and whose guaranteed destructive power is the surest way we know to deter any nation in the world from waging war against us.'

Peter lay back at one end of the sofa in the living-room, staring at the ceiling.

'Does that mean you've just been promised a job for life?' Belinda asked warily.

Peter smoothed back the hair from his forehead. For a long time he just stared at nothing.

'I don't really know,' he answered eventually.

JAVA SPIDER

A British minister has been kidnapped. His abduction does not fall under British jurisdiction and the authorities in Jakarta claim that he has been seized by a guerrilla movement. But their investigation makes no progress as horrific satellite pictures of him are released on national television.

The government sends one man to rescue him – Nick Randall has served in the Far East before. He knows that nothing is as it seems in the land of masks. Greater forces are at play than even he suspects. Together with a lone woman TV reporter he penetrates a remote island, where a powder keg of armed local rebellion is threatening to explode under the repressive regime.

'A plot constructed with devilish cunning.'
Daily Telegraph

THE BURMA LEGACY

The jungle still holds bloody secrets.

Fifty-five years after the end of World War Two, Tetsuo Kamata is a wealthy businessman, but he was once an interrogator in a Japanese Prisoner of War camp. One of his victims, Peregrine Harrison, recognizes him. Harrison never got over his maltreatment at Kamata's hands and has dreamed of killing him ever since. Now he has his chance.

But if Kamata dies, so do the livelihoods of hundreds of car factory workers. MI6 officer Sam Packer is diverted from his hunt for an ex-SAS drug trader in Thailand and given the order to stop Harrison. The search takes him deep into Harrison's past and to the poppy fields of the Golden Triangle. To save Kamata from execution Packer must penetrate an alien and hostile world, a quest which brings him face to face with the very drug lords who have sworn to kill him.

FIRE HAWK

A whispered secret in a Baghdad hotel lobby leads to Sam Packer's kidnapping, torture and expected execution. His paymasters have given him up for dead. Only the intervention of his ex-lover, Chrissie, and a hostage swap get him released. But days later Chrissie is murdered. Perhaps she knows too much, knew of the secret Sam had uncovered – that a biological terror weapon codenamed Fire Hawk had been smuggled from Iraq for use against an unknown target in the West.

Personal motives of revenge clash with the priorities of State Security as Sam follows the weapon's and his dead lover's murky past through the Middle East, Cyprus and the Ukraine. At each step the mystery of the ultimate target deepens and the fanatics who control it become ever more elusive.

'The suspense is sizzling. Geoffrey Archer has again used his ITN experience in a sinuous mix of international threats that are coming to have the same chill-factor as the fear that underpinned the best Cold War thrillers.'
Daily Telegraph

THE LUCIFER NETWORK

A deadly secret whispered by a dying gunrunner on a lonely road in Zambia sets MI6 agent Sam Packer on a frantic race against time. A terrorist gang has acquired a horror weapon but before Packer can discover more, the man dies.

Packer is on his own, faced with sceptical colleagues and the gunrunner's daughter Julie, who may hold the key to the secret but who also suspects it was Packer who engineered her father's death. Betrayed and compromised, Packer follows a faint trail of coincidences that began with his own father's disgrace twenty-seven years before.

As Packer fights desperately to win Julie's confidence, the unlikely pair follow the trail of murder and deceit from Scotland to Vienna and on to a lonely island in the Adriatic; there they will find not only the weapon but the identity of the sinister organisation known as the Lucifer Network.